. . . Lover reaching out, her arms pale and ready to encircle Zoe's back as she moved to lie on top of her, their mouths meeting first. The softness of their breasts touching, spreading, fusing. Groins, sweet contact! met, blended, warmed one another as they moved in the slow first circles of desire. Their tongues, strong travelers taking turns. To feel hers entering her mouth, to receive it and press it with her own, wanting it deeper, wetter, then to change, to thrust and gain full entry, explore moist surfaces within. And then? to separate, knowing, to pull back, because it was going to happen, and they could afford to take time, to build slowly, sure of what would come.

zoe's book

a novel by Gail Pass

NAIAD
1987

First Naiad Press Edition, 1987

Printed in the United States of America

Cover design by The Women's Graphic Center
Typesetting by Sandi Stancil

Acknowledgments. The author gratefully acknowledges the following sources: *Beginning Again* by Leonard Woolf (New York: Harcourt, Brace & World, Inc., 1963); *Virginia Woolf* by Quentin Bell (New York: Harcourt Brace Jovanovich, Inc., 1972); *The Literary Life*, edited by Robert Phelps and Peter Deane (New York: Farrar, Straus & Giroux, Inc., 1968); *Lytton Strachey* by Michael Holroyd (Baltimore: Penguin Books, Inc., 1971); *Diane Arbus* (New York: Aperture, 1972).

ISBN 0-930044-95-9

Jean, thank you.

ABOUT THE AUTHOR

Born in Toledo, Ohio, Gail Pass attended Smith College and graduated from the University of California, Berkeley, in 1962. After working and writing in the San Francisco Bay Area for 15 years, she moved to Portsmouth, New Hampshire. It was during this 1975 transcontinental car trip that *Zoe's Book* was first accepted for publication.

Living in New England for the next four years, she taught fiction writing at the University of New Hampshire, Department of Continuing Education; worked to establish a shelter for battered women; and wrote her next novel.

Surviving Sisters was published in 1981. For the next several years she commuted between Montreal, Quebec and her home town, continuing to write and work. Resettled in Toledo, she is currently writing nonfiction.

I

SHE MUST BE close to eighty. Reclining on a chaise longue, her little figure wrapped round with a blanket from the waist down, she sees me hesitate in the doorway. I must cross the room to meet her and have about twenty closely watched steps in which to prepare myself.

She'll be frail. The hand I shake will be palsied; her voice will quaver. She'll have rheumy eyes, and a faint odor not very pleasant. Old age. I should never have agreed to this.

"Ah, you've come," she says in a voice hearty enough for any playing field. "Good, good." Her hand is offered, "I'm Zoe Mohr," and my hand finds itself embarrassed at having to increase the pressure it mistakenly withheld at the start. "Sit down, sit down. Over there if you like. Or there. It makes no matter. Little details never do."

I sit while she rearranges the robe over her legs. The contours, I notice now, are not smooth but abrupt, angular. Perhaps the wool plaid is covering leg braces.

"You've noticed, I see. Doesn't matter. Happened, hm, over a decade ago. One has to expect these things if one's going to live. It's all part of dying you know. Tea?"

She doesn't wait for me to respond but pulls a rolling cart closer to her and begins the English pouring ritual. Her hands are heavily veined but still quite lovely. There's no wedding ring.

"I believe what the Hasidic Jews say, that man's both the carrier of life that he is and the corpse that he'll be. At seventy-six you bloody well know it. Are you Jewish? Neither am I. But I know what it means."

To be a Jew? No, to watch oneself age. She appears to be doing all right. Hair's healthy looking, thick and white, perhaps black in its youth. Must have been, her eyes are almost black. Handsome woman, once. I can imagine her face without those dozens of little grooves, the nose less fleshy, chin squarer. Very handsome. I wonder.

"Do you stare because you're American? Or because you're young. Or is it just your nature? Perhaps there's another reason. Yes, I prefer to think that. We'll see."

I take care to look elsewhere while she pours more hot water into the teapot. It's a comfortable room. Bookshelves on every wall. Good reading areas, soft light and comfortable chairs, a few small tables. No pictures, though, no little objects; just books. Strange, I should think a woman her age would have more clutter about her, things one picks up in a lifetime.

"There's a telescope under that cloth by the window. Have a look." A telescope, and I'd thought it was a birdcage. So much for knowing my seventy-six-year-old women. I don't do much better with the younger ones either.

"Entrance to the British Museum. I've quite a good view of it, don't you think? Helps pass the time, watching the types that go in and out. Noticed you first about a week ago. Sent my assistant over, to see if there was more to you than an athletic walk."

Thanks. It's startlingly clear: the steps, the columns, the people looking satisfied and scholarly. There, leaving now, it's the girl who always sits across from me in the Reading Room, the one who plows through the books in front of her with such confidence it makes me sweat, the way she fills out all those little index cards on, what is it, Anglo-Saxon hagiology.

"I needn't tell you that you've been arriving later and leaving earlier since the second day you started. But perhaps you're not aware of how gloomy you've come to look. Worried in the morning, sad in the afternoon. It shows. Even from here."

I'm sure it does. Even from here. Dissertation blues.
Everyone says it'll happen. You get too tired, too strung out,
too bored and unsure of yourself to make the final effort and
finish. Yet you have to face it, day after day, for months,
months, years. Some people don't ever finish. They crack.

"Now it could be just the usual. I've seen many a doctoral
candidate drag her feet up those steps and eventually come
down smiling. But my spy tells me you've barely begun, she
says you seem unsure how to start."

Does the world really need three hundred and fifty foot-
noted, bibliographed and cross-indexed pages on Lawrence's
moon imagery? Forget the world; will they get me a job?

"It must be very difficult for you. Very taxing. The
tensions must be quite horrible."

Oh no. Yesterday, got on a bus and a woman's face turned
to bone right while I looked. A grinning skull. Nothing to it.
Went to buy a chop for dinner, saw strings of fingers in the
sausage case. Everyone says it'll happen. Just learn to live
with it.

"But I suppose you've reached some accommodation with
yourself. Found some way of coping with it all. You look a
strong girl. And surely you must think the suffering is worth
it, mustn't you? Though frankly I never found Lawrence
worth a moment of discomfort, let alone anguish."

Yes, well, many people don't like his work. She's probably
not what I thought at all. Can't confront sex in a book, let
alone life.

"Why a girl like you, or what I suspect a girl like you to be,
is writing about a man like him I'll never know. You'd have
disliked him intensely had you ever met him. But then,
considerations like that mustn't matter in the objective world
of academia. Whether or not you like a person should have no
bearing on your critical estimation of his work. Of course
that's quite impossible in real life."

What is she saying? Had she met Lawrence? It's possible I

guess. No, she's probably just a dotty old lady. Lonely and crazy as they come.

Still, the way she's looking at me, waiting for me to react. There's a little smile around her mouth. She's testing me.

"I did know them. To be honest, Lawrence only slightly. And then merely because I was trying to help Lesley Moore through a very difficult time." She reaches for a teacake and chews it slowly. She must know I want her to go on. But she has to wipe her hands on a napkin; place it on the teatray. Push the cart back a few inches.

"Mansfield was treating her abominably, as usual. But Lesley took to suffering like a duck to water. She always was a bit of a wet." Laughter. I can't listen to that exuberant kind without joining in. "But a friend nonetheless, even though her selflessness was a bore more times than I care to relate. That particular crisis had to do with Katherine going off with Middleton Murry, I always called him Muddleton Mary but never to his face, going off to Cornwall with Lawrence and Frieda in search of the idyllic country life. Leaving behind heartbroken Lesley. No good telling her Mansfield would realize how much she needed her, she always did eventually, and would call her to come running, which invariably happened.

"Once, just once, I would like to have seen Lesley show a little backbone and not let herself be thrown out and begged back. But she never did, she never said no. Mind you, it would have been hard for anyone close to Katherine to deny her. She did have the most beautiful brown eyes."

I can't believe it. She actually knew those people? Can talk about them as I would an old friend? This woman is a find!

"Nineteen fifteen I think that was. But you can check it out in any number of books if you care to. It's well documented, the London ménage, the two couples in Cornwall. The fact I tell you about it doesn't necessarily prove I knew them, does it? I may just know about them."

But, why is she saying this now to confuse me? Why tell me these things if they aren't true? I mean the facts are true, it's her participation that's open to question. If she's lying, then she's gone to an awful lot of trouble to find an audience.

"At this point, it isn't my desire to supply you with countless anecdotes about the past. No. In due time, due time, I will share with you some of what I know. The Woolfs, Carrington and Strachey, Duncan Grant, the Bells, the Nicolsons, Ottoline Morrell. Gertrude Stein briefly, and Alice of course. Roger Fry, Saxon Sydney-Turner, Radclyffe Hall. Friends some, acquaintances others. Oh there are things I could tell you. But not now, not now."

No, I really must draw back. This old lady has just said she knew an entire galaxy of Bloomsbury stars, and their satellites, in addition to Gertrude Stein off in an orbit of her own, plus Lawrence and Mansfield in their separate worlds. No, this just can't be. Virginia Woolf, Lytton Strachey, Radclyffe Hall — friends, or perhaps they were among her mere acquaintances. No. I'm being taken. I've never heard of Zoe Mohr before today. She can't have known those people and not be known to us; we've read their manuscripts, edited their letters, researched their milieu. She couldn't have been there and escaped our attention.

"Would you like to see a letter addressed to me and signed by, say, Virginia Woolf? Ha, ha, I bet you would. Well I don't have one. Would you know her signature if you saw it? Ah, you could have it authenticated, certainly. Virginia, who careened from one mood to another, often from one moment to the next, Virginia, who pulled herself out of madness time and again to create what she had to, was compelled to. Do you think her handwriting never varied through all that? That out of all that wild fluctuation her signature remained the same? A black line of sanity? Yet I'm quite sure if I were to produce such a document it would do much to increase your faith in my credibility. You would believe a piece of paper. You would trust a few scratchings of the pen."

It's true. I would. She makes me feel the lesser for it. Why am I gripping the seat cushion?

"Or a photograph. Yes, a photograph. You'd like a photograph wouldn't you? Carrington and I blinking in the sun at Tidmarsh. Or Leonard with his arm through mine in front of Monks House. Something easily verifiable, so that even if the faces are a little blurred, you can be positive about the house, or if the architecture seems faint, the people stand out. Something clear. Something real. Evidence.

"Of course I needn't remind you what experts in your country did to certain photographs in the McCarthy era. Very convincing evidence. Lives ruined on the basis of it. Absolute proof, a picture of two people talking. Behind the picture, there must be reality. You see the picture and assume the event. If you want to. You have a choice. Look at flying saucers. Hundreds of pictures, but only a handful of people believe them.

"Well I have no photographs. I have never needed a physical reminder of my own past. I don't need to reread a letter, or hold some faded photo in front of my eyes to remember.

"Oh I know what you can say, that they were mad for writing letters in those days. No telephone service for ever so long. Three, four, five letters a day were nothing; in fact, they were a way of life. And the photographs! My dear, such a sense of history they had. So many pictures the world would want to see some day. But it went deeper than that; there was also the great friendship they had for one another. Yes, deep friendship."

What is this woman doing? She brings me to the brink, then turns me around; gets me going and then tries to stop me. I don't know what to believe, or why it's so important to her that I come to some decision.

"This setting of the scene seems to take forever. Shall we have the tea hotted up?" She produces a small silver bell and shakes it several times. In walks the spy. I thought she'd looked out of place in the British Museum Reading Room. That flat face and those huge hands. "Ah Briggs, we'll have some more tea please."

Most muscular forearms on any woman I've ever seen. Not the most adroit emissary either, I'd barely understood a word when she approached me. It wasn't at all the proposition I thought she had in mind; sheer relief must have made me say yes. So here I am, drinking tea with an old shut-in whose only passion is for twentieth-century British literature.

"You've met Briggs. Been with me for years. Helps me with my therapy. Not overly bright in comparison, say, to someone like yourself, but good at her job. And loyal. Loyalty is such an admirable quality." Back comes loyal Briggs with the makings for fresh tea. She sets them down while managing a badly hidden glance in my direction, checking me out to make sure I'm not up to something dangerous with her employer. "Thank you, Briggs. That'll be all." Out she plods.

"Now, where was I? Oh yes. I'm afraid I may have misled you a bit earlier. You must realize, we were considerably younger than they were, fifteen or twenty years in some cases, less in others. That in itself would have been no great barrier, but we were also not quite of their class. In England that is a unique and far from comfortable experience. People like Mansfield and Lawrence were never really accepted by the others, you know. Yes of course you know that."

Indeed. The Midlands and New Zealand could never gain entry into Cambridge and the Civil Service. No literary credential in the world would get you admitted into the inner circle if you were a miner's son from the North or anyone's daughter from around Down Under. That was England by God, and Bloomsbury by choice.

"But I did tell you they were my friends and acquaintances. And they were, to a degree. It was possible. Quite possible, to see them, talk with them, go to the country or ballet with them, even to sleep with them. Without being of them. One could do such things if one had certain gifts, if one were amusing, attractive, or curious in some way. Brilliant, immensely talented. Being rich didn't count on its own; one had to carry at least one of these other qualities along with one's fortune. Then the doors would open, the outer ones at least."

What was her entry card? Looks, I'll wager. Money too? What did she bring?

"Oh dear, I hadn't really meant to go into all this now. I'm trying very hard to get beyond these prefatory remarks, but they want to go on and on. I must learn to exercise more control. Well, I'll just finish up this bit and then we can get down to it.

"England, you may not have surmised, is my adopted country. It was meant to be Portugal, as it was for many middle Europeans. But my parents never got there, and since I was already here for schooling, I hadn't much choice but to stay.

"So I could be excused, you see, though never totally accepted, for lacking certain proprieties. In addition, I have never wanted for funds. And, to be perfectly honest, I possessed a few other attributes somewhat in demand." Modesty was probably not one of them. "I listened well, learned to gossip wickedly, and cut a rather striking figure. Understand, we had many philosophies of . . . life, in common. Shared certain beliefs about personal relationships, individual behavior, that sort of thing." She checks to see if I'm following her. "You seem to know what I mean. We made a cult of rational bisexuality."

I hope she realizes that not everyone with an "athletic walk" would have been receptive to this.

"We believed in it. In theory and practice, though some found it easier to hold with the former and not the latter. And vice versa in a few cases. Actually most leaned much more in one direction than another. They did a turnabout occasionally, sometimes from whim or passion, but primarily when it was expected of them. Naturally, there were combinations, many of us involved in ones which were more or less comfortable, depending on the degree of our rationality.

"There." She fusses with the robe over her legs, sort of squares her shoulders, clasps her hands in her lap, then turns those sharp black eyes on me. "Well? Am I to be believed?" She must feel she's done her part and it's up to me to do mine, for there's an impatient insistence to her voice now that I find pressuring. "Come, come. I know quite well you've been sitting there all this time doing nothing but trying to make up your mind about that. First it's one way, then another, now yes, now no, it could be, it couldn't. Your face, child, reads like a book. At the moment a not too interesting, rather slim volume. I wonder now if you've enough experience to appreciate . . . perhaps I've made a mistake."

If I were six years old, my legs would dangle and my feet wouldn't touch the floor. This huge armchair would have expanses of green silk untouched by my little body. It would hold me, my small weight would mean nothing to it, while the stern lady scowled at me and said I had to choose.

"Do you think it was easy? Finding you and getting you here? Have you any idea of the patience, and thoughtful planning it took? The number of times I've waited here, by the window, waited for Briggs to appear. The countless disappointing moments of seeing her leave the Museum alone. Another failed day gone by. Another unrewarded vigil. But there would be a new day, and my hopes would rise again, only to be crushed again, and again, until they barely lived at all, and I despaired of your existence."

Something in common there.

"Oh, and the time so ripe! If the time were not so ripe, the agony would have been diminished, the frustration not so

great. It would have . . . what is it, Briggs?" She had come
in and is hovering nearby, a bottle of pills and glass of water in
her hands. "What, time already? Oh very well, give them
here." Briggs hands them to her and bends to straighten her
blanket, tuck it in, fluff the pillow behind her back. "Don't
pother over me so! Here, take this away." She thrusts the
empty glass in Briggs' direction. The faithful attendant
hesitates, looking down at her charge with worried eyes. "For
heaven's sake, Briggs, do take this away. I am fine, perfectly
all right, a bit of agitation is not going to kill me. Not yet."

Reluctantly, Briggs takes the glass and leaves, but not
without a silent, somewhat menacing glance at me first. Loyal
she is, but it's I who could use a little protection at this point.
Though from what I'm not exactly sure. This woman is
drawing me in. She is pulling at me. I feel the strain, and it's
so tiring, this holding back.

"Perhaps I'm being unfair, requiring an answer of you now.
Yes." She frowns, staring down into the plaid blanket.
"Perhaps it is too soon. I had thought . . . perhaps you
needn't . . ." She lifts her head. "Right. It comes from
planning too much out ahead of time. Robs one of flexibility.
Let's continue, shall we?"

You mean I've been reprieved? Nothing's required for the
moment? Well then, by all means. Let's continue. Who
knows, maybe I'll even begin to understand what this is all
about.

"I'd thought it absolutely essential that you believe me
when I said I knew people from that era who came to be
recognized by the entire world for their profound influence on
literature and the arts. I thought, you see, that if you believed
me about them, you'd have to believe me about a relationship
with someone I'm quite sure you've never heard of. Someone
whose existence is almost impossible to document. Yet
someone whose influence on literature would have been, had
her work survived, every bit as profound as Virginia's. Yes, I

am convinced of it. Julia Carroll was a literary genius, and had she not married Edward Gordon, the world would know it today."

Oh now really. What's she trying to hand me, a Lost Bloomsbury?

"Have you ever considered, though I suppose it's idle speculation, how many of Virginia's books we wouldn't have today were it not for Leonard? Oh, I don't mean just that he set up Hogarth Press primarily with her needs in mind — it was a cunning form of therapy you know, in addition to its publication benefits. No, I mean the way in which Leonard controlled Virginia's environment in order to nurture her genius. Some say Virginia never had a chance to get well, with Leonard putting her to bed at the slightest sign of exhaustion, keeping everyone away from her at the merest trace of irrationality. Not being a psychiatrist, I'm no judge of that. But I do know that without such care, such dedication to her genius and sensitivity to her mood, it's a good bet many of those books would never have matured to completion. Born? probably, her brilliance couldn't be contained, but completed? not likely. Not without Leonard there to turn their every dwelling into a hothouse, where Virginia's writing could flourish and her fragile stability be protected. Mind you, Leonard had his faults, indeed he did, but I must give him credit for this, for relegating his own needs to second place. Where they assuredly belonged. He could have done much worse with his life than be handmaiden to Virginia, but nothing better that I can think of."

I'm inclined to agree. Zoe Mohr and I seem to share more than one bias. Still, what of Julia Whoever and her nasty husband — was that a bombshell or a dud?

"I fully recognize, of course, that not every sort of genius requires such treatment. Yet I can't help comparing Julia's circumstances to Virginia's. Both of them so gifted and tormented, fighting what were basically the same battles.

Except Virginia had Leonard for an ally, while Julia had . . .
only me. And I wasn't enough. It wasn't me she married."
Silence. Her eyes are on nothing here. I'm afraid the reverie
will last a long time, but no, she's shaking herself out of it.

"In any case, a discussion at this point on the conditions
under which the creative potential thrives or dies is not
something I wish to pursue." Oh yes, she's recovered. "I'm
certain we'll have occasion to talk about this and many other
interesting topics at a later time. Once you've agreed, we'll
have ever so many of these afternoon chats to look forward to."

She will go along dropping her little explosive charges won't
she. Now it's once I've agreed. Agreed to what? What? Will
she never get to it? Much more of this and I'll be so worn
down I'll have no resistance to anything.

"Once you've agreed, as I say, to take on the task, we'll be
working very closely. We'll help each other delve into the
past, discover what's there, and report the findings. The
results, of course, will go out under your name, I wouldn't hear
of it any other way. The transcription, the actual writing, will
be up to you; that's as it should be. That, after all, is why you
are here."

She leans back, looking quite proud of herself, thinking no
doubt she's explained everything, and what's more, explained
it to my satisfaction as well as hers. But I've got news for . . .
her face starts to change, to lose its smugness. "Painful as this
will be for me, I'm glad it's going to happen." The lines
around her mouth seem to have deepened. "Unearthing the
past, bringing these people . . . to life. Seeing them. Their
moments of beauty. Desperation. The world will see too.
We'll show them, we'll illuminate the truth. And Julia, Julia
will have what she wanted. At last." She thrusts her head
forward, as if I dare to deny her words. "And I will give it to
her. I will."

She relaxes, apparently freed from her visions. "With your
help of course."

I am beginning to see. Talk of illumination. Oh ho, the woman must be mad to think I'll drop everything for this, this questionable little project of hers.

"You will do it, won't you." She makes it a statement. Takes a lot for granted, she does. Thinks I'll drop my work on Lawrence just like that. Chuck all my preparation, to prowl around on the track of some lost literary giant. Some crazed genius who traipsed in and out of Bloomsbury without a trace. Some woman who just happens to have been her lover.

"Your dissertation, your book." Yet, if she really were all that, "I am offering you a life, four lives, hidden until now." The earth would shake in more than a few circles. "Even if my estimation of Julia Carroll Gordon's literary achievement were incorrect, if she were less than I say," it could still create quite a stir. "Even then, wouldn't it be worth it? The opportunity, the chance to explore, to see for yourself? To live another's life, in addition to your own? Can you afford not to accept?" I don't know, I'm wondering. "Is the step I ask you to take so very frightening?"

Frankly, yes. It does scare me a little, the whole idea seems so free-floating. Just her word, and off I'd go. Nothing to fall back on, nothing for support. No assurances. No reality, but what she'd offer.

"Think of the rewards, if you must, if the excitement of discovery isn't enough for you. Think of what you'll find, what you can learn, and of what it might do for you personally. I mean in addition to if you publish. Think. Imagine. Feel." I am. I am.

"Say you'll do it."

I don't know.

"You'll do it."

I need time.

"You will."

This is crazy. "You'll do it."

Yes. I will, I'll do it.

"I knew you'd go along! Briggs!" Much ringing of the bell. "Briggs!" What does she mean Old Faithful to do — lift me onto those broad shoulders and march me triumphantly around the room? I only intend taking a week or so to see if there's any truth to the tale. "Briggs girl! Cause for celebration, break out the gin!"

II

For two afternoons, I've sat in an armchair and listened. Now I find myself sitting on a train that's heading south of London. Zoe Mohr has suggested that I might want to visit the boarding school they attended, where it all began. She doubts there'll be any records I can verify; either a fire in '28 or a stray buzz bomb in '44, she's not sure which, destroyed the administration wing. But she thinks it's worth a visit, and I've no reason not to agree. I seem to have suspended reason for a while. The sense of going, moving, doing almost in a vacuum is a strange one; I literally do find "me" on a train traveling to an English boarding school two girls might have gone to sixty years ago. I don't feel foolish, but there is a weird absence of ego, temporarily making me a willing object to be pointed in any direction.

Rolling past my window are endless segments of houses and wires, suburbia with an accent. It's hard to remember that in 1912 and for many years thereafter, the school grounds actually were in real countryside, remote from the city.

Another world. Hills, spacious lawns with trimmed box hedges, trees, paths, and on a rise the country manor. School for the select, home away from home for the daughters of privilege. In those years sent away to learn, not the Latin, Greek, history, of their brothers, but certain of those domestic and drawing room sciences befitting young ladies of birth. If solicited, there might be a tutorial for the daring few who demanded their right to an education, though they might never find a university willing to accept them into its sanctified halls. For the rest, there was some form of studies, and for all, a strictly regulated life.

"Because the weight of the Empire did not rest on our shoulders," Zoe Mohr had said, "because the very backbone of England was not forged from our spines, because, in short, we were women, we were spared a few of the Eton-Harrow horrors. There was, for example, very little of that nasty sado-masochistic brutality the English seem to think is so good for a man's character. We had no 'fagging' equivalent, no apple-cheeked youngsters made to toast our buns — forgive me, it is not my words which make the image so blatantly sexual — or clean our boots. There was no proof of womanhood required on the playing field or in the locker room."

But they were more restricted, had less privacy, fewer privileges. Nor did they escape the inevitable. Status, power, knowledge all dispensed by one sex. Affection, sympathy, excitement all to be found in one sex. The farthest horizon was the nearby town, the closest source of comfort perhaps the bed next to one's own. What secrets were shared. What passions stirred, to be sated or frustrated, depending.

I decline their offer of a girl guide. Having found their grounds and massive oak entry hall on my own, I want to continue that way, without having some sixth-former chosen for her good grades or ability to meet the public getting in between me and the environment. They assume I have some architectural-historical motivation for wanting to walk around: the main house is centuries old, and I won't find stables like theirs being built anymore; though the coach house has been remodeled into a little theater and the sleeping quarters, naturally, have been renovated, the library and classrooms are much the same as they were at the turn of the century, except for the addition of electricity. The latter three areas are restricted to students, but I'm free to see the rest if I so desire. Which is fine, because all I really want to do, now that I'm here, is get a sense of it.

This is the port of entry, the place where Zoe Mohr and Julia Carroll first came into each other's lives. Weathered

The council of prefects, convened to pass judgment on fellow-students found violating school rules.

"I for one am prepared to treat Fielding-Smythe with leniency. It's her horse had to be put down, and she is a new girl. Carroll, on the other hand, has no fit defense that I can see. It's just like her to do something like this."

"Quite. She's never had much regard for the rules here or those of us who live by them."

"What d'you mean by that?"

"Surely, Mohr, even someone with your limited sense of propriety can't have failed to notice how Miss Julia Carroll comports herself." Always going off alone, never joining in or pulling her fair share. "Miss Julia Carroll need only keep a faraway look in her eyes and commune with the rabbits."

"She does love animals, Byrnes, that's why she's in this mess. Why do you think Fielding-Smythe turned to her in her grief?" Because Carroll would understand. She'd know the girl's need was more important than any rule. So both of them were out after lock-up, keeping vigil over a dying horse. To Mohr it was a lovely and sensitive thing to do, to ease someone's grief regardless of the consequences to oneself. She didn't know Carroll well, but she would make an effort to after this.

"What you seem to be forgetting, is that Carroll is a sixth-former who willfully broke the rules, whether to suit herself or out of some brave compassion doesn't matter."

Obviously, Carroll and Fielding-Smythe had to be made examples of. They debated subtle variations of punishment until Fielding-Smythe's was agreed upon.

"The chair will so recommend. Now, what's to be done with Carroll?"

"One month Sunday shut-in, and one month restriction to grounds."

"That's hardly severe enough to my mind. Why not combine the both for two months?"

"No, no one should be restricted to grounds for that long. Not to get away from this place for eight weeks would drive even the strongest into a lunatic asylum."

"I'm with Mohr. We only get but one skimpy afternoon in town as it is. Tell me I'd not have even that for two months, and I'd throw myself off Sealey's Peak."

"That was a savage thing to say."

"What? Oh for heaven's sake, Mohr, I was not referring to Jennie Hilbreth."

"Our only suicide in over a decade. It does seem that whenever Miss Carroll chooses to involve herself with someone in distress, they end up worse off than they started. Lucky for Fielding-Smythe the groom didn't shoot her by mistake, if Jennie Hilbreth's fate is anything to go by."

"Byrnes! That happened over three years ago and bears absolutely no relation to the problem at hand."

"As I recall, Mohr, you were the one who reacted to an innocent remark and made us all think about poor Hilbreth's fall. The fact that Carroll happened to be with her on Sealey's Peak when it happened . . ."

"Are you trying to say she pushed her?"

"Nothing so gauche as that. But Carroll didn't stop her, did she?"

"You don't actually think she knew Hilbreth was going to do it?"

"Well they were the closest of confidantes." And after Hilbreth's accident with the oil lamp, Carroll was just about the only one who could stand to look at the girl, let alone spend any time with her. "That hideous, scarred face, I don't know how Carroll could bear being near it."

"It's obvious Hilbreth felt the same way, isn't it? What makes you think Carroll could have saved her? D'you think Hilbreth just kissed her on the cheek, said 'Well, guess I'll be off now,' then turned around and leaped?"

"I'm sure I've no idea, Mohr. The kissing on the cheek part certainly sounds credible."

"I swear, Byrnes, if we were allowed to duel like the Germans I'd call you out for that!" Sheer principle kept her rising to the defense.

"Careful, Mohr."

"You'd best calm down, Mohr."

A decision was reached, the terms laid out to Julia Carroll. She accepted them, the confinement to room and grounds for whatever period the committee had agreed upon, "as if we'd actually done her a favor. As if our restrictions fit into some plan of hers, or were precisely the sort of thing she meant to do herself. She listened to the penalties being read to her with a look on her face of . . . serenity, or perhaps it was triumph, a quiet triumph. Byrnes was furious." And Mohr was enthralled.

She'd never really "seen" Julia Carroll prior to then. Mohr had her set of friends and Carroll had, it seemed, no set at all. She was a floater, disinclined to membership in any group; she was odd, apart, yet reachable. Once or twice she'd let herself be drawn into brief attachments of an intensity no one was ever quite sure of, including the other girl involved. It was rumored that Miss Pitt, the drawing instructress, had resigned because of her, but if so, Julia Carroll seemed not to know. Ever since Jennie Hilbreth, she was accustomed to attracting a rumor whenever it had no other place to settle. Being looked upon as a "noble" creature was something new.

For Mohr's eyes had truly beheld, and they would not be turned aside. Unfortunately, this person she had stupidly never paid attention to was now too often hidden from view. Sundays she couldn't see her thin figure moving in its distracted fashion from sitting room to terrace, or along the pathway to a favorite bench in the woods. She couldn't watch her hair turning to amber in the sunlight. Those eyes that liked to focus inward to hidden places. The aristocratic nose. Cheekbones that gave structure and shadow to her face, the lips that suffered from being chewed during meditation. All, locked inside a dim, badly heated room. Mohr came to hate the sound of church bells; they signaled a day of deprivation.

She was determined to become Julia Carroll's friend. "But I felt rather like a Saint Bernard lumbering after a young giraffe. It wasn't easy. I was afraid to interfere with her solitude, afraid to speak lest I say something totally inappropriate, afraid for this, afraid of that. All the usual fears one has in these circumstances. One's own inadequacies become so glaring, while the other's perfections never cease multiplying.

"On Town Days she liked going on long hikes rather than giggling around shops with the others. I used to follow her when I could." Staying far enough back, she thought, to escape detection, she'd watch the tall, long-skirted figure make her way over creeks and through meadows, up dusty hills, sometimes all the way to Sealey's Peak. The girl moved awkwardly but always, it seemed to Mohr at least, with a sense of purpose. Trying to keep pace was difficult; on several occasions she felt the hiker meant to walk herself into exhaustion. Other times the girl would throw herself onto the ground and lie for hours without moving, yet not be asleep. Some days she'd take a walking stick and beat at every weed or bush she passed, as if it were an enemy, or reminded her of one.

The special time was when Mohr lost track of her in a grove of pines. It was a tiring, uphill trek, the last part done almost in a crouch. Reaching the treeline, Mohr paused to catch her breath, head down, hands and knees sinking into years of fallen pine needles. When she looked up, there was Julia Carroll not a dozen feet away, looking back at her and laughing. Standing in a clearing, the sunlight full on her. The smell of pine. The sky. Sound of laughter, throaty but full, open, enjoying itself in the rarefied air.

"Well, come on then." She was holding out her hand.

From then on, whenever weather permitted, they hiked together. Sometimes, though, Carroll gave the impression

Mohr wasn't there. Her face would be tight, closed, and Mohr would look at her apprehensively, wanting to break through to her, to help, but reading all too clearly the warning she mustn't even approach. Yet on other walks the girl would talk and laugh and make Mohr feel so glad to be alive, so happy to be there with her, blessed by her voice, her eyes, that she would have to fight back the unmanly impulse to cry.

"Whatever's the matter?"

"Nothing."

"You are a silly girl. Come, I'll show you the Isadora Duncan rock. Look, stand here by me, look, d'you see? Her profile on top there, so Grecian, staring off over the valley with such sublime composure. Then the way that glisteny vein of stone seems to drop in folds down that narrow part like some ancient toga? Oh surely you see that. And look, look, that small outcrop, that's her foot, poised for the next movement which will spring so naturally from the one she just did. Or so the theory goes. I never could get the hang of it. After one excruciating month of lessons I persuaded Mother to let me stop. She would put me through such dreadful agonies, determined that this singularly angular body of mine would somehow transform itself into the epitome of grace if only I put my obstinate little mind to it. But I mean, Mohr, can't you just see me? ten years old and leaping through the grass in my small white tunic like some wounded stork?" She proceeded to demonstrate, contorting her body into a classic pose of grief, then springing outward in a great leap that was never meant for the display of hiking boots. She landed with knees bent and elbows at the most awkward of angles, then bounded off again. What made it all absurdly funny was the regal carriage of her head and the look of haughty self-possession on her face.

If Mohr's stomach didn't burst she might recover. Carroll dropped to her knees beside her, rolled over laughing, and lay back with arms behind her head. She had small, even teeth. Eyes looking at the sky were flecked with green and brown, and yellow. Mohr wanted to touch the blush on her cheek.

"Oh but Mohr, to be able to control one's body. Really control it. How grand it would be. To dance. To be able to express that moment of joy one sometimes gets, when only dancing will do it justice. Haven't you ever felt that way? I have. Choreographed an entire ballet while sitting in a chair, feeling my body do the most intricate and abandoned movements. Yet I don't know the first thing about dance. But in that moment, I know. Like in a dream, Mohr. You know the sort of dream where you seem to have the answers to all sorts of things you never knew you even understood before? Then you wake up in complete ignorance. And you feel such a dreadful sense of loss. Like that."

She sat up and picked at the grass. Ripping it out, throwing it away, blade by blade. "Have you seen the Russians? Last year, the Ballet Russe? They know. They are magnificent. They know how to . . . to bring together everything that's important. They keep only the essence, Mohr, and discard anything that doesn't illuminate the core. It's so pure, and vital. Everything's made to work for them, for their idea.

"And Nijinsky. Oh if ever there was a god. His body. For half an hour I watched one muscle in his calf. One muscle. The way it moved." She was looking at it in the distance, Mohr supposed. Resting on one arm, a forgotten blade of grass in her mouth. In her own time she would return. "Do you know, Mohr," Carroll was actually giggling, "I think I've developed a passion for Nijinsky's leg? I want to take it home with me and lavish caresses upon it! I can hear Mother now, 'Well, dear, at least it belongs to a man and I suppose one must look upon that as some improvement.' "

More laughter and noise, the both of them giving in to it, unable to stop, not wanting to. It exhausted them, and for a while they were forced to lie quietly while chests stopped heaving and stomach muscles relaxed.

Carroll turned to look at the girl beside her. "But you can

do it, Mohr. You can control your body. I've watched you."

"You have?" Mohr's face; from inside her head she felt it get hot. To hide, yet stay and hear more.

"Often. Playing at sports. You're glorious on the field. Yes, you are, don't you know that? Lithe, powerful, your arms and legs going precisely where you wish them to, your body all at one with itself." She sat up abruptly. "Dance for me."

No sound from Mohr's mouth, gone slack.

"Mohr?"

"No. I couldn't."

"Yes. Dance for me. I want to see you, Zoe."

"No. No! I can't."

"Yes you can. Stand up. Stand up, girl." Reluctantly Mohr got to her feet and stood before her. She felt heavy, her arms hung like weights at her side, and she couldn't look at the eyes moving over her shoulders, breasts, legs.

"Show me, Zoe. Show me your body."

Startled eyes. "What?" It came out strangled.

"Your body, you silly goose! Show me how it moves. What did you think I meant?"

"I, I . . ." She had started to shake. Never could she control the shivers of anger when they chose to take over. She could have hit her. She could have yelled at her and let ugly tears gush about. Instead, she wheeled around and walked away, taking her red face and clenched fists out of sight.

They tramped back to the school in silence. Just before going in, Carroll said, "You know, Mohr, you really should stay out of the sun more. You're positively brown. It's most unladylike." She went up the steps, leaving Mohr behind to deal with it.

But there were other days.

"Mohr! Mohr! Come, you must help me! You must pose for me. But you must! Middle of term and my portfolio is empty. Empty! I must be mad to've let it go so long. I'm in a state, Mohr, and you shall just have to put aside your silly shyness and let me draw you. We're off to the meadow, I can do you and a few landscapes this afternoon if we hurry."

Carrying an easel and a folding stool, Mohr obediently followed the agitated girl. The sun was wrong. The shadows too vague. The grass, why must the grass be so straggly on the very day she meant to capture it in gentle waves? They'd set up here. No. There. No. Over there. Oh very well, here then. "Do be quick, Mohr. And take off that ridiculous hat, I can't see your face. Why ever are you wearing that thing, anyway?" Carroll had started in making quick movements over her sketch pad. Gradually she looked at her model with decreasing frequency, growing absorbed in her work.

"Won't I get too much color sitting out in the sun like this?"

"What?"

"My face, won't it . . ."

"Oh twaddle. You're a lovely nut-brown. You must have the courage to go against convention, Mohr. Look at Isadora. Look at Nijinsky. Look at my lovely 'crazies,' as old Pitt used to call them. The way she'd lean over my shoulder, breathe a breath decidedly unpleasant, and say 'You must learn to draw to Royal Academy standards, Carroll. I'll not have you putting those "crazies" from Paris and their artistic abominations up on a pedestal, d'you hear?' And half the time she'd rip the sheet off my pad, crumple it up, and command me to 'Begin again, young lady, and this time do it properly or I'll have you sent before Head Mistress.' "

"And would you?"

"Sometimes. Other times I'd force out a tear or two, clutch her hand and sob, 'Oh please, Miss Pitt. Please, just for today let me be Cézanne?' Or some such thing. Van Gogh for an hour. Matisse for a minute. It always took her quite aback, those pleas of mine. She'd get this odd look on her face, rather like fear, and give in, as if she were placating a distraught stranger who at any moment might turn upon her."

"Poor Pitt. Where is she now, I wonder?"

"Living with a cousin in Cornwall. I get little notes from

her now and then, all about discipline and the soul, art and the spirit, God and the Royal Academy. There. Finished, I think."

"May I see it?"

"Later. I shall do two or three quick landscapes, and then give a grand exhibit, with you my single viewer."

Mohr lay on the grass and watched her. The weather really had been kind to them lately. There'd been so many of these outings together, with Carroll deciding their goal and Mohr happily going along with whatever she'd chosen for them to do on their Wednesday "specials." As long as they could be alone, as long as she could look at Carroll and listen to her talk, Mohr didn't care where they went or what they did. In those hours Carroll was hers. Carroll had given her the gift of her thoughts, knowing Mohr would accept them with all the regard such a trust merited. For her own part, Mohr had silently given her entire self over to the girl; she was attached to her, they could have been sewn together and it wouldn't have made the two more into one. So Mohr felt, idling away the hours while Carroll sketched.

"Well? What do you think?" The sketches were propped against a rock, three landscapes and the figure study fluttering in the breeze. Mohr walked up to them and looked at each one closely while Carroll looked at her. "Well? Give me an opinion."

"Well. They're, uh . . ."

"Mohr. There are times when I wish you to lie to me, and there are times when I wish the truth. This is a truth time."

"Yes, I know."

"Oh. Then they're no good, are they?"

"They seem . . . muddled. Not one thing, not another."

"I was rather hoping you wouldn't notice that."

"I'm sorry. But . . . you know the 'idea' you talk about, the 'core'? Well, it's not there, I don't get any sense of it in the drawings."

"Oh Lord, Mohr, I don't ask your opinion about much, but

when I do . . . You're right, there's no vision behind them. None. No illumination, no essence. Everything I admire is missing."

"Aren't you expecting too much of yourself? After all, you haven't studied for that many years, and Miss Pitt was certainly no master artist."

"Help me gather everything together, will you? Watch the easel leg, it doesn't fold the way it should."

"Wait a moment. I hate to see you getting so depressed. They aren't bad sketches, you know."

"They are insignificant scratches on a page. When am I going to find it, Mohr? I can't dance, I sing atrociously, absolutely no ear at all, I've tried very earnestly to master the piano and can't get beyond the simplest Handel sonata. And it's clear I'll never be a painter either."

"What about the stage?" Mohr asked half-jokingly. "Bernhardt can't go on forever."

"Acting, Mohr, is something I do every day of my life. People certainly aren't going to pay to see me do it on the stage when they can knock on the door for free. It's my second nature, or perhaps my first, I'm not sure which."

They were walking back, Carroll with her head down and Mohr anxiously looking at her. Had she only known how much was at stake, she would have handled it differently, somehow. But Carroll had acted as if, well there it was, Carroll had "acted" as if the important thing was to finish her portfolio on time. She hadn't given Mohr a clue that it was also some sort of test of her talent, and that she meant to make a permanent decision on the basis of it.

"How can you be so sure the vision won't come to you later? After you've worked on your technique some more, or something like that?"

"Mohr, when you're tone deaf you don't need to be told. Well I'm, I don't know what to call it, the graphic equivalent, and I . . ."

The grass rustled, and suddenly Carroll was shrieking and clinging to her. "What is it? Julia, what's the matter?" The girl's fingernails were digging into her arm, her eyes were wide with fear. "Julia! Tell me what it is!" She was sobbing, shaking her head, unable to talk. Instinctively Mohr put her arms around her and held the quivering body against her own. "Julia, it's all right, sshh now, it's all right," and without realizing, she began to kiss her hair, her neck, blindly trying to soothe her.

As the sobs lessened, Mohr became fully conscious of their bodies' touching. How small the girl's shoulders were, how easily they fit into her arms. Breasts pushed gently against her own. Groins, soft mounds, nudged each other. Heat there. Throbbing.

"Julia." Her mouth was so dry, "Julia." She held her tighter.

The girl drew back. "I'm all right now."

Mohr had never felt that lonely so quickly; the front of her body turned cold. She tested her voice, "What was it? What happened?"

"It was a mouse. A field mouse. It ran right in front of me, I almost stepped on it."

"I don't believe it. You? You love animals. I can't believe you became so utterly terrified because of a little field mouse."

"Believe what you like." She stooped to retrieve some of the equipment they had dropped.

"Don't be angry. It's just that I would never have suspected it of you."

"I hate them. I loathe mice of any kind."

"If you say so. But I never . . ."

"Mohr! Let's not go on about it. Here, take these. We'll have to run or they'll take away our tea."

Before going to bed that night, they met in the hallway. Carroll looked haggard and Mohr became worried. "Are you sure you're all right?"

"It's an omen, Zoe. I know it. Seeing that . . . creature. Today, when I've been hiking round there for years without ever spotting one before."

"It's the weather. You know how unusual it's been this year. It was probably out looking for water."

Carroll was staring at the wall. "No. No. It's an omen. I feel it. Something horrible."

"That's just superstitious nonsense. You're talking yourself into it."

"No. I know what I see." She laughed halfheartedly. "Life. That this should be the vision I'm granted. Either I garbled up the message, or it's the Fates, trying to be funny." She walked toward her room. "I really wish they wouldn't do that."

While Carroll waited for something to happen, Mohr was constantly going back to what had taken place. She relived the meadow scene over and over, altering it to her desires. At the point where Julia pulled away, she had her stay instead, and say with total trust, "You'll always protect me, won't you." Arms crept behind Mohr's neck.

"Yes. Oh yes." Such a firm back, skin so smooth beneath the blouse. Hand moving slowly, seeking. Soft flesh, nipple, her thumb felt it rising.

"Dearest Zoe, I always want to be with you." Lips on Mohr's ear.

"I love you, Julia." Bodies pressing. "I love you." Their cheeks slid apart, mouths found each other.

The kiss. It always stopped with that. She'd never experienced a truly passionate kiss and her imagination didn't quite know what to do with one. But she tried to really feel the sensations that came to her, directed by the mind.

Weeks spent that way, the two of them knowing different tensions, drawn to opposing times, yet still sharing the same external world. Then the news came proving Carroll correct. Her brother Jordan was on the *Titanic*, intending to join up with their American cousins for a grand tour of the United States. A graduation present.

Mohr was given no chance to see her before they took her away. The school couldn't be expected to cope with her when she got into those states, and quite frankly, they hoped Mrs. Carroll would find instruction for her elsewhere, after she recovered. If she recovered. Once before, when Jennie Hilbreth had died, she'd been taken out of school for a few months. Mohr remembered; it hadn't mattered to her then. Now, she felt her life destroyed.

The school has since been surrounded by the town so it's difficult to be sure. But to the north, there are some development homes which wind along what might have been a decent-sized hill before it was graded into streets. If that is what's left, then I shall have to go back to Zoe Mohr and tell her Sealey's Peak is gone.

III

"I'M NOT SURPRISED." She seems quite perky at the news.
Hands me my cup of tea, her black eyes sparkling. "The fact
there is no Sealey's Peak merely adds further support to my
theory about the past. It's one's mind, not things, that keep
the past alive. Things break or get lost. They fade, crumble.
Now you report that even mountains can disappear. Ah, but
not one's memories. Over the years they grow and become
richer, more precious. They indeed last a lifetime, my dear,
some of them at any rate. Those that one needs."

If I'd thought to shake her by the news, I've failed.
Evidently there's still some residue of doubt in me that made
me want to try. A little testing of her reactions. An attempt,
perhaps, to undermine her story. I can't help feeling there
should have been something at the school for me to verify,
some "thing" to measure against her word. All I found were
implanted memories; very real ones at the time, strangely real.
But now that their immediacy has receded, I'm looking for
proof again.

"One thing you can be sure I'm correct about is the
'openness' of your face. I can see you're still not fully
convinced about any of this. All I can suggest, really, is that
you give me time. However, I don't mean to spend it
constantly engaged in little games of proof. I am not a
scientist, far from it. If you continue to persist in this
quantitative attitude, requiring items that can be tested or
compared or measured in support of what I say, then you
belong in a laboratory, far removed from these proceedings."

She so easily manages to place me on the defensive.

"I wish there were something to show you. Before the last war, that is the last European war, I used to have a Giles Carroll pot that I was very, very fond of. It would be lovely indeed, for both our sakes, to have it still." Her hand trembles as she puts her cup back on the tray. "Dear Giles. He was a kind person, sweet. Julia's eldest brother. He, too, had talent, but he was able to enjoy his. He accepted it for its own sake. Didn't feel compelled to search beyond it, or through it. The difference, you see, when there is no genius behind one's artistry."

Silence for a while. Thinking about Julia? I don't know, I'm no good at second-guessing her.

"Giles was fortunate enough, while studying at the Slade, to get to know Duncan Grant. The nature of that relationship was never quite clear to me; I think, however, given Giles' preference for stalwart young men outside his own class, there was nothing sexual to it. But, whether there was or wasn't isn't really important. What did matter was that through Duncan, Giles got involved with Roger Fry's Omega Workshop, designing ceramics. Pots, plates, fireplace tiles. Others were doing furniture and textiles; anything man was likely to need, someone in that workshop was eager to design. Marvelous enthusiasts. They saw themselves at the forefront of the arts, engaged in a sublime combination of the artistic and the functional, actually influencing man's environment rather than creating in private for themselves and a select few.

"Giles and I used to argue, though, about whether they'd really succeeded in defining the artist's role in relation to society, as he thought, or had actually found new outlets for the artistic impulse, as I maintained. But to my mind that was by no means a lesser achievement. Which would he prefer, I'd ask, a new art form or a new definition of the artist?"

She seems inclined to ramble today. Not at all disposed to getting back to her relationship with Julia.

"Well. At any rate, Giles remained a loyal supporter of the

workshop, even after he had split with them over the issue of pacifism. In those days everything was related."

And by now I should be used to it. But I still can't get over the way everyone knew everyone else, and all of them were involved in the most important movements of their day. Art, literature, economics, politics — they were either changing it themselves or sleeping with someone who was. That they should all have known each other seems as fantastic to me as Zoe Mohr's having known most of them.

"Fact is, I first met Giles in a French hospital shortly before the Armistice. And if I hadn't, I honestly do not know if Julia would ever have come back into my life. Meeting Giles was an instance of something I suppose everyone experiences at least once, when time and chance seem to conspire to create a turning point. November, nineteen eighteen — I'm not likely to forget mine."

It takes several afternoons to tell me about that "momentous chapter" in her life. The story clings to me as if my own mind had created it. Not an entirely pleasant sensation. There are moments when I feel my life has been taken over, and I must fight against it.

Yet even London doesn't give me sufficient relief. I find myself choosing a G. B. Shaw revival instead of the latest West End production, knowing "they" might well have seen the same play. Visit the Tower; the Thames is cleaner now than it was to their eyes. At Buckingham Palace they could have watched the changing of the guards' grandfathers, though I doubt they would have. Big Ben must be ringing the same tone. Parliament's the same, Chelsea isn't. Comparisons are unavoidable because "they" are always hovering around my awareness.

When parts of the story come to me, it doesn't matter where I am. On a walk, at the theater, in a pub or museum, parts of it simply come to me, and when they do, it's not Zoe Mohr's aged face I see, but a young one belonging to her. Not her voice I hear, but their voices.

Giles', a little high and lacking in timbre: "I ask you, Zoe, how could I be expected to pass up all those uniformed country boys longing for the comforts of home and dear old Mum? 'Never fear, dear, Mother's here!' became a welcome cry in more than one trench, I can tell you. I wrote Strachey saying he was an absolute fool for getting those medical releases, that by March I expected to have buggered my way across half of France. And all those C.O. fellows spending the best of their years plowing potatoes — potatoes! at Philip Morrell's place. When they got my letters about what I'd been plowing over here, they must've turned green as spring peas!"

"I'd no idea it was such a dangerous pastime," her laugh clear, low, yet too young to be mellow.

With the Armistice near, many women from the Ambulance Column had been sent back to London. She'd managed to stay on, although more and more her duties centered around the hospital rather than the field. There was a great deal of sorting to be done now that the number of men freshly mangled or killed had been reduced. The time had come, or so it was thought, to see just who the survivors were and what was needed for them and their families. It was on some list or other that she'd seen the name Giles Carroll. Merely reading it had made her stomach react the way it did on those awful night runs, when wounded men screamed as she jolted them over shell holes no driver could avoid.

She'd gone to see him. It might have been Julia's face lying on the pillow. Julia with a broader forehead and darker eyes, features a bit harsher, chin longer. Damp hair ringed his face; she'd held back from pushing the strands away. They said his lungs had suffered permanent damage from the gas, that his shattered right arm would heal eventually but would be slightly shorter than the left and never as flexible. Compared to most of the other men in his ward, Giles was lucky.

She visited him daily. Beneath Giles' cheerfulness was another level of man it might have taken years to reveal, but war tends to grant a unique lapse of caution between people who have no time for drawing room games of retreat and advance. Since coming to France they'd both learned how to get down to intimacies quickly. "To my way of thinking, pacifism is one of the few luxuries in life I never had. I think, Zoe, I would have traded a great deal for it, the ability to regard war in a principled, impersonal manner." He was sitting up, looking better, his face no longer waxen. With his hair brushed back from his forehead, he seemed younger and very vulnerable. "I detest violence. Human life is the only thing we've got, really. But it seems I wasn't free enough to act on that. As if my mind couldn't detach itself from other . . . forces I guess, forces working in me." He kept his eyes averted. She wanted to touch him, take his hand, but knew he wouldn't want her to. Later, perhaps.

"They say, you know, the military makes a man of you. And ever since Jordie died . . . He was always the athlete, liked shooting, good head for finances; all those things. While Jordie was alive it was all right. I mean I could let him be the boy my parents wanted and not feel terribly guilty about being . . . something else. Then when he wasn't there anymore, I felt . . . I joined up."

"Giles, please."

He raised his hand to stop words she didn't really have. "Some proof, eh Zoe? Here I lie, the arch bugger of the regiment. Lungs bad, arm. Health's too delicate now for sports or shooting or much of anything, really. But that, that doesn't make for grand irony. D'you know what does, though?" He looked up at her with watering eyes. She shook her head. "They made me kill. They made me take a human life, and . . ." She waited, knowing of no gesture equal to his anguish. "I thought, you know, I was giving their idea of manhood a try, and all the time they were taking away my humanity. Now that's ironic, Zoe. Well isn't it?" Even then, with both allowing the tears to show, she didn't touch him. It wasn't comfort he wanted, it was a witness.

Of course they talked about Julia, who was "fine, much
better, has been for years." A little "delicate" now and then,
but on the whole, really fine. Had started weaving. "Sent me
this — shawl, I think it is. I do hope for her sake it's one of her
earlier efforts." Was even reading to convalescent soldiers and
"being quite brave, according to Mother, about their various
gruesome injuries. Speaking of which, I have decided, and
you are the very first to hear of it, to take up needlepoint! The
doctors say that the dust, you know, from the clay, will prevent
me from ever throwing a pot again. So I've the ideal excuse
for embarking upon a ladylike project. Cunning, eh?"

He was waiting for her reaction, something appropriate in
the line of affectionate sarcasm. But "How immensely daring
of you," was all she could come up with, her mind concentrat-
ing on Julia. Julia, who had never left her thoughts. Pushed
to the side, yes, but out? Never.

They'd taken Julia away from her at school, and she'd
waited, hoping to be called for. Wanting to be with her,
helping. Surely someone would have realized this and called
for her. Maybe she ought to have written, offering herself, but
she couldn't, afraid the Carrolls would read between the lines.
See her secret, the two of them joined as they might have been.
Summer had come without a word. Somehow, the life ahead
of her had to be filled without Julia.

And somehow, it was. At that age one can be desolate for
just so long. After a while the original object of frustrated
passion starts fading but the passion keeps on growing. Soon
one is looking at imitations of the original, then at persons
vaguely reminiscent of her, finally, at opposites. All the while
tension builds, physical need gets more and more insistent.
Eventually the past loses its hold, and whoever happens to be
there, sympathetic at the right time in the right place, gets the
benefit of all that desire pouring out at last. Unfortunately,
the lover is only a surrogate recipient, and one usually feels
compelled to move on.

There'd only been four or five. Until now she'd thought

herself honorable in telling each at the start she had no
intention of getting involved. But seeing Giles forced her to
recognize it was Julia, not honor, made her say it. She sensed,
however, he wouldn't appreciate such a revelation regarding
his sister.

"How many, would you say, all told?" he was asking her.

"Now I could give you a definite answer to that if only I
hadn't lost my tally card during a raid. Really, Giles. Must
one keep count?"

"I'm not completely sure you haven't. It's extraordinary,
actually, how like a man — I never realized that women did,
too."

"Well I may have acted rather like a man, but at least I
never dressed like one."

"But you would have made a smashing-looking lad! Walking suit, cap and regimental tie. I can see it now."

"Giles, control. Please. I was merely a bit of a rake, that's
all. I may've wanted to be like a man sexually, in a way, but
I've never wanted to look like one physically."

"Never?"

"Well, not in the last fifteen years at any rate. Perhaps
when I was six or so you could've accused me of harboring
such transvestite thoughts, but certainly not recently."

"Pity. I like dressing up. You should have seen me in the
Slade Follies. A vision of loveliness in pink tulle. That's t, u, l,
l, e." They laughed and Giles' turned into a cough. "Oh blast
these bloody lungs, am I never to giggle again?"

"If the shell that got your arm had hit you elsewhere, Giles,
you'd have been left with a perpetual giggle and little else."

"Zoe, I beseech you, don't be moralistic with me. I gave up
thanking the ruddy Lord for his small favors a long time
ago."

"You have an absolute knack for turning any conversation
around to the subject of Giles Carroll. Give me a turn, will
you? Lie back. Rest. Save your energy for Paris. That flat
I've been trying to get is almost mine."

"What grand news! However did you do it?"

"Remember my telling you about the strange but helpful woman I met who drove for the American Fund?"

"Vaguely. Older, wasn't she? And rather like — something peculiar."

"A watchful bird. Well, peculiar or not, she's kept her word, and it looks as if I'll have a fairly decent place for us to stay by the end of November. I'm sure we'll be able to move you by then. And you're going to recuperate in no time at all with Paris surrounding you. Think what fun we'll have exploring the city together. Radclyffe Hall always said I had to see Paris, unfortunately it took . . ."

"Radclyffe Hall? What's that? Sounds like something out of the Brontës, 'And there he brooded, his dark brows lowering, the Master of Radclyffe Hall.' "

"Master Radclyffe Hall; I must tell John next time I see her, she'll like that. It's because of her, actually, that I'm here. She's the one who got us involved in the ambulance corps. An old friend."

"You mean friend-friend? Or just friend, friend."

"Do I honestly look the type who'd be attracted to a Master Hall? Though I must say John and I, on occasion, had similar tastes; in friends. Anyway, it was she who used to argue with me so heatedly about dress. 'You must own up to it like a man, Mohr,' she'd say, 'own up to it. Your position is untenable. You can't be a little bit of both; you must be one or the other. Otherwise you're not accepting the male in you. You're shilly-shallying around being untrue to your real nature. One can't pick and choose what one likes about men and discard the rest; that's superficiality of the worst order. One must confront and fully accept one's masculinity.' "

"What a horrid idea. And what did you say?"

"I asked her what were we to do with the woman in us, that all the suits and ties and cuff links in the world wouldn't change the fact we were female. Why not fully confront and accept that? And if we followed her logic, we couldn't allow ourselves any feminine tendencies, such as tenderness for example. Yes, I know, Giles, men can be tender too, but the world isn't accustomed to thinking of them in that way. She didn't like any of it, she'd humph and haw, then give me one of her choicest cigars and send me away, telling me to think about it some more."

"Which, of course, you did."

"Of course. And I went right on picking and choosing."

"Good girl. Never let them box you into one corner or another; corners are such airless and unhealthy places. One should always be free to dance about and be what one chooses, now one thing, now another. Otherwise, boredom. And boredom, my dear, is one of the greatest horrors the world has ever devised. You must promise me, Zoe, that if ever I'm dying, slowly and hideously, of boredom, you'll do everything in your power to end my suffering."

"I cannot envision that crisis in your future, Giles."

"No, I can't either. I expect I'll even manage to make marriage amusing. Who knows, perhaps one day you and I will marry. Each other, I mean."

Even a second's afterthought would show him he didn't mean it. When Giles married it wouldn't be to someone like her. No, he would turn to a woman who complemented the masculine side of his nature, not competed with it. Someone who offered contrast sharp enough to stimulate him into husbandly concern, and husbandly performance. He would not marry her; nor, she knew, would he wish Julia to.

On November eleventh the Armistic was signed and two weeks later she'd completed final arrangements for securing the Paris flat. Her American friend had been very helpful during the search and negotiations, but the practicalities of getting both herself and Giles released, their belongings and persons transported, and at least a few amenities supplied fell entirely to her. Everything was monumentally difficult. Not only had a war just ended, a flu epidemic had begun, making her last few weeks at the hospital even more harried than before, and causing a crucial bribed official to be absent from his job on the very day they were to receive priority tickets to Paris.

If only they'd been able to get on the train, she might have survived the ordeal unbroken. The bodies, she was so tired of them awkwardly sprawled over yesterday's battlefields, cramped onto ambulance tiers, sweating under grey hospital sheets. First the dying and wounded, then the sick, so many bodies, crowding in on her, demanding something from her. Now escape, planned, paid for, but denied! Because the train, her train, was jammed with bodies, sick and healthy crushed into stifling compartments which would take them to Paris. Leaving her behind, Giles dependent, all her efforts . . .

She actually felt the sickness attack her. One moment, healthy; the next, deathly ill. She remembered marveling at the swiftness of that attack in the same instant she succumbed to it.

There'd been fever, frighteningly high. Pain, pain in her back so excruciating she'd looked down at her spinal column from inside her body, where she was hiding in a hot red cloud, and seen the pieces of bone break apart. She knew that if she could reach the splintered chunks to put them back together, it would be all right again. But her arms were indifferent; they wouldn't move a muscle to help her. And it was then she noticed her legs, too, had come away and were simply lying close by, waiting for her to do something. Logic told her that once she gathered up her spinal column, her legs would come back of their own accord. So the very tips of her fingers were the first things she must work on; get them moving and she'd soon have herself back together again. From inside her cloud that was so bright, so red, it was almost suffocating her, she worked on her fingertips, ceaselessly sending them messages to move, move.

Later, it might have been years, she opened her eyes and

saw Julia's face hovering above. It wasn't fair. After all she'd
been through, a cheap trick like that simply wasn't fair. She
felt tears running hot on her cheeks. Let them! She'd worked
bloody hard to fight her way out and open her eyes; and not to
be faced with this, another damn illusion. The tears were
tickling her chin. She raised a hand to wipe them away, but
another's got there before her, dabbing at her face with a cool
white cloth. Julia's voice said, "Hello, Zoe." But she wasn't
going to be trapped into responding; she was going to go to
sleep again, and when she woke up that face and voice had
better not be there.

"But of course I'd known for weeks," Giles was smiling at
her from a bedside chair, "that Julia meant to join us here.
The reason I didn't tell you, and in no way deserve your anger
with me for not doing so, was that Julia wanted it to be a
surprise. A present. We would arrive in Paris, you see, and lo,
there on our doorstep would be Florence Nightingale, come to
nurse *me* through recuperation. Fell-swooping, she would
release you to the charms of Paris." He sat back, looking
satisfied, as if everything had gone according to plan. "Now, I
am not complaining that I have been abysmally ignored by
Florence, who has tended you most devotedly since her arrival,
which, incidentally, was days late. However, I'm not altogether satisfied with referring to this flat as 'our own little
Crimea.' But I suppose the main thing is we are all quite
comfortably ensconced here. Florence is out right now but
will be back soon, having heard there is a fresh vegetable to be
found in the vicinity."

Her hand picked at the blanket. "How is she, Giles?" She
hoped he would be serious, tell her the truth without knowing
how much the truth meant to her.

"She's . . ."

"She's fine." And there she was. Smiling, beautiful, taking
Zoe's hand, entwining its fingers between her own. "Hello,
Zoe," impossible vision, "welcome back."

Brother and sister seemed perpetually delighted in each other. There were countless anecdotes to tell, an endless supply of stories about friends, events, the other had missed. Watching the two of them, same eyes flashing, cheeks blushing to identical pink, delight bouncing back and forth between their faces, she might have felt excluded. Instead she felt exhilarated; to be surrounded by their gaiety, in the center of it, was like being in the middle of that children's game where one must intercept a ball tossed between two players. Without the third person, there's no zest to the sport. And whichever way she turned, toward one or the other, she could see Julia.

At the moment, Julia's reflection was staring at her in mock horror. "I simply don't believe it of Duncan! Why, just yesterday," he looked to Zoe as if for help, then back to Julia, "he was deserting both Strachey and Keynes for some gorgeous Cambridge undergrad, crew I believe, can't remember his name but it'll come to me in a moment . . ."

"Yesterday to you, Giles, but much in the past to Duncan. He's utterly devoted to her and has been for, it must be, two years at least."

"Tosh. I can't imagine Duncan Grant utterly devoted to anyone, even the beauteous Vanessa Bell. Though she is lovely, and now that I think about it they were always putting their heads together at the Omega and coming up with clever new designs for Roger."

"Well it's quite obvious they are now putting together more than their heads. He did find time to ask after you, however. In fact, as I recall, both he and Vanessa and that fey little acquaintance of yours, Carrington, made much of your absence from the party."

"Carrington! Not the Impossible Carrington? But I haven't seen her since a still-life course at the Slade, when she got to class before everyone else, covered herself with flour, and knelt bare-breasted behind the fruit bowl table. We were all dutifully sketching this dreadful plaster bust, when suddenly it blinked its eyes and burst into the most raucous laughter. That was Carrington, and you will please tell me how on earth she managed to be invited to a 'do' for Leonard and Virginia Woolf."

"For one thing, she did the woodcuts for the volume being honored. It really is a lovely little book, Giles. A story by Virginia, very good, one by Leonard, he should never have left the Civil Service, and some rather strong illustrations by Carrington."

"Yes, but how? To be asked to illustrate; why not Duncan, or Lamb, or sister Vanessa for heaven's sake?"

"Here we come to the other thing, though I'm not sure you're ready for this little bit of news. Your friend Lytton Strachey and Carrington are living together."

"What? God's tooth! Is this what I fought the war for? Have I risked precious appendage so that His Most Royal Bugger may stay at home and set up house with a woman? A woman?"

"Giles dear, they live together, but they are not *intime*. Of course it's because of Lytton that she's allowed to place toe one inside Hogarth House, let alone collaborate with the Woolfs on their first publishing venture. Though she can be quite enchanting."

"Oh? Can she indeed?" He looked toward Zoe for an appreciative reaction, but none was forthcoming. She felt chilled.

"Yes, when she's not boring one to near death about the virtues of Lytton, the main one being, evidently, his total disinterest in the state of her sensual charms. Knowing how much he cared for you, my dear, she went about saying to anyone who'd listen how sad it was you couldn't be there, for Lytton would so enjoy talking with you."

"I see. Strachey, of course, said nothing of the sort."

"Of course."

"She's not . . . pandering for him, is she?"

"I don't know, I'm sure she would if he asked her. However, I doubt Lytton would ever admit he needed any help in attracting handsome young men to his side."

"Well what the devil has he got her for? Strachey, who is so finicky; I just can't picture it."

"Naturally he's never confided in me, but I imagine he looks upon her as a faithful, totally adoring dog who has cleverly learned how to cook and keep house. Very convenient to have around, and on those occasions when one wants a bit of affection, or feels compelled to bestow some, there she is, wagging her . . . tail, and offering up her cute little bobbed head for patting. Something like that, I should think."

"Hmf. Well, tell: what did you think of your hostess, the Enigmatic Virginia?"

"I thought — she was very late, hardly anyone noticed her walking down the stairs — but I happened to be looking in that direction, something made me turn around actually. And I thought, she is the most beautiful person I've ever seen. But . . ."

"What's to be done with you?" He turned to Zoe. "Virginia Woolf has, if nothing else, the most equine of visages." The appraisal brought her no comfort; she could tell Julia had not even heard him.

". . . underneath, I could see . . . she was using up part of herself to hold the rest of herself together. It was so self-consuming. Each moment, there seemed to be less of her in the room. I felt she would, turn into a wraith; join the ones that haunt her."

"I do wish she'd take her tongue with her, wherever it is she's going. That part of her body, at least, is very much flesh and blood. And sting."

"Don't, Giles. She has touched me."

"Oho!" He raised an eyebrow expecting Zoe to return the gesture, but all her muscles were concentrated on sitting there, sitting through it. "I'd heard rumors of that, you know, but never until now . . ."

"No. Though I would of course, gladly. But it's not through body that we meet."

"Well how then, through the looking glass?"

"Maybe. Why should I have to explain? The room was crowded, I was introduced, she said something, I don't remember the words, and then she looked at me. And we met, within that. A moment later she moved on, greeted other people. I left the party and have never seen her since. But, I've not stopped being with her."

"Extraordinary. I must be the only person who isn't instantly smitten by the green-eyed lady of Paradise Road. Although I do prefer her to her husband. Leonard is so-o-o correct. And with none of Virginia's sort of bawdiness to offset the bitchiness. Leonard, however, will never loosen his stays for fear of some outrageous pederast popping out. Still, I do miss them all. Everyone seems to have been so busy getting on with their potential while I've been gone. Painting, writing, even constipated old Strachey's had a biography come out, while I, I've been off heroically learning to stomach horse-meat, fighting the War To End All Wars."

"Giles, I absolutely refuse to pity you. What you are feeling is envy, and that is hardly a tragic emotion. You know perfectly well that Roger and Duncan and the rest are going to welcome you back with open arms; you'll be immediately enclosed within the artistic circle again. And whether it's pots or tapestries, whatever the project, you're going to succeed. Not because your hands are innately adept and your mind has all kinds of designs, colors, shapes milling about. But because you are an artist with friends, and their critical opinions happen to be the only ones which count."

"You talk as if we're the R. A., heaven forfend. And it's not quite as easy as you make it sound. The secret, sister dear, is to make it 'look' easy. Sweat is something best saved for the bed, where it becomes a mark of passion, not labor. A gentleman does not labor, even for his art. At least not in public."

"Maybe so, Giles, but to be able to make such a distinction seems to me significant."

"Significant of what? Would you rather we were tortured all the time? Twisted gnomes working in isolation and shoving an occasional masterpiece outside the door? Must I suffer to prove my intentions, or my talent? It strikes me that you are the one guilty of envy here, Julia, not I."

"No, I don't envy you, Giles. I don't want to *be* you. I admire your talent, but I suspect you don't take it seriously enough."

"Perhaps it's not worth any more than I give to it. One must recognize one's limitations you know."

"At least you have found what is there, what it is that lives between your limits, even if you don't choose to challenge them. The horror is, never finding it. What if one never finds it?"

"There are other horrors in the world, worse than that."

"Yes." She went away from them then; Zoe recognized the look. A glance at Giles told her he too was aware that Julia had gone elsewhere, leaving them behind to question each other silently until she returned. "Other horrors." She spoke quietly. "For a moment, I'd forgotten."

"Yes, well," Giles rubbed his hands in simulated heartiness, "the horror before us now is that Gordon may arrive before we've dressed for dinner. There are certain friends who would forgive such a lapse on our part, but not, I fear, dear Edward."

It was Edward Gordon who had helped Zoe and Giles reach Paris. The two men had known each other since public school, where Giles' flamboyance had attracted its opposite in Edward and they'd become friends, though their admiration was not mutual. Giles had felt he could turn to Edward in those rare boyhood moments which required good sense and a level head, qualities he admired in a friend but never aspired to himself. Edward, though he would admonish Giles and feign irritation at being called upon, was never happier than when he could be of service to this boy whose recklessness he

wished he were capable of. With them it was respect on the
one hand versus idolatry on the other; it was to be expected
that they would drift apart in later years. Fortunately Giles
had heard of Edward's recent regimental promotion and
assignment close by, and of course the old school tie was strong
enough. Within hours of Zoe's collapse, she and an exhausted
Giles were on their way, having been bundled into a staff car
thoughtfully equipped with both driver and brandy flasks.

"Bloody spot of luck for us," Giles would say sometimes,
"old Gordon coming through like that."

Yes, Zoe wanted to reply lately, but must he keep on
coming through? Every day? Ever since demobilization,
when he'd called on them and been welcomed by a grateful
household, Edward had been in Paris. It was either two
cousins once-removed or one cousin twice-removed who put
him up, but their degree of closeness didn't matter since he
seemed to spend all his time with his friends and none with his
relatives.

Good old R. F. Gordon, our Regular Fixture, Zoe and Julia
had taken to calling him in private. Tickets to the Ballet
Russe? how thoughtful of our R. F. Our R. F. says a new
bookstore's opened called Shakespeare & Co. and we simply
must take it in. He's been busy, our R. F., finding all those
little clubs in Montmartre where the women dance with each
other and the men are so beautiful.

Eventually our R. F. was reduced to simply "Arf," and
anyone overhearing a conversation would think it was about
either dogs or cockneys, Zoe couldn't decide which. Frankly,
she was getting tired of both Arf and Edward Gordon; the
others, however, didn't seem to mind. She appeared to be
alone in thinking him a bit too courteous, a little too
thoughtful, too agreeable, too helpful. Such behavior was
extreme, really, not quite human. And while he was unfail-
ingly kind to her, she sensed it was more for the Carrolls' sake
than her own; because she happened to be their friend, by

chance was sharing their life at the moment, she was included in Edward Gordon's attentions. Furthermore, she felt Julia and Giles were too ready to use him, taking advantage of his desire to please by allowing him to do all sorts of rather menial tasks. It was always Edward who pushed through the crowd to get them drinks, or saw to the baggage, saved seats, hailed taxis in the rain.

Since neither Julia nor Giles supported her in these opinions, she was inclined to doubt them. "You mustn't," Giles had said to her on the only occasion she'd tried to approach him about it, "let Edward emasculate you, Zoe. However, next time I'll try to see you're the one who whistles for a motorcab." "Oh bugger off, Giles." She'd had to force herself to smile.

Julia's reaction, especially, exposed her feelings for what they were. "Well what of it? What is so terrible about taking advantage of Arf when that is what the man so obviously desires? It seems a most mutually profitable relationship. Anyway, he suits me. Haven't you noticed?" That was it, of course; she had noticed, couldn't help but notice. The two Carrolls, Giles darker, taller than Julia but sharing the same angular grace. In the middle, Edward. Precise, contained, a body between two flapping wings. When they took off, he was their balance, their support transported. They could count on his sense of the ground; without them, he would have been treading it forever, a mere pedestrian.

Physically, too, he had a delicacy about him that belonged with theirs although it was totally different. Whereas they lounged, he perched; they strode, he paced. But Zoe lumbered. At least that's how she saw it. Zoe's body served her best when engaged in some strenuous activity; inside most rooms it threatened clumsiness. She was always conscious of how easy it would be to break a china teacup, or drop the scones. Not that she did, but she was too afraid she would. Just as she feared accidentally stepping on Julia's sensitivity, or colliding unintentionally with Giles' latest enthusiasm. She wanted to protect, but mightn't she trammel instead?

Edward seemed to have none of these reservations. Fair-haired, slender, impeccably dressed, he accompanied them with total confidence, as if it were his destiny to be there. So it was jealousy she felt, no point in trying to call it something else. Edward appeared villainous in her eyes only. And, he had a way of making her feel particularly inept.

"I still can't believe it," Edward said again after they'd arranged themselves in a cab, "one of *the* people to know in Paris and she's used her as an estate agent!"

Lord, she hated being referred to in the third person like that. "Who did?"

"Why you did, by your own admission!" said Edward, prepared, no doubt, to file legal brief in support.

"I did not employ her as my agent," damn his teeth, "she offered to help me find a flat. Just as she offered to help me change a tire that night during the war. When it was raining buckets. And Alice Toklas could've been the Queen Mother for all I cared, so long as she could hold a torch. At the time, her canteen of spiked tea was more important than her social credentials."

"Yes, but what we," Giles gestured to the three of them, "are still marveling at, Zoe dearest, is that you knew Devoted Companion to American Eminence sufficiently well to benefit from her friendship, yet you didn't think to pursue it until recently."

"Incredible." More shaking of Edward's pomaded head. "I have been trying for weeks to get us an invitation to Twenty-seven Rue de Fleurus, and all the time she . . ."

"Who?" Only Edward could make her want to be this way, difficult, like a child purposefully thwarting its parents in public.

Other things she would remember abut that night. Gertrude Stein's solidity, the way she actually occupied space, took it over. Her mistake in assuming it was the men who would be most interested in following her through the narrow alley to the back, where Picassos, Cézannes, Matisses filled the room. How Alice recognized her friend's error, gently pushed Julia forward knowing her interest to be the greater. Julia entranced. Giles delighted, Edward removed, seeing himself. Soft touch at her elbow, Alice guiding her to the settee, thin wrists pouring wine. Alice B. Toklas, with her sense of where each belonged, artist unseen, subtly maneuvering people to place. Glances never returned from Gertrude Stein, talking, talking, masterpiece who had the floor, let others have the walls. While Alice, who chatted, watched, saw, said to her, about whom? always a fixture, dear, and never a fact. Take care.

Important names drifted in and out, heads to remember beneath paintings destined, too, for greatness. Let others take notes and describe the scene for posterity, Zoe couldn't. She felt immersed in shifting currents, caught in the flux of relationships winding about the room. Perhaps she'd been overly sensitized by the gaunt woman at her side. The hollow-eyed lover relegated to the background for so long she eventually saw everything about the creatures cavorting in the fore. Had Alice been referring to herself, then? Edward? had she sensed it about him? Or did she mean Zoe to take care, to assert, lest she disappear into a well-loved chair.

The balance was changed. Saying good night, Edward took Julia's arm. They had arrived as four, and left in twos. Either Julia was aware or she wasn't; both interpretations were equally tormenting.

Deep voice. "But this color, color that is not color, for color can be known by the absence of color." She was sitting on the edge of Zoe's bed, her legs bent apart, feet resting flat on the floor, one hand on a knee, the other fisted under her chin. "This color, which, if not a color, must then be Color, this color collar cully . . ." Julia tried to maintain it, but was forced by her own hoots of laughter to give up the imitation of last night's hostess. Laughing, arms on her stomach, she rolled back into Zoe's bed. Tears scrambled out of her eyes; eventually she wiped them away, lay looking up at the ceiling. Zoe saw sunshine and Sealey's Peak; she couldn't stop her throat from closing up.

Julia, still smiling, turned her head around to look at her. "What's the matter, Zoe? You've been so quiet all evening."

Sitting in the chair an arm's length away from her, Zoe forced a smile that she knew must look rueful. Closing her eyes in denial that anything was wrong, she opened them to find hazel eyes staring at her.

Julia stretched out her arm; fingers barely touched Zoe's sleeve. "Listen, Zoe, you mustn't."

Her skin was burning where the fingers had touched. She couldn't look at her, must turn away.

"Zoe, please. Don't. You mustn't."

She wanted the fingers to come back, to caress. Facing the wall, she closed her eyes and concentrated on that shivering patch on her arm. It waited.

"You mustn't love me that way, Zoe."

She whirled around. "Why?" So she was crying, her face ugly, so what? "Why?" And her fist was gripping the air as she sat twisted in her chair barely seeing the woman in front of her, "Why? Why can't I love you? I do love you! Julia, please, let me love you! You've got to let me!" What did it matter if she was sobbing now, unable to say words she'd dreamed of?

Julia said nothing, did nothing.

Zoe was hiccupping, her nose was running, she needed a handkerchief. "Don't you . . . love me . . . at all?" The words came out in little nasal dollops.

Silence. She opened her eyes, forced herself to look at Julia, who was holding out a white cloth. She took it, blew, busied herself blowing, folding, wiping. She'd been a fool, she should never have . . .

"If I go to bed with you," Julia asked softly, "would that be enough?"

"What?" What did it mean?

"I will, Zoe, if that's what you want. If that will make it easier."

What was happening? Pity? Charity? Could she offer her body the way she did a handkerchief? something to stop the flow? Florence Nightingale come to bandage the wound? It was her guts, her heart . . . "Oh God, Julia. Don't play at indulgence."

Julia pushed herself off the bed, began striding around the room. "All right, then, all right!" Bureau to bed to window, angry strides. "Christus." Teeth clenched, cheeks burning. "This is not . . ." Back and forth. "I simply refuse, I will not allow . . ." She stopped in front of Zoe's chair, looked down at her, turned around and walked two steps, came back. "Why must you be so impossible? Why must you complicate?"

Zoe looked up at her mutely. Her anger was gone, she was too puzzled to feel angry.

Julia dropped to her knees in front of her. "Zoe. I can't bear for you to despise me. You did for a moment, I saw it in your face. Don't you think I've seen everything else in your face too?" She took her hands, held them between her own. "Zoe. Did you think I didn't know? years ago? Your love is my pillow, I rest upon it. I must have a place to rest, Zoe. No one else can give this to me but you. And I need it, this, you, so desperately, I can't, I won't jeopardize what I have. I know how horribly selfish this sounds, I admit it, it is supremely selfish of me. I need your love to be there, for me to draw upon, to use. But, only when it's necessary. Otherwise my pillow, my precious pillow, would . . . smother me."

"But I wouldn't! I promise!"

"Oh Zoe, you can't make that promise, you know you can't. And even if we were to, you'd start resenting me for not giving you all the things one should. Your love for me would change, and I wouldn't have it anymore. Because I can't, Zoe, I can't take the time to love the way you'd want me to. 'In Love' is not where I want to be. If I were to stop now and love you, it would be a detour and that's all. Because the condition or the state of love isn't what I'm looking for, what I mean to find. It's not Love that lies there within my limits, waiting for me."

"How can you be so sure, Julia? What if you're wrong?"

She sat back on her heels. Her hands, though, were still on Zoe's. "Well if I am wrong, my precious Zoe, then I'll need you more than ever. Won't I."

"Yes, but, I don't know if I can. If I'm strong enough. Julia, am I never to have you?"

"You do have me. More than anyone ever will." Her hands moved to Zoe's face. She leaned forward, kissed her mouth.

Zoe felt those cool lips on her own. She gave them no chance to withdraw, raising Julia's body with hers, moving them both toward the bed. It would not be enough, it would not make it easier, but if that's all she was meant to have, she would certainly take it.

IV

DECREPITUDE DISSOLVED into suppleness, and withered flesh became smooth. Perhaps the voyeur in me made it happen, transforming Zoe Mohr into what she might have been, then. Was it perverse to see slender limbs flexing and stretching? Watch the shadows ripple over well-toned muscles. Follow taut, unblemished skin as it glistened on the curves. Such a youthful body.

"I'd already seen what could happen if I wasn't careful. I'd be another Lesley Moore, and Julia would be my Katherine Mansfield. Except I would, most likely, have been given more bed privileges." Face lined with seventy-six years of living, she rings the bell for tea. "So I wasn't sure, you see, exactly how I felt when the four of us came back to England in nineteen twenty and had to decide whether or not to get a house together. But," she waits, body shriveled, legs immobile, while Briggs sets the things down and then withdraws, "the decision did not have to be made immediately on our return. Julia's parents were kind enough to let us stay at their home in Hampshire until we knew what we should be doing." She sips her tea, and I, eyes burning, turn to mine. Is it as hard for her as it is for me, the contrast? Harder, surely. It's her loss; my own is ahead, coming closer every day. "I learned a great deal in Hampshire."

A large house, displaying to the outside world an iron gate between pillars of stone which rose from the high stone fence fronting the estate. The name Stone Hedge had been supplied by Julia's father, a man whose dry sense of humor would have entertained his family more frequently had his mind accompa-

nied his body to the dinner table. Usually the conversation
flowed around him in little eddies and lapped at him
inconsequentially, as if, Julia used to think, he were a raft in
the sea, on the water but not of it. Tall, very thin, with
thinning sandy hair, he would sit at the head of the table
mildly grinning at his wife and children, looking at them from
behind thick lenses but rarely seeing them, glad, however, that
the five of them were gathered together at mealtime. One had
learned early on not to take offense at his inattentiveness, his
distracted air. It was simply "Father's way"; his mind, you
see, was so busy on other things, inventions and the sort, that
he didn't appear to care, but of course he did. No one could
fault James Carroll on caring, in the abstract, for his family.
Had any of them come to him with a grievous problem, he
would certainly have responded, wrenching himself away from
his latest creation without hesitation, putting their well-being
ahead of any scientific breakthrough he might be on the verge
of. True, the practical, everyday problems of raising a family
were left in the capable hands of his wife, but "I want you to
know, Rebecca, that I am here to be called upon," was a
phrase he was fond of using, never seeming to realize that she
rarely took advantage of the sentiment.

"You are not to bother your Father if I am at hand," Mrs.
Carroll would tell the children, "unless it be the most dire of
emergencies." Fortunately Mrs. Carroll always was there, the
children had never known her not to be. So Mr. Carroll was
free to spend his days in one of the estate's cottages he'd
converted into a workroom, where he could concentrate on
many intricate problems the Industrial Revolution had raised
about gears and cogwheels. Several patents were in his name,
but none of them, he felt, sufficiently important to bear
mentioning; his ambition was "to equal the invention of the
safety pin, now think about that for a while and you'll see the
ingenuity, the enormity of such an accomplishment." Not
that his every waking moment was devoted to achieving this;

Julia could remember his emerging from the cottage into the
sunlight and suddenly swinging her onto his shoulders,
laughing and holding her high, high off the ground. Giddy
and frightened and pleased all at once, she would grip his
jacket collar as he skipped through the garden bouncing her
up and down. She remembered the strange mixture of fear
and delight which could turn giggles into screams as the
motion, speed and height took hold of her. Once her father
tripped over a root, pitched forward and let go one of her legs
to free his arm for balance. She felt her terror come true, saw
the ground rushing toward her as she jounced off his shoulder,
falling, her mouth open too terrified for sound, the ground,
squeezing her eyes shut not to see it when she hit, waiting for
pain, death, heaven. And the miracle, arms lifting her up and
away just in time. Her mother's arms.

She was a small, strong woman who often appeared larger
and weaker than she really was. Her slight frame seemed
mismatched with the full breasts that had caused her a great
deal of embarrassment until she married, discovering then the
pleasure they gave, and received. Her face, too, was full,
almost moon-shaped, with dark, slightly slanting eyes. "The
Cossack in me," she liked to say, partly to hear one of her
children reply, "But Mother, Cossacks don't come from
America!" and she could say, "Ah, but they were horsemen,
and I like the idea of a Russian cowboy roaming among my
forebears," to which her husband, if he were around, might
respond, "More likely there was a Ukrainian princess, the
most beautiful in the land. And she had to flee her country, to
avoid the Czarina's jealousy, for her beauty was so great that
even in St. Petersburg they heard of it." And the two adults
might smile at each other above their children's heads,
excluding them. It embarrassed Julia to look up and see them
like that, her mother's neck going red, her father's mouth
parting slightly in a strange sort of smile. Giles might spill
something to get their attention again, or Jordie, ever the little

man, would get up from whatever he was playing at to put his arms around Mrs. Carroll and kiss her cheek. One of them, usually, could be counted on to break the spell.

No one outside the family would have thought Mrs. Carroll a beauty, and few people other than husband and children were exposed to her warmth. When eighteen she'd been sent to England to make a match, the classic case of wealthy American parents wishing to join distinction to money. A title would have been preferred, but James Carroll, whose family went back only two hundred years, would do. After all, Rebecca's parents were first-generation Americans, and to them two centuries were impressive enough to offset the fact James was Church of England; anyway, they'd known from the beginning that chances of merging with a Jewish family who went back far enough were too small to be counted on. Under different circumstances the Carrolls, of course, would never have agreed to such a pairing, but family fortunes had suffered extraordinarily sharp reversals, and the American money, however new and Jewish, was eminently spendable.

And so the two became one. James, for his part, was quite pleased; there was something exotic about marrying a Jewess, and this one had lovely breasts. Not stupid either, no, Rebecca had a fine mind, it simply had never been used much, her parents had given her no chance. The major thing, though, was that he was free now; he could work on his inventions for the rest of his life without having to worry about family and fortune.

If that's what James meant to do with her money, it was fine with Rebecca. Her agreement to the marriage had never even been sought; she'd obeyed her parents' wishes because it was unthinkable not to. But she was determined to turn necessity into romance. All the practical arrangements in the world weren't going to deprive her of passion. She would have it. Even if she had to conjure it up, pasting its likeness onto the everyday in her life, she would know it. She was going to adore James Carroll, and by God, he was going to love her so completely that living would be impossible without her. They were going to fulfill each other, in every way. This was her life, and she was not going to go through it with half her mind and half her senses asleep. They wanted marriage? very well, she would show them Marriage.

She gave everything to it, to being wife and lover. Mrs. James Carroll, tastefully yet modestly attired. Contributing both her name and her time to the proper charities. Able to oversee a household with calm efficiency, whether confronting an obstreperous cook or dealing with a gardener prone to kicking dogs. She sewed, she could follow a conversation, she even read poetry.

And to her husband she evidenced an eroticism that had, at first, made them both abashed. She was the only one who could dislodge him instantly from abstraction. He was her "Beast," the very last epithet friends or family would have applied to him. But she did, delighting in her power and the rewards of bringing him forth.

In the beginning he'd been inclined to regard his wife's sensuality as a racial characteristic, rumor having attributed it to the Jewish people. But that sort of thinking went against his grain, and necessitated seeing his wife as separate from himself, at a distance which he no longer felt after a few months of marriage. For long periods of time he actually forgot she was a Jew, and when she said or did something that prompted him to remember, he would quickly think of another explanation for her behavior. She was Rebecca, his wife, unique, and whatever she did was because she was Rebecca, not because she was Jewish.

Neither society nor his relatives, unfortunately, saw things the way he did. When, for example, Mrs. James Carroll had been asked to head the local fund for Widows of the Boer War, because "Your people are so very good with money, my dear," she'd had to fight down the impulse to decline. She not only accepted, she saw to it that her campaign raised more money than any other in the county. "We are so very grateful to you," the ladies had said, "for devoting so much of your time and energy to helping our poor victims." Showing the ladies a gentle, modest smile, she'd refrained from saying, "Thank you, but I didn't do it for your people, I did it for mine."

And her people were most definitely not his. When Julia had her first "upset," the Carrolls could be heard muttering about Jewish emotionalism running in the family. Possibly inherited. They'd been warned about it before, money no substitute for breeding. Those people knew nothing about restraint, and try as one might, the Carroll genes comprised only half the child. The better half. Of course they failed to mention James' sister in this regard, but then the family never mentioned James' sister. She'd been in a "home" since childhood, well cared for and almost forgotten.

But it didn't matter to Rebecca what the Carrolls were saying; she'd managed to wall herself off from such attitudes. It had been quite simple, once she'd realized that only in her home would she find the love and appreciation so necessary to her life. The knowledge had been like a wave knocking her back onto shore, commanding her to stay out of an element where she didn't belong, to build castles in the sand instead. So she had, turning to her husband with even more intensity, determined to create with him a perfect world to be lived within the tiny radius of their own home. Within it, as My Sweet Rebecca, she would be worth much more than Mrs. James Carroll could ever be outside it.

A little circle of love, with warmth and light, passion, tenderness, and recognition. James could have lived that way forever, just the two of them, but naturally there were children. A child would not, she assured him, detract from what they had, but contribute to it. Their circle would be enriched by expanding. Think of a child's love; what could equal it? A child's total dependency; who was more needed than a parent? The opportunity to form a young mind, an innocent being to nurture, one whose growth was theirs to oversee. "Yes, but you and I . . ." James would mumble, his voice drifting off. "You and I, my darling, will always be to each other what we are now," she would say. "Nothing can change what we have. Don't you believe that?" He supposed that he did.

First had come Giles, followed by Jordan, then Julia. To the roles of wife and lover, Rebecca Carroll was capable of adding, with equal devotion, that of mother. It was Mother they turned to, Mother who saw to their education and training, Mother who started the dinner table conversations and insisted that each of them, Father excepted, must carry his part. If Caesar's wife was not beyond reproach, then his children would be. Art, music, literature; the dance, the hunt, games of skill and agility. She exposed them to all of it, convinced that each would find his métier. "Approach every field with an open mind," she said to them, "for in it may lie your source of excellence, just waiting to be discovered. But if your eyes are closed, your thoughts drifting, you might very well walk by it, and never find another to take its place. Then you would be very sad, wouldn't you, and so would I." The first time she'd heard this, Julia had cried for over an hour, her young imagination creating vivid pictures of loss.

And once, on a nature hike with one of their tutors, the children had found a weakened, obviously stray young dog under a gorse bush. They'd taken turns carrying him home. Jordan had spotted him first and wanted to name him Source of Excellence. "That's silly. That's not what Mother meant at all," his less literal minded brother and sister tried to argue. Jordie, however, threatened to beat them both bloody if he didn't get his way. They compromised on Sox, but in private Giles and Julia referred to their favorite pet as Benjamin Dog, in honor of the late Prime Minister their Mother held up as an example of achievement.

"Naturally I knew very little about any of this when I met Mr. and Mrs. Carroll in nineteen twenty," Zoe Mohr says somewhat cautiously. No wonder. I have just issued a challenge. Yesterday afternoon she told me all about Julia's parents, and not till three o'clock this morning did I realize she told me too much. So I have walked into her flat demanding an explanation, and I don't care whether I appear rude or not. I want to know how she came to know so much about them.

"Even a dullard couldn't have failed to notice almost immediately what a really demanding woman Rebecca Carroll was. And the extraordinary intensity of her need to be the center of her husband's and children's lives. Petite, yes. Charming? most definitely. But manipulative? my goodness, we . . ."

Look, don't give me yesterday's information all over again, just tell me how you got it. None of this old-news-in-new-words routine. I've no intention of getting sucked in today; I am going to sit right here, outside it all, and wait as long as I have to.

She breathes deeply, lifts her chin. "Now you listen to me." And her voice is cold, very cold. "I will continue to tell this my way. Not yours. I am perfectly willing to deal with any responses you come up with, but they are not going to alter my method. If I want to slowly reveal Julia Carroll to you, to have her evolve for you as she did for me, why must I treat her parents the same way? They are not the main people in this, they are background. Background! It has taken me years to compile information on the Carrolls, and by presenting it to you all at once I am saving you a great deal of effort." As far as it's possible for her to draw herself up, make herself taller, she does so. Rigidly haughty, that is the way I'd describe her right now.

Nonetheless, I am not going to be intimidated. Questions still remain. For example, the Carrolls' sex life.

Overplayed astonishment. "Did I ever say that what I told you about the Carrolls was due to direct observation? Either mine or Julia's? Or Giles' even? Of course some of it, most in fact, was. However, there were other sources."

Like what.

"Guesswork. After-the-fact interpretations. Recollections filtered through time. None of it entirely trustworthy, but then, what is? Truth is no more an absolute than anything else."

You'll have to do better.

"If pressed, I would have to say that Julia's diary revealed the most."

Now we have it. Julia's diary. What diary?

"Julia started it while she was still in school. The project, though, was no girlish fancy, she kept it up for most of her life."

And?

"And, I have absolutely no intention of introducing it as evidence at this point. The diary comes later."

I won't accept that.

She looks at me, perhaps testing her will against mine. "Very well. Julia kept a diary. It was not, however, a series of common little entries, such as 'Today we had fishcakes for dinner.' For Julia it was an instrument of both search and release, full of imagination as well as fact. Eventually, it became a springboard for her other writings. But that was not until later, much later. And whether you like it or not, I will not let you rush me into further exposition about that." She fusses with her old-fashioned blouse. Head down, chin pressed into the ruffle under her neck, she lifts invisible crumbs from the fabric and speaks so offhandedly that it takes me a moment to realize she's started in again. ". . . free to leave if you wish. I can't stop you. Can't keep you here under force. If you don't like what is happening, you can walk out at any point." Her attention moves from blouse to teacup without so much as a blink in my direction. "Our agreement has always been assumed, nothing signed. If you want to close the book on the matter, all you'll have lost is a little time."

Now wait a minute, did I say I wanted to stop? She needn't get so huffy over a challenge or two. I mean I know I'm replaceable but still; I've got a little more invested here than just time. I've brought some interest and imagination and willingness to the proceedings too. And not just here, but on my own I've thought about these people. My mind hasn't exactly been asleep. I've been helping, doing my share, and if she doesn't see that — I can't believe she doesn't care whether or not I come back. Maybe she doesn't know how much I look forward to . . .

"Shall we continue? Good." Her body relaxes, she smiles and would probably pat my hand if I were closer. Silly, I guess, to have felt so hurt there for a moment.

"Mention of Julia's diary," she's reverted to her normal chatty tone, "always reminds me of the similarities. Of course Virginia Woolf's diaries, at least a few carefully edited selections from them, are known to the world, while Julia's . . . Well. It has always seemed to me that both women had an almost compulsive need for that particular outlet, and they used it for purposes each would have recognized in the other. Another link between them." Her head nods in self-agreement, then she sighs, the corners of her mouth turn down. "In Hampshire, I learned about the possibility of something, a childhood experience, that might well have been yet another connection."

It was unthinkable that the Carrolls meet them at the station, in public, where anyone might witness the family reunion. They waited in the privacy of Stone Hedge, but Mrs. Carroll, knowing that Julia might well be tired of the noise and motion from the train, and that Giles had inherited some of his father's fascination with machinery, had thoughtfully provided them with a choice of conveyance. They could travel the remaining few miles by car or by carriage. Julia immediately went for the horses, and somewhat to Zoe's surprise, Edward did not try beating her to the second seat. Instead he gaily waved to them from the open car and seemed totally pleased at the opportunity to tear off with Giles.

A sense of peace flowed through her as she reached for Julia's hand beneath the blanket that covered them both. Thighs touching, their bodies swayed to the rhythmic trot of the horses. They passed places where the trees formed a canopy, a serene enclosure over the road. Dense thickets on either side contributed to the pleasant illusion of security. She looked at Julia, the dappled shadows on her face softening its angles, obscuring the tension around her mouth and the worried frown that would come and go ever since the channel crossing.

Going home was always a bit nerve-racking, she supposed. One's parents, no matter how well-loved, were bound to be difficult at moments, to grate and treat one as a child. Worse, the temptation to revert to childhood when irritated or threatened, to find one wasn't as mature as one liked to think. The same old things could still have their hold.

She hoped, for Julia's sake, that the months spent at Stone Hedge in illness were vague memories now, and not the cause for her increasing the pressure on Zoe's hand. Zoe returned it, reassuringly. She was looking forward to meeting Julia's parents, to seeing the house where she was born, to walking with her to favorite landmarks, secret places. She was no different from any other lover in wanting to share her beloved's past.

"Will our bedrooms be joining?" she asked.

"No."

"Oh." Her disappointment had to be temporary. "Surely you could change the arrangements? Without Mother . . ."

"Surely I couldn't." Julia withdrew her hand. "And Mother has nothing to do with it. I specifically asked that you be put down the hall from me."

"Why?" She couldn't keep her voice from faltering slightly

on the *y*. But she would hear Julia's explanation, and it would do away with the apprehension beginning to crawl around inside her.

"Because." Julia struggled to keep a hold on severity. She lost; her shoulders sagged. Her fingers trembled as she pressed them along her forehead. "Because I just can't there. I'm sorry, Zoe. I just can't."

"Is it your parents?"

Julia shook her head, "No. It's, it's silly. A quirk. That's all." She forced herself to smile, squeezing Zoe's hand as she did so. Her eyes, though, couldn't join in the pretense. Zoe saw Julia trying to force them to meet her own in a test of the truth. She could only get them as far as the blanket covering their bodies, separate and moving steadily toward a house that was going to put even more distance between them.

Suddenly Zoe wanted the journey to be over. The horses' gentle gait was maddening. The trees were barriers, hemming her in; she longed to see an open field. Foliage, shadows, gloom, everything was oppressive. They should have taken the car; Giles and Edward already must be warming themselves with a brandy.

She didn't know what to expect next from Julia, but the laughter surprised her. Julia was laughing, not hysterically, not in a forced way, but in little hoots, the way she did when she was truly amused. "Did you see, the way Arf went scampering to the car? He couldn't wait to, jump in with dear brother Giles. Hoo," she was wiping moisture from the corners of her eyes, "poor Edward. Giles has been cruel to him, really."

"What are you talking about?"

"Don't tell me you haven't been aware of Arf's Grand Passion?"

"For Giles?" Zoe was incredulous.

"Oh Zoe! I'm surprised at you, you're supposed to know so much about these things. He's been positively panting for

Giles. Has been since public school. They had to take those ghastly cold showers in the morning, all the boys prancing around naked, their little things turning blue. Edward always managed to get into Giles' group, and 'drool at me through the spray' according to Giles. Oh poor little Arf. If only he were a stableboy or a sailor. Wait till he finds out his bed is not only three doors down, but one floor up!"

For the first time since meeting Edward Gordon, Zoe felt a positive emotion toward him. It disoriented her, this feeling of compassion for a man she'd grown to dislike and distrust. If what Julia said were true, then he was indeed poor Edward. But if it weren't . . .

By the time their carriage pulled up in front of Stone Hedge, Zoe was thoroughly confused. Finding Mr. and Mrs. Carroll waiting to greet them on the broad stone steps unhinged her even more. She'd expected to meet them later, after she'd freshened up and changed from the traveling clothes she so desperately wanted to get out of. But there they were, Mr. Carroll very tall and somewhat stooped, grinning at them benignly from behind the small but very erect body of Julia's mother. She was smiling too, but her smile had a peculiar, triumphant cast to it, as if she were a general, Zoe thought, welcoming home the loyal troops.

Of course at the time Zoe hadn't really "seen" all that, she'd been too busy painfully bumping her kneecap getting out of the carriage. "Don't drop the scones," Julia had whispered to her before hurrying forward to embrace her parents. And that had been the final turn for Zoe, that joshing indication from Julia that she was totally aware of what Zoe was going through, that despite homecoming and quirks and parents a part of her was still with Zoe, knowing her and saying it would be all right. Had she whispered her undying devotion instead, the moment would not have been more intimate, and Zoe could not have loved her more.

Still, meeting Mrs. Carroll for the first time, Zoe most

definitely had not been at her best. Lying alone in bed that night, she wondered why the initial confrontation had been so important to her. What had Julia or Giles said about their mother that made Zoe want to meet her from as strong a position as possible? The woman's handshake, the apparent warmth of her greeting — all that had been fine. But in her eyes, in those eyes that were darker than Julia's, Zoe had seen, what? Something supercilious. Zoe felt that in the instant of being greeted, she'd been summed up and dismissed. No threat, nothing to fear; Rebecca Carroll had made her decision, and her face had shown what it was.

Well, she was wrong. And unjust. It was stupid to judge people on first impressions. Zoe thrashed around, searching for comfort between the foreign sheets. She wasn't weak! She was flexible. Flexible. The woman had made a major error in mistaking her flexibility for weakness, there was a difference. Damn! People would insist on tucking in blankets so tightly there was no room left for one's feet at all. How was Mrs. Carroll to know she was so ruddy flexible when she'd been nothing but flustered all day? The woman wasn't stupid; she'd shone at dinner; everyone had been entranced. Giles treating her in such a courtly way, so amused by his mother's wit, so responsive to her every word. And Julia, obviously pleased at giving way to the woman's charm, shyly enjoying her, proud to be her daughter. Mr. Carroll, did he ever stop grinning? No, he did not, perhaps there was something wrong with his bite. And Edward. Poor Edward, blast his little blue balls. Would he always be on cue? laughing at the right time, witty when called for, never short for words, always with ones exactly suitable. How she could have wasted a moment's compassion on him — what was the matter with this pillow? Then, of course, there was herself, Zombie Zoe. Every English country home should have one. She shines, she sparkles! She is a dolt. Perhaps Mrs. Carroll was on the mark after all. Maybe it was Zoe who couldn't tell the difference between weakness and flexibility. No, she mustn't think that, she must try to sleep.

But the bed was so huge. Lonely. Was Julia sleeping? Or was she lying awake, staring at shadows and thinking of Zoe just a few doors away. Zoe, taking up only a quarter of the bed, hugging her shoulders for comfort, straining to see if the door handle had really turned or was it her imagination. Julia could come if she really wanted to; she had in Paris. The bedroom door slowly opening, Julia's white-clad body, almost ghostly to Zoe's eyes, gliding across the room to her bed. Only then, when she could feel the covers sliding back, another body's weight on the mattress, could Zoe be sure it was no apparition, but Julia in the flesh, Julia come to her. Lover reaching out, her arms pale and ready to encircle Zoe's back as she moved to lie on top of her, their mouths meeting first. The softness of their breasts touching, spreading, fusing. Groins, sweet contact! met, blended, warmed one another as they moved in the slow first circles of desire. Their tongues, strong travelers taking turns. To feel hers entering her mouth, to receive it and press it with her own, wanting it deeper, wetter, then to change, to thrust and gain full entry, explore moist surfaces within. And then? to separate, knowing, to pull back, because it was going to happen, and they could afford to take time, to build slowly, sure of what would come.

Kneeling, Zoe slowly raised her gown. Julia reached out, stroked her thighs. Her groin, Julia's hand moved up and spread across the damp triangle, one finger disappearing to rub its length along the cleft. Stomach, Julia's face caressed it, her lips made a wet path across Zoe's hip. The ribcage, Julia drew back to see it rising, taut, her hand moving among the shadows to feel the bones beneath. And Zoe's breasts, perfect handfuls, they were nuzzled, kissed, the nipples made to tickle Julia's palm as her hand moved lightly around first one, then the other. Shoulders, not to be denied, but caressed, fingers sliding to feel along the breastbone, trace its prominent curves.

The gown off, hands behind her for support, Zoe still knelt, while Julia's lips trailed down her neck, biting where the shoulder joins, leaving her mark, her bruise of possession. Throaty noises of delight and pleasure shared. Zoe in control, pressing Julia back against the pillow with the steady pressure of her kiss, her hands working to lift the flimsy gown. Julia stretched before her, long pale legs, dark love mound, gentle belly, sweet sloping skin and the undercurve of breasts just visible. Her own swaying against Julia's leg as she knelt to run her tongue among the toes, to nibble at the anklebone, the knee. Mouth never ceasing, she slowly spread Julia's legs and moved between them, her lips working to the inner thigh, her breast rubbing against the moist cleft as she kissed the creases on either side, her hands moving along the flanks, the stomach, up to cup the breasts raised in welcome. She climbed, they lay together in rapid beat. Hands searched, parted other lips to stroke and explore the everchanging flesh within, the ecstasy point grown beneath their fingers, urging them to move faster and faster. To go in deep, deep, one finger, two, faster, rougher, deeper. Moving, heaving. Bodies hands breath. And then?

Would Zoe be the first to break and thrust her mouth against that other mouth writhing to be kissed, to feel teeth and tongue and lips against it and in it and moving, moving, moving, making bringing until until — Or would four mouths, head to toe, lips mixing, softer wetter, harder higher, do together. Highyer. Too . . . geth . . . er. High. Togeth . . . together!

The pleasure was limited but all she had on nights when Julia never opened her door. And though isolation lay on the other side of fantasy, sleep could overcome it.

Days were easier. Sometimes with Giles and Edward, more frequently just the two women, hand in hand roaming the countryside. Julia was fond of wearing her brother's old shirts rolled to the elbow; they made her seem even thinner, but Zoe liked the look. She liked the way everything was, out of doors.

On hot days Julia would sweep her hair up, twisting its honey strands and sinking pins haphazardly as she walked. Zoe would fall behind to see the delicate, long neck revealed, made more vulnerable by stray tendrils curling against it.

Such an innocent part of the body, she must hurry forward to kiss it, loving the slightly salty taste, the smell of fresh air and leaves that came from the skin.

"What are you doing?" Julia asked her softly, leaning back into Zoe's body so that she should put her arms around her.

Zoe whispered behind her ear, "Getting back to nature."

"Oh!" Julia pushed through her arms. "You must be one of those horrid sapphists from the city! One of those nasty, unnatural creatures who haunt our Empire's byways!" She skipped away, laughing. "Come on, you little lecheress, I'll show you nature!" her arm a swooping arc urging Zoe to follow. "Come on, city girl, to the brook! The brook!" She went leaping over hillocks and thrashing through the tall grass, her skirt catching on the stalks, her shirt coming untucked.

When Zoe caught up with her, Julia was motionless by a bank of wild flowers. She was looking at something beyond them and quietly singsonging to herself, "That's not the brook. I want to see the fish. Where are the fish?"

Puffing from the chase, Zoe followed her gaze to a wooden shack fifty yards away and managed to gasp, "What's that?" before bending over to ease her lungs.

She was breathing easily by the time Julia responded, her voice gone very flat. "That. That is nothing."

Zoe peered at her quizzically, "Julia, what a strange thing to say. What do you mean it's nothing? It's here. Surely it was used for something at some time." Julia continued to stare at the old shed, her body moving from side to side as if she were becoming mesmerized. Her eyes began to glaze. "Julia?" Zoe shook her arm, "Julia, for heaven's sake, what is going on? What are you thinking? What's happened?"

"I hate it. Tear it down."

"What?" Suddenly Julia was sinking fingers into her arm and moving about excitedly. "Yes, tear it down, Zoe, tear it down!" Her face was flushed and her eyes were shining with the vision of destruction. "Oh please tear it down, Zoe. You can do it. You're so strong, you can tear it down. For me, you can tear it down, tear it down." Julia jerked away from her and began dancing about, singing "Oh gardener's shack is falling down, falling down," twirling her body into smaller and smaller circles, "falling down, Oh gard . . . shack . . . ling down," her voice getting breathless, "sha . . . ss . . . fall . . . ingdown. Yes!" She stopped just as suddenly as she'd begun and stood with hands on hips a few feet from Zoe. "Do it!" "Julia, please, I . . ." Zoe's arms were wide in helpless supplication, begging Julia to stop, to bring herself back from the frightening place she'd worked herself into. She watched as Julia's face contorted; stood by impotently as Julia screamed "DOOO . . . IITT!" And found movement restored when the sobs began, Julia slowly falling to the ground sobbing unintelligible words as Zoe rushed to lift her sagging body. For a long time she held her and murmured sounds meant to soothe, waiting for comfort to take hold.

It was pointless to ask Julia what had happened. Immediately on their return she was put to bed, everyone silently having come to agreement that she'd suffered from "too much sun." A few days' rest and plenty of liquids would set her right again; there was no need to call the doctor because that is precisely what past experience told them he would prescribe.

Watching Mrs. Carroll come down the stairs from having seen to her daughter's needs, Zoe half expected the woman to turn on her with accusations of stupidity or neglect. She did feel responsible for what had happened, knowing at the same time that her guilt was an absurd instance of breast-beating, for there was no possible way she could have either predicted or prevented what had occurred. Still, she was prepared for Rebecca Carroll to be angry with her; but the look Julia's mother allowed to flit across her face was not one of anger. Instead, it seemed to say "Even you cannot help her, you and your precious love are powerless too." To Zoe's eye, Mrs. Carroll experienced a certain satisfaction in relaying that message.

The evening's dinner conversation was more than a little constrained. Zoe couldn't bring herself to even attempt holding her own, while Giles and Edward worked doubly hard at filling in the gaps. Only Mr. Carroll appeared not to find Julia's empty chair a source of discomfort. Zoe discovered herself resenting his "life must go on" attitude, because it was his life, of course, that he meant, not Julia's. His own little sea must continue unruffled; the raft, as Julia liked to think of him, must be allowed to bob contentedly, protected from any waves that might upset it. Probably she was being unfair to him, for surely the man cared; they all "cared." But what were any of them doing about it? She felt a foot tapping against her own, looked up to meet Giles' eyes asking her to see it through, make some effort. She tried eating the food on her plate, but it simply would not go down. "Would you like another glass of claret, Zoe dear?" Mrs. Carroll inquired. Zoe shook her head and managed to smile at yet another instance of the woman's being overly solicitous; all during dinner Mrs. Carroll had been too considerate, thinking, Zoe knew, that she could afford to be, now that she had proof of Zoe's limits. Edward spoke up, "I say, this *is* a fine wine," and began a discourse on vintages he had known more for Mrs. Carroll's benefit than hers.

After dinner Giles came up to her. "Stroll?" Dear Giles. "Yes, please." She took his arm as they moved out onto the terrace and down into the garden. "Can you tell me about it?" he asked after they'd been walking for a while. This was the Giles she trusted, the one usually in hiding underneath all the brittle sarcasm. She squeezed his arm, saying, "Those are the words I wanted to say to Julia, but didn't. Because she wouldn't have known what to do with them. I'm not sure I do either." "I'll wait," he said, and without warning she was crying, leaning against him, crying from the strain.

"There now, there now," his arms around her, "poor little Zoe." "Oh Giles," she was so grateful for the shelter, the understanding, his arms. A body to lean on, to — she felt it pushing against her leg. No, still crying light tears. No he couldn't be, but it was mounded, growing. She stepped back, "I'll be . . ." pretending she hadn't noticed, "all right now. Thank you." He acted as if nothing had happened; perhaps she'd been mistaken. They walked on.

"You mustn't think you're to blame, Zoe. Because I get the impression, you know, that you do. Don't forget Julia's been through these sessions before, and most likely she will again."

"Yes."

"We don't know what brings them on. I'm inclined to think it could be anything, really. What seems perfectly all right to us, can be absolutely horrific to her. It's as if she literally doesn't *see* the way we do. As if her eyes, or her brain, are registering totally different images from those the rest of us see."

"Mm." They'd reached the front gate. Without discussing it, they started up the road rather than turn back to the house.

"The doctors are quite useless, you know, when it comes to something like this. One says to feed her, the other to give her emetics. A third one says rest, she must get rest and more rest, while yet another tells us to send her out every day for a constitutional, rain or shine. I tell you, it's the doctors drive one mad." '

"Giles. You know that, shed I guess you'd call it, near the border, the southerly end of Stone Hedge?"

"Oh, the one our gardeners used for storing some of their tools. And a bottle or two. Yes, what about it?"

"Well did anything ever . . . happen there?"

"Happen? Uh, let's see. The gardeners had it, then the

three of us started to play around there for a while, secret
clubhouse sort of thing."

"By three, you mean you and Jordan and Julia, right?"

"Right. But then, you know, Jordie and I, we got a bit
older and the age difference between Julia and us seemed,
suddenly, terribly important." He laughed, "So we excom-
municated her. And, yes, I remember, we forbade her to come
within a hundred yards of the place. Turned it into . . . The
Order of the Royal Mouse, knights only. Silly."

"The Royal Mouse? Why did you call it that?"

"Zoe, must we talk about past stupidities?"

"Yes, I think so. What did the name mean?"

Giles cleared his throat. "Well. It's different, you know,
with boys. I mean, they can do things that, don't mean
anything other than sport, or fun, or just physical . . ."

"I know what you're trying to say."

"Lord. All boys do it, it doesn't matter if you're related or
not. Before you know it you're not just measuring the curve of
your urinary arc, you're doing other things as well. And
they're just as significant as the number of feet you can pee,
they mean just that much."

"Giles, enough. I'm not accusing you of harboring deep
incestuous desires for your brother. The name, I assume,
referred to?"

"The old bald-headed mouse; not very clever of us, I
admit."

"No, but you weren't thinking of cleverness at the time. Did
Julia ever . . . see you at it?"

"Good God, no! Zoe, I swear you have a definite bent
toward the perverse."

"Well could she have snuck up on you, seen you two
without your being aware of it?"

"Why are you persisting in this line of questioning? No,
absolutely not. We always tied up one of the dogs outside the
door."

"Now there you were being clever." They continued along the road, Giles perplexed and Zoe trying to see her way among the possibilities. If she could only find the place, the point where things came together. "And you were how old?" she asked Giles.

"Oh the usual age, eleven, thirteen, what does it matter? It was only for one summer, Zoe, an almost forgotten summer a long time ago and not in the least unique. My God, eighty percent of the entire male population — I've simply no idea what you're trying to get at by pursuing this."

"Julia would have been, what? Seven or so?"

"Yes, Julia would've been seven, or six, or eight or five. What difference does it make? I've told you, Julia had absolutely nothing to do with it! Jordie and I played around some, then I went back to school and that was an end to it."

"But Jordie was still here, at home, wasn't he? Still being tutored at home? He and Julia both?"

"Well yes, but so what? What of it?" Giles halted. He took hold of Zoe's shoulder forcefully enough to make her stop and have to face him. "Zoe. You will tell me, right now, what all this means." His long tapered fingers did not leave her shoulder; he was determined that his demand be honored.

"I don't know what it all means. That's what I'm trying to — Giles, if you could have seen the way Julia reacted to that shed today. With such a strange mixture of hate, and fear, and, mania. It reminded me of another time, similar though not so excessive, when we were at school together, hiking. Like today. She saw a mouse. A tiny field mouse, and it sent her into hysterics! Then, maybe she'd been building up to it and that was just a warning, but soon after, the news came about Jordan, and total collapse. So I must wonder if . . ."

"No." Giles had been looking at her steadily. He turned, walked away a few paces. Then he swung around, his face contorted by emotions too complex for Zoe to disentangle. "No," he said softly. "That's monstrous. He wouldn't have. Not to Julia."

"But if you and he had, perhaps Jordan thought he could with Julia, too."

Giles thrust his arm forward as if to stop her words from coming to him. "No, Zoe! I tell you no! Even Jordie would've known that wasn't the same thing at all. Good Christ." He scuffed the dust; began pacing back and forth, head down, fists on his waist. "I mean he was a bully at times, and he could be incredibly insensitive." Still not looking at Zoe, he continued to walk about within a limited area. "Ask him something that didn't have to do with shot or saddles or cricket bats and rugger scores, and Jordie'd . . ." Aimless gesture. "Even later, when he was grown. When he was A Man." Giles stopped, staring at Zoe with a puzzled expression. "What am I doing?"

"Whatever it is, you're not making a very good case for him."

He looked about him at the ground, distractedly ran a hand through his hair, grimaced. Zoe spoke to break the chain of reaction, "Let's go back, shall we?" He nodded.

They walked back the way they had come, but silently this time, each separately busy with the past. So much to be sorted out. Pieced together without sure knowledge of the pattern. Every item something to be decided over, accepted or discarded, perhaps put aside to be picked up later. Sifting, shifting, what was, what could be, what could be faced as having been. And everything colored by private needs, some known, some not. The truth, or at least an acceptable alternative to it, was in there somewhere.

Reaching the terrace, Zoe prepared to climb the few steps leading to its broad stone flooring. "Zoe," Giles had taken her hand, was holding her back. She hoped he didn't want too much from her. Even her smile was ready to collapse. "Yes?" What was it about, what did his expression mean? she was so tired, the day had taken all her strength. "You are a good friend," Giles spoke looking into her eyes, "and I am so very fond of you." He kissed her, fully. From a distance she felt lips, soft but persistent, on lips that were hers. The sensation lasted, how long? Before Giles drew back, hesitated, then hurried into the house. Leaving Zoe alone at the foot of the stairs, wondering how to react.

V

WANT TO SEE the mouse? the cute little mouse? Oh yes, show me, show me the mouse. You'll have to promise not to tell anyone. Why? Because it's a very special mouse and it doesn't want anyone to know it's here. I promise. All right, but don't scream or anything when you see it or you'll scare it away. I won't, I won't make any noise at all. I'm going to blow out this candle because it's frightened of the light; now give me your hand and put it here. There? Yes, I have a special pocket for my little mouse; if you reach inside you can feel how warm and furry it is. It feels funny. Go ahead, don't be afraid, you can touch it again, you can play with it. Why is it so wet? It gets that way when you pet it, it's showing you it likes to be petted. It wants to come out. Yes, help it, put your hand around it like that. It's a big mouse, you shouldn't keep it in such a little place. Oh it gets smaller when it goes back inside; it's just stretching now because it feels so happy when you stroke it. It doesn't have much fur, it might get cold out here. No, no it won't, it likes what you're doing, it might even let you kiss it if you wanted to. I don't want to. Okay, then just rub it up and down like that, like that.

Out of everything Zoe Mohr has told me recently, this is what lingers. This possibility, or variations on it. A scene she hinted at but never described, leaving the details to my mind with the strong suspicion it would fill them in. As it has. Versions of my own making; evidently all I'm meant to have. Just as Zoe was left to conjure up her visions of the truth, never ascertaining it from Julia. Never really trying to.

Why? Why hadn't she confronted her with the possibility?

Had I been in Zoe's place, I think I would have. Gone to
Julia and asked her, right out, if Jordan had molested her in
the shed. If she'd blocked the memory, then I'd have helped
her, forced her, if necessary, to remember. To bring it all out
and deal with it.

Provided there was something to be dealt with. At least I'd
have tried to find that out. It's possible the whole thing was in
Zoe Mohr's mind and had nothing to do with Julia's mind at
all. But I doubt it. Either way, I'd have wanted to be sure. I'd
like to be sure, now, too.

"It seems to me you are assuming three things," she says
when I approach her — no, reproach would be a better way of
putting it — with the idea. "One, that Julia would've been
able to remember, whether assisted or unassisted by me doesn't
matter. Two, that she could have done so instantly, or at least
in a matter of days. And three, that the act of remembering
would not have damaged her further, but would most
definitely have helped her. The magic of catharsis, isn't that
what you have in mind? A little Freudian abracadabra?
Coupled, of course, with a great deal of determination. When
it comes to will power, the Prussians and the Puritans have so
much in common."

Freud was an Austrian, and not every American is a
Puritan. What is more, that is totally beside the point.

"I refuse to believe," she shoots piercing little looks at me,
"that you are basically simple-minded. Sometimes, however,
you make it very difficult to sustain such a refusal. I think I
could treat your assumptions more graciously if they were not
founded on a larger, much more dangerous one. You seem to
think Julia was raised in a vacuum, that one day she went
walking in the woods, rather like Red Riding Hood, and
Jordan, with his Big Bad Mouse, leaped out at her, traumatiz-
ing her for life. Just get her to relive that horrible scene, and
presto! she'd live happily ever after.

"What, may I ask, ever happened to heredity and environment? Are we to dismiss Rebecca Carroll's influence? Should we forget about James Carroll's sister simply because his relatives managed to? You take a possible genetic predisposition, parents who were neither one exactly free from neurosis, siblings on the inside, society on the outside, and all you can come up with is a fairy tale!"

Well, dammit! At least I'd have tried to determine if it was truth or fiction! It's one thing I could have done, some kind of action I could have taken. You can talk heredity and environment all you want, they are no excuse for sitting back and not trying to make things better.

"My dear, no generation has a monopoly on idealism. I did what I thought was best, armed with what knowledge I had at the time. And consider, please, both the times and the knowledge.

"The words we've been using, 'trauma,' 'catharsis,' 'neurosis,' they're so everyday now, so easily spoken and applied. You were born with them already swimming about in the cultural stream for anyone to fish out when he chose. While I, I can remember when they didn't exist, and then when suddenly they did, strange objects proliferating around one, to be approached with suspicion, or ridicule, or fear.

"I remind you the year was nineteen twenty. Sigmund Freud was far from a household name. I, like most people, had never read his book on dreams, which was the only one available in English, nor do I think it would have helped me in this case if I had. Yes, the London Institute of Psychoanalysis existed, but so did a thousand other groups and cliques and cults concerned with various arcane or esoteric causes. If Lytton Strachey's brother James hadn't gone to Vienna and got himself analyzed, I don't know how long such a state of naïveté would have continued. He and his wife came back determined to quite literally spread the word, and proceeded to pour out translations as fast as they could. Then Leonard Woolf, ever the cautious one, decided several years later that it would be all right for Hogarth Press to publish Freud's entire works. But to Leonard, as well as to most of us, these were intellectual pursuits, nothing more. Virginia, for example, was never psychoanalyzed, even though her husband was publishing Freud and her brother Adrian was practicing him. Nor did Lytton, with two analysts in the family, attempt to get Carrington onto their couch any more than he tried getting her into his bed.

"How can I explain it to you? Nothing is comparable to such disparity today. Everything is so popularized, perhaps that has something to do with it. This mass culture of ours would have made Bloomsbury shudder. To them, culture was a class privilege, and they were its foremost arbiters. Today's culture has no boundaries; the Bloomsberries, however, spent a good deal of time erecting boundaries and seeing that they were maintained. Leonard could publish Freud as his contribution to a select fund of knowledge, but that didn't mean he had to apply the ideas themselves to his private life. The boundary, you see, was respected; work and wife were separate.

"And to us, James Strachey and Adrian Stephen were acquaintances, involved in endeavors either interesting or dubious depending on our bias. What they did with their lives had little to do with how we handled our own." She stops to drink a glass of water. A pause for dramatic effect? or is it simply that the words have made her dry.

"Perhaps I did err in not confronting Julia the moment she'd recovered. But," she puts down the empty glass as if merely holding it made her tired, "I was afraid to. Far from minimizing the experience, I was afraid that any reference to it might cause a relapse. I thought it better to wait, and in the meantime to get Julia away from Stone Hedge as soon as possible. So I pressed for a decision about London. My reasoning, such as it was, led me to believe that once we were settled, I would have time and opportunity to help her get rid of whatever horrors were living inside her. That I wouldn't be able to, or would be prevented from doing so, never entered my head. I was, you see, twenty-four years old."

She continues to talk, I to listen. Briggs comes in looking very stern. Silently, she points to the large watch strapped around her wrist. "I'm afraid I must rest now," Zoe Mohr says. She does look fatigued. I forget how taxing these sessions must be for her, how much effort it must take to guide me through a world she is so intent on revealing. I think, sometimes, it borders on compulsion, this need of hers to make me see and understand. Recreating, interpreting — dealing with all that and me at the same time can't be easy, even though she usually makes it seem so. And I do forget. But, perhaps she wants me to.

"You will visit the address I have written down?" she asks. I turn at the door to assure her, see Briggs lifting her off the couch. I'm shocked; I would rather not have seen, I don't want to know. It's a violation, whether of her or me, or what we have established together, I'm not sure.

For we are joined now; I am involved. Walking past the British Museum confirms it: no guilt, I feel none at all in front of Imposing Entrance. Pass it by. How simple. Little white index cards, gone! Lawrence? Lawrence, I'll get back to him sometime. Maybe. Who cares? The important thing right now is — I'm on my way to Taviton Street.

Bloomsbury. God, to have lived here then. With them, all of them at some time or another. Bedford Square, the Morrells. What parties! What scenes and passions, triangles and bitch fights; Lady Ottoline, presiding. The talent she had for bringing them all together. Pity a poor outsider at one of those gatherings.

Gordon Square, where the action was. Everyone here at some point. Virginia and Vanessa, Thoby and Adrian first, Stephen clan setting the pattern at No. 46. Then Vanessa married Clive Bell, Virginia and Adrian moved down to

Fitzroy Square, Thoby went off, died. Brunswick Square came next, but it's gone now, the house where Virginia and Adrian, Duncan Grant and Maynard Keynes, that other economist Gerald Shove, and Leonard Woolf all lived together. Wonder about Gerald and Leonard. No ambiguous relationships in Gordon Square, though. Lytton Strachey's mother and sisters lived in one house. Duncan Grant, how that man got around, eventually shared several with Vanessa Bell. Clive joined them now and then, when he wasn't busy elsewhere with his own loves. James and Alix Strachey rented off floors of their place, Lytton, Carrington, and mutual attraction Ralph Partridge sometimes staying on one. Lydia Lopokova practiced on another, then pirouetted into Maynard Keynes' life and over to No. 46, displacing several men there, at least for a while. Adrian Stephen and wife psychoanalyzed down the block, sharing, I think, with Arthur Waley from the British Museum. Other friends, cousins, lovers, moved in and out, back and forth. Leonard and Virginia weren't far away in Tavistock Square, but that house, too, is gone, struck by a bomb in World War II.

Many of the Gordon Square houses, however, are still here. Perhaps they were camouflaged. Maybe all the intertwining matings over the years embodied themselves into a massive grapevine, and it covered the area, incestuous circles coiling overhead. A magic grapevine, if you were protected by it. A detestable growth if you weren't, if you were outside its reach looking on with fear or envy.

But strip it away, and only the Georgian terraces remain. The four-story houses sedately linked together, presenting to the street a barrier of muted façades. Not that all of Bloomsbury is so quietly sure of itself; many parts are downright tacky. But here there are iron railings on the ground floor, and narrow balconies off the first. Every balcony shields three French windows, each capped by a small triangular roof. Above these are two rows of somewhat shorter windows; though roofless, they look secure within their substantial wooden frames.

Zoe Mohr has directed me to a sister building on Taviton Street, one block from Gordon Square. It's where they lived, the four of them. "A perfectly natural decision for us to make," she'd said, "and a perfectly natural place in which to carry it out. We hardly debated about it at all, actually. As a group, we simply gravitated to the Bloomsbury district as if by instinct." To this house, bricked creamy yellow, with — no, I'm sure none of them would have allowed that geranium plant to live outside the third floor window. The building must be broken up into eight or ten apartments now. But when they were here, the four floors were separate yet connected, so that they could be either blocked off or opened into one huge dwelling.

"What a marvelous house!" Julia was whirling around the sitting room. "It's perfect. We shall be very happy here, I know it." They decided Edward should have the ground floor; cook and maid the small rooms off the main living area on the first; Zoe and Julia would split the second, and Giles would have the third, but not entirely to himself. "We shall have our workrooms here. Giles must have a place to paint . . ." "And to tat," Giles interrupted. "And this room here will be ideal for my Projects to Save the Soul. The Past over here, you see, piano, easel, loom." "Must the piano go up here?" Edward groaned. "It's a symbol, Edward, I need my symbols around me." "But it's also a bloody heavy fact, Julia. Couldn't you have just this one symbol in the sitting room?" "Yes, Julia, do," Giles pleaded. "I promise to paint you a superb picture of it. We'll label it with huge gothic letters 'Piano' and put it right here in the corner. A symbol of a symbol, of a symbol. That's much neater, don't you think?" Julia looked at Zoe, who agreed. "Oh very well, but surely there's a more attractive alternative to dictatorship than this beastly will of the majority." "Well," Edward offered, "we could all take turns being Enlightened Despots. However I doubt our socialist friends would go for it." "My dear fellow," Giles turned to him, "everyone knows socialism is an excellent system for the masses. But we are only four."

At first, they all did participate in making decisions about the house, but gradually the task of running it day-to-day fell to Zoe. Edward would have continued his involvement, out of a sense of duty if nothing else, except his connection at the Foreign Office "practically offered me my choice of cubbyholes the moment I'd walked in the door. Hastings, you remember Hastings, don't you Giles?" "Not 'Tubby' Hastings? God's foot, Edward! if old Tubby's in charge we can expect another war momentarily." Giles had already been "lured away by Roger Fry and Co.," as Julia put it, and was busy helping rebels against the Slade organize an exhibition of London post-impressionists. Julia, initially the most enthusiastic of them all, began drifting away earlier and earlier to spend more time in her workroom.

"I guess I was destined," Zoe Mohr had told me, "to stand in other people's corners rather than create some area of my own. I didn't mind, really, because I was often quite useful to them. My days were very full, very busy. Even Edward and I managed to work together on occasion, compiling statistics, reports for the Foreign Office. And Giles frequently asked me to pose. We'd be in his room, the light streaming in, our voices rising and falling; it was very pleasant, in the beginning." Brief pause, emphasis noted. "As for Julia . . ." She'd smiled, ruefully; remembering.

The climb to Julia's workroom. It had been weeks since Zoe had been up there; she'd actually had to schedule an afternoon off for herself. If she weren't careful her whole life would go by, consumed by little projects that took away her time and left behind no monument to mark its passing. Julia, she knew, was up to some great and mysterious endeavor. There'd been many tradesmen's deliveries at the door, brown paper parcels she'd insisted on unwrapping in the privacy of her workroom. Much thumping and whirring from within, long hours spent there alone, humming, cursing, occasional shouts of — joy? anger? wafting downstairs to everyone's curiosity. They would have been more concerned by the strange noises and Julia's secretiveness, but she was so lighthearted of late it seemed to the three of them that everything must be all right. Julia had agreed, after some persuasion, to a "free day," or at least an afternoon's ride in the park, and Zoe was to knock on the door when ready to go.

"Come in!" Julia yelled in a peculiar voice, as if she'd lost the power to enunciate.

Zoe opened the door. "I'm . . ." Julia, hair disheveled, her mouth full of straight pins, sat hunched over a sewing machine. She was swathed in what must have been an entire bolt of red velvet. Blazing streaks of satins and taffetas hung from the walls. Fur pieces and laces and ribbons swirled over the floor, coiling around table legs, clinging to Julia's feet. And paper, huge sheets of flimsy white paper with strange blue markings on them were pinned to the wall in untidy bundles, while what was once smooth brown wrapping paper lay crumpled wherever it had been dropped. Noise, what had seemed like whirring from outside was in here a screeching whine that raced and slowed, raced and slowed, controlled, erratically, by Julia, who was trying to speak above the clatter and through the pins sticking between her lips. "With you in a minute," she must have said.

Zoe made herself nod. She stepped over an unopened bundle and closed the door, noticing then the tailor's dummy behind it. If she just gave herself time, if she refused to be overcome by the bizarre appearance of things and went slowly around the room examining each item on its own, she would make sense of it. This was a scene of creation, not devastation; she must keep telling herself that. Here, these sheets of paper were patterns, "rt slve," "bdce," other abbreviations faintly discernible on the blue-edged shapes. And those ribbons, they weren't grouped haphazardly, they matched the trim lying underneath. The lace, did the lace go with that black velvet hanging beside it? Buttons, braiding, hooks and eyes, all in little heaps scattered about, but they were sorted heaps. Yes, everything in its . . .

"Well?" The noise had stopped, the pins been removed. "What do you think?" Julia was looking at her expectantly.

"Julia, whatever are you up to? You must have enough fabric here to clothe half of Bloomsbury."

"Do you really think so? I was worried about that, it was very hard to estimate, but perhaps I've done it correctly after all."

Zoe tensed, body preparing itself for danger. "I . . . don't understand."

"If things go at all as I expect them to," she went about picking up a hat here, a dress there. "I really shall be making clothes for half of Bloomsbury. The amusing half, at least." She laughed. "Oh Zoe, it's going to be such fun! I hardly know what to show you first. Here, one of my best creations. Shall I model it for you on my very own body? Yes, of course I shall. Wait here." She disappeared into the small room adjoining.

Surely she did not intend becoming a dressmaker. That was preposterous. It would be like Giles' announcing he was going to, sell paints in a shop somewhere. Ridiculous. Designer maybe? That didn't seem right either. It still smacked of trade. What's more, Julia had never cared a fig about fashion before. Zoe couldn't imagine her suddenly caring enough to want to dress other people in addition to herself. And the fabrics, no one had worn bombazine since Queen Victoria; velvets, furs, there certainly wasn't much call for that sort of thing anymore. What could it mean?

The door was flung open and Julia entered, twirling. She looked like a barber pole, or a giant peppermint stick, all red and white satin stripes. She stopped in the middle of the room. "Don't you love it?" Her arms were open expansively and she was grinning, waiting for Zoe to say yes, she adored it.

But Zoe couldn't. She couldn't say anything. They were all to blame, letting Julia lock herself up in here, leaving her to — Everything's all right, certainly, everything's fine. Look at her. Look at that . . . garment, she's so proud of. The ugliest — they'd laugh her off the streets if she dared . . .

"Zoe? What's the matter? It's a gown, not the end of the wor . . ." She stopped. Arms lowered, body drooped. "Oh. I see." Her face had lost every trace of animation. "You thought . . . this was real, didn't you? You actually thought I was, going to wear it." She walked to a table, picked up a spool of thread. "Where, Zoe? To the ballet? Did you think I meant to wear it there?" She threw the spool down. "Or the opera? The symphony perhaps?" She'd turned. "Or maybe," she slammed her hand on the table, "maybe just down the street. A little night's stroll in all my finery. Was that it, Zoe? Did you think I'd visit our friends and leave tatty strips of satin as my calling card?"

"Julia, don't. Don't." Zoe looked around her for support. "I didn't know what to think, what to make of it. All this," she gestured at the disarray, "then that," her hand indicated the dress, "I just didn't know. You never said. You just let me come in here and . . ."

"And jump to conclusions. Very flattering conclusions. Very." Julia pushed herself away from the table and began walking about. "Friends. I'm so fortunate to have such . . . trusting friends."

"Julia, you know I . . ."

"I know nothing!" The veins in her neck stood out. "Nothing! Except that you walk in here, into a place where I have been . . . working so hard," trembling voice stopped her for a moment, "so hard, and right away you . . ." she rubbed shaking fingers along her forehead. "Anyone else and you'd have, waited. Been Giles, you'd have laughed, waited for him, to explain. Instead of jumping, right away."

Zoe sat down on the floor. She couldn't stand it anymore, having Julia attack her like this. And it was true, it was true, if she'd walked in on Giles instead of Julia she'd have played along, amused, waiting for the Grand Announcement of what it was all about. She shielded her face.

The lower half of Julia's body came into view, walking slowly closer, sound of satin shooshing the only — no, breathing too, hers, Julia's. Body stopped, stillness except for breathing. Julia's voice, "Zoe," oh God how sad her voice, "am I really insane? Have I been so mad, there's no hope?" Without looking Zoe could see the tears falling on Julia's cheeks. She reached out, embraced her legs. "No, Julia, no, no. Don't think that, don't." Julia's hand rested on her head. "Then why, Zoe? Why did you, why've you done this to me?" Zoe pressed her face into satin legs.

Forgive. Something they both must do. The emotionalism passed, cleansed, prepared the way. There was so much stress to be lifted. Julia, degowned, cleared a space for herself on the floor next to Zoe and they sat, touching. "Are you all right?" Zoe asked, taking her hand. "Yes, don't worry. I can handle this. This isn't the same, it's not like what happens when I . . . lose control; it's different." "How? How is one supposed to know the other isn't happening?" Julia shook her head indicating she had no answer. Zoe pressed, "If only we could tell, if only there were some way to. That's why I acted as I did. You have to realize how hard it is. When we see you — when I walked in, I thought the worst. Because I had no way of knowing."

"Yes, it's unfair of me, isn't it? Not to be able to myself, but expecting you all to. Sometimes I think I'm . . . testing. I'm testing how much you really care. Perhaps I did trap you today. For some perverse reason, knowing you'd be bound to think — But it doesn't make sense, Zoe. I know you love me.

And Giles, my parents. Why would I suspect you of something I must be sure about?"

"Well were you, aware of feeling that way? of purposely wanting to trap us? Me? Did I do something, or say . . ."

"No, no. If only it were that simple, if only I *were* aware. Anyway, today was different. Today was so . . . surface-like. I mean, I didn't break down, did I. We had a fight. Maybe I wanted us to, I don't know. But I didn't lose contact, I was here through every bit of it."

"Could you tell beforehand? That this wouldn't be the same?"

"No. No, except for this, sense of surface. The other times, it's like going under. Like a huge wave towering over me, my back's to it and it comes surging up from nowhere, sweeping me under and, down to its depths. And there's this horrible churning and choking, I can't breathe or see, I'm fighting, struggling, there's no air, no air. And then, peace. I'm in a water world, under the sea, and it's safe. Everything's filtered green and wavy, everything undulates because I'm seeing it through a curtain of water. And I, I like it there, at first. I'm a little girl, exploring, playing, protected all around me by the water. But it starts to get darker. A wind, somehow there's a wind under there, churning things up again. Darker, green goes to black and I'm cold, I'm frightened, I want to go home, I'm not safe. And I turn around and around, trying to see my home, the light, trying to swim, moving my arms and my legs trying to swim but not getting anywhere. I'm trapped, can't breathe, I'm so frightened, swimming, swimming and not getting there, getting sucked back or down. I scream I scream! I . . . wake up screaming, they tell me I . . . come back screaming."

They were silent, both sitting cross-legged; Julia picked up a stray ribbon and began tearing it into tiny threads. Zoe watched her, as if the action were important, held some code that would make sense of it all. "And you've no way of knowing when, or if, the wave will come?"

Julia frowned. "Not really. If there is some warning I don't seem able to pay attention to it. Maybe something in me knows, but if so, I still can't get out of the way."

"Do you think it's brought on by the same thing? I mean the times when you have gone under," she hesitated to mention either Jennie Hilbreth or Jordan, unsure of her way, "was there some connection between them? Were they related in some way?"

"Hmmm, I've tried, you know. I honestly have tried, in my lucid moments, to puzzle it out. It's so strange to be split like this, to have one part of me removed, trying to be objective, about the other. Sometimes that other is a total stranger; her past, her history belongs to someone else. Not to me, I'm just a point in space looking down at her, a little enclosure of air with two eyes."

Zoe smiled, placing her fingertips on Julia's temple. She loved those eyes. Julia's hand closed on hers and pressed it. She brought it to her lips, kissed the palm. Zoe felt her concentration draining away and desire flowing in to replace it; too soon, she must recapture her line of thinking. "Julia? Did you? Did you ever notice a connection?"

Julia was rubbing her cheek against Zoe's palm. "Death," she said lightly, "but death connects everything, doesn't it." Still cheek to hand, gentle strokes, "So tired, take me to bed, Zoe. Hold me, let me sleep in your arms," her words lilting in a strange lullaby.

Zoe obeyed, undressing her as she would a child and putting her to bed. Julia held out her arms for Zoe to lie down next to her; within a few moments, she was asleep. Here, for an hour at least, Zoe could protect her. She pressed the thin shoulder closer and told herself when Julia woke up, she must ask her what the dresses were for.

Julia called it Project Number Twenty-one; the number may have referred to the year or the latest in her series of soul-saving attempts. Zoe was aware of Julia watching her read the sheet of paper she'd retrieved from her workroom, leaping out of bed and scurrying back to sit knees up on the blanket. Robed, barefooted, she perched near the foot of the bed while Zoe sat, in judgment, with her back against a pillow. "Julia, I cannot concentrate unless you dim your beady little eyes." "Sorry." Julia bent her head and pretended to examine her fingernails, peeking from under her brows whenever she thought Zoe wouldn't notice.

Although the printing was beautifully done, Zoe had trouble reading the Elizabethan script, never having been comfortable with the *f* look of the *s*. It always made her feel buck-toothed until she could read it correctly:

THE TAVITON LAYER*f*
prefent
WORK*f by the* BAWD

Fir*f*t Production: Rolmeover and Jellyit, a Turgid Farce anent the Mountaewe and Copulate kid*f*.

*f*econd Production: Mickbe*ff*, the Arre*f*ting Foible of a poor Iri*f*h lad who wanted to be Queen.

Third Production: Richard the Turd, an Hy*f*terical Drama in which the Humping King give*f* hi*f* all to a Hor*f*e.

All private part*f* will be di*f*creetly covered. The ca*f*t will di*ff*emble every third Tue*f*day, 8 o'clock p.m.

"The idea," Julia was saying, encouraged by Zoe's laughter, "is to form our own sort of repertory company, rather peculiar and very select. We'll perform every month in the drawing room downstairs, and then, when we get better, we'll challenge the Strachey-Bell-Woolf circuit to a competition. A Festival, with a prize for the Best Bawdy Playlet Written For Family Members. Mem — bers." She rolled over, hooting, and they giggled about on the bed. "That's why, you see," she eventually managed to continue, "I am cleverly making the dresses first. I've got to have something to lure Giles and Arf into the project."

"D'you think," Zoe asked her, "Edward Arf will go along? Dress up? What would the F.O. say?"

"Most of the chaps in the F.O. would be damned jealous," Julia protested. "After all, red velvet, purple brocade, cunning little furs and absolutely miles of crinoline — you don't see much of that around anymore. And Arf will love it. He can hide behind the theatricality of it all and yet indulge himself, rather like doing it with official blessing or under government auspices, something like that."

"And what about me? It's perfectly all right for Giles and Arf to stuff themselves into corsets and crinolines for art's sake, but I'd hate to have to put myself through that kind of torture. I don't know what they see in it, really."

Julia leaned over and shook Zoe's knee, "You, my love, will not have to worry. I shall see to it that you are always in breeches. As author, producer, director, stage and costume designer, I have some control over these matters." She hopped up and straddled Zoe's lap. "In fact, little lady, I can make you . . . a star. If you, play your," she was slowly bringing her face closer, "cards right." An inch from Zoe's lips, she stopped. "Well?"

"Breeches you say?"

"Breeches. Nice, snug ones," Julia whispered.

"Show me," Zoe had taken her hand, "how they'll fit."

They'd only just finished when Giles' voice came hurtling up the stairs, calling to them that he had news. Zoe grabbed her clothes and dashed back to her own room. Though it was quite all right to do what they'd been doing, taste dictated one not get caught in the act. Giles, particularly, preferred knowing in the abstract, sensing their relationship rather than being confronted with physical proof of it. Zoe would have liked many more instances of such proof, but Julia didn't seem to need, or want, them frequently. In her mind, there was nothing to prove. No relationship. They could make rapturous love, because Julia was not about to live any experience to less than its fullest. But she was not Zoe's "to have" whenever she wanted. Julia did not belong to her, that was the Paris Agreement, she must be left alone. If she weren't, then no matter how much Zoe looked after her and took care of the practical things in her life, Julia would live without her. For certain, she wouldn't hesitate to try, tomorrow, if necessary. While Zoe knew, about herself, that she would never care to try. Even though she would be able to do it and Julia, probably, wouldn't. Very confusing, determining their degrees of need and independence. Better to simply enjoy the lovemaking when it happened. And hope the next time would not be far off. Giles could have come home unexpectedly every afternoon for the last month and not run the risk of having his sensibilities assaulted.

"Julia? Zoe?" His boots were clumping along the hallway. "Come out, come out." Simultaneously, they emerged fully dressed from their rooms. "Ah, there you are." He put an arm around each. "No riding today? Cook says you've been in all afternoon."

Julia kissed his cheek, saying, "I preferred a horse of a different color." Zoe had to turn her head aside to hide a face gone telltale red. Fortunately, Giles was not paying much attention, walking down the stairs between them and burbling on about "connubial bliss" having "struck again!"

Over sherry, they discussed the marriage of Carrington and Ralph Partridge. "Not surprising, really," Giles said, "though whether they did it because Lytton was afraid of losing Ralph, or Ralph was afraid of losing Carrington, or Carrington was afraid of losing either or both of them, I'm not quite sure. At any rate, they are all three still living at Tidmarsh, so nothing's changed in any practical way." He sipped his sherry. "Except, one presumes, dear Dora has finally conquered her fear of the male appendage and been truly deflowered at last."

"That certainly is a change, then. Partridge has succeeded where other men failed. Mark Gertler and Gerald Brenan must have tried hard enough, and long enough." Julia held out her glass for Giles to fill again.

"Evidently not hard and long enough though." He laughed, standing over Julia while the decanter wavered precariously above her skirt.

"Giles, you're snickering into my sherry." She pretended irritation. "Don't be a schoolboy, and pour."

Watching them, Zoe remembered Giles' facile account of youthful measuring games with Jordan. She didn't know whether or not he'd ever penetrated a woman; for a fact, Julia had never been with a man. The result of other "games"? Yet both could sit easily discussing in ribald fashion the antics of others. Intellectually, they could countenance everything; nothing was forbidden. Personally, none of them, including herself, was nearly so free.

". . . a few women, too, who're lamenting the loss," Julia was saying. "Carrington didn't confine herself to teasing just cocks, you know."

"Never say 'just,' Julia, as if they were mere nothings. A man's most precious treasure is not his money, nor his wife, or his lover, but his . . ."

"His what?" Edward walked in. "Ah, sherry." Poured himself a glass. "His what, what are we talking about, hm?"

He was told about the marriage, and then the four of them began embroidering on the reasons for it and the history behind it. They amused themselves for half an hour alone with variations on the wedding night, having Lytton pop up in the middle of the bed at odd, extremely odd, moments. Zoe's arms hung at the sides of her chair; she was too feeble from laughing to move them. Giles started to lift his glass, burst into more giggles, and had to put it down. Julia was balancing her glass on her stomach and grinning crookedly. Every so often, she would chortle. Edward, wiping his eyeglasses, said, "Yes, well, laugh while you can, children. We'll all of us be married some day."

VI

"That prediction of Edward's made me feel very uncomfortable," Zoe Mohr says the next afternoon. "I remember it
hanging about in the air after he'd said it, stifling our good
humor, isolating us, each from the other. From then on we
seemed to be almost waiting for change, knowing it was going
to come but not when. As if in the background there were
something threatening, a distant wind which might come
upon us at any moment."

She gazes into the past. A stillness surrounds her. There'll
be no sparks today; I doubt she has the energy. I think she
wants only to poke among the ashes, tormenting herself with
visions of what had been.

"I know how my relationship to Julia must seem to you.
That I was weak, allowed myself to be exploited, suffered
because of her and got little back in recompense. Perhaps, you
think, I enjoyed suffering, and that I wanted to be used. That
underneath my posturings of strength and efficiency, there lay
a doormat, the real me willing to be walked over if the feet
were those of my beloved."

No, my judgment has not been so harsh. How could it be?
I know too well that helpless feeling.

"In fact," she continues, "you probably think my every
encounter with Julia ended in tears or upheaval of some sort.
That we couldn't meet without either Julia going mad or me
breaking down."

It could seem that way, I suppose, to someone else. But not
to me.

"And in between such meetings I spent most of my time

coping with severe sexual frustration. So that anyway you looked at it, I was either a fool or a masochist."

Who isn't familiar with those roles? One can hardly give oneself over to adoration without playing them. Sing hallelujah. But don't confuse worship with love, don't let the foolish masochist take over.

"It's so hard to know what's best. We spend so much time trying to determine what we really feel, where we really stand, how we really ought to go about things. Only to look back, years later, and see we were operating from totally wrong premises to begin with. And we've put ourselves through all those agonies for nothing." Usually her back and shoulders are very straight, but today she sits like someone in need of comfort, or encouragement. She is slumped, sagging. "But," she rubs her hand up and down on the armrest, "I refuse to believe that was the case between Julia and me. I can't afford to." For the first time this afternoon, she looks at me. Directly, as if I must read in her eyes the truth and tell her yes, you are right to do this. "If I agreed with such a description, of myself and of what we had together, I would be invalidating my life." Unsure, her face still asks me to concur. "I loved her." What more would I have her say?

Nothing. I've been there, I've been in love. And the person I am now refuses to belittle the person I was then. Though I would do things differently if my present self were placed in the past's opportunities, I won't ridicule what that earlier girl lived through. Her pain and her happiness are safe from my worldly retrospection.

"And she loved me, though I never confronted her with it." Again, her hand goes slowly back and forth on the armrest. "Hard as that may be to believe, it's true. Julia was more capable of love than she realized, but she needed to think she was not weighed down by 'the usual human baggage.' To my mind, love transported one, but to Julia's, it tied one down. And she felt that without freedom, she would never find whatever it was she was meant to discover, the thing that would release her from those dreadful pressures. To me, if she thought she was free, then in fact she was free, so I was not going to step in front of her with petulant demands she acknowledge her love for me. If I had done so, it would only have shown that I did not respect her needs, that I did not truly love the person Julia was."

I find that a bit too noble to swallow. Really. She never once put her own needs ahead of Julia's?

"It wasn't too hard, you see, because actually Julia gave me a great deal. The secret was not to say 'Thank you.' Somehow Julia always replenished my love sufficiently to keep it going. My worst problem was not with her capacity for loving, which held enough for me provided I was never too greedy. It was when I had to share it; then I found things acutely distressing."

She talks, and what a strange experience the afternoon proves to be. When she is through, we both sit silently. I have never felt closer to her, to Zoe. I sip my gin. I could have handled things no better; nor was she more capable than I. Not when it came to jealousy.

Imagine having Virginia Woolf as a rival. That part of her story made me shiver; my body wouldn't stop shaking while she talked about Julia's extravagant devotion, her passionate yet chaste commitment. Poor Zoe. For a short time, the pain was hers alone; I was too excited, too interested, too captured by the scene to empathize. I had the luxury of choice and I chose to listen without identifying. The distance faded soon enough. When she began talking about the aftermath, then I wasn't just Zoe Mohr's listener; I became Zoe, too. Audience and actor both. And that, was strange.

Leaving her house I'm in one of those uncomfortable buzzing states. Can't get my mind, my vision, to connect with what's outside me. The gin, I guess. Plus all the emotions I've been put through. Get to my flat, no recollection of how I did it, no memory of streets, people, traffic. I really can't take gin. We both needed a drink, though, Zoe Mohr and I. But I'm not drunk; just buzzing, disjointed. Fall into bed. I need to recoup or I'll never get to Sussex in the morning.

In summer, 1922, they christened their country house The Crannies. There were so many little rooms joined together in haphazard pattern, that to get from one to another it was necessary to go up or down small flights of stairs, or turn a corner built for no sake other than its own into one of the several hallways. Giles insisted a "deranged doll" had a hand in designing it. Julia, naturally, was charmed by its peculiarity. Zoe's desire to find a place in the country where they could escape for weekends of fresh air and simple living outweighed any other reaction. Edward's main concern was that it was in the "right" place. Virginia and Leonard Woolf were only a few miles across the downs at Rodmell, and the Bell-Grants, Vanessa and Duncan, were busy growing vegetables at Charleston not many miles farther on. The neighbors had already passed judgment on the area, and lo, it was good.

The house backed right onto the Sussex downs. It was possible to walk over the rolling hills in several directions without encountering villages or people. Toward Rodmell, the River Ouse cut a channel, deep in spots, that wound among the knolls. One could listen to water flowing over rocks, and dream in solitude.

In good weather the others often joined Julia on her hikes, but if they did, she would always take a later walk by herself. Even in winter, Julia hiked. The cold and drizzle didn't seem to bother her. Zoe would watch her tall, bundled figure striding away, walking stick for companion, and often think of other times. Of trailing a long-skirted girl through pine forests, or over the Hampshire countryside. Her hair was cut short now, no tendrils on the delicate neck, but nothing had really changed. Following with her eyes, Zoe would feel the same pain, the same desire grip her; Julia still took her breath away. Today, she'd found wild white flowers growing under a bush somewhere and plaited them into a wreath for her hair. Despite the boots and layers of sweaters, she looked like a winter nymph at one with her domain — grey January sky, mistlike rain, hills disappearing into fog.

To the woman walking along the riverbank, Julia must have seemed more a ghost than a nymph or fellow human. There'd been no warning, no sound in the fog, no noise for hours but river and her own breath changing places with the air. Suddenly, through the mist, a figure had floated onto the bank, lifted her arm and drawn flowers from her hair.

Some of the stems were caught and Julia had to pull out several strands of hair to get them. Wincing, her hands chapped, ears throbbing from the wind, she felt far from a spectral figure. It was rather silly of her to have walked this distance in such weather. She doubted half an hour's solitude by the river was going to be worth it.

"Katherine?"

Startled, Julia twisted her body toward the voice. There was someone downstream. A tall — a woman, approaching slowly through the wisps of fog.

"Katherine?" the voice asked again, disbelieving.

Julia's hand hadn't moved from her head. "No," she said, lowering her arm, "no, it's not Katherine." She waited for the woman to come closer; she knew this person, the shape and walk were known to her.

And the face, looming gaunt in front of hers. Virginia Woolf. "Katherine," the mouth whispered. Eyes, sad even in repose, were stricken now, sunk deep in mourning. Attenuated fingers reached out to pluck the last wilted flower; Julia felt it being gently lifted from her hair. She watched a petal rub against lips pulled down by sorrow. Green eyes were turned away from her, toward the ground. Julia knew not to speak.

"Often I see you," the voice was quiet, factual, "putting on a white wreath and leaving us." She pivoted, still cupping the flower in an elegant hand. "And you say the words you wrote me. 'Do not quite forget Katherine,' you say. Then you dissolve." She looked down at the flower, and let it drop. Her hands plunged into huge sweater pockets. "When she was alive, I often wished she would dissolve." A cheroot and matches were brought out. "But she knew that. Mansfield and I had no secrets." The cigar was lit, acrid smoke wafted back, signaling to Julia she was free to move. Virginia no longer needed her to be someone other than herself; she walked to a rock and sat, still electing silence. "I even told her once that her scent reminded me of a civet cat taken to street walking," Virginia said, throwing her head back, snorting. She dragged on her cheroot, plumes of smoke floated from her lips. "She laughed and said she liked playing the tart, why did it bother me so? Quite suddenly, I envied her her atrocious scent. But," she bent down and pushed the cheroot's glowing tip into the earth to smother it, "only for a moment." Her body straightened, a hand came up holding two small stones; she looked at them resting in her palm and did not speak for several minutes. "Much alike," she said then, staring at the stones, "yet, not the same. Not at all." Her hand began to tip, "One is gone," a single stone fell to the ground. "And one, is here." She placed the stone in her pocket, keeping her hand around it. The other hand went to her chin, its fingers kneaded her lips as she walked slowly up and down. Stopping in front of Julia, she pushed both fists deep into the pockets of her long sweater and distractedly stretched it further out of shape. "Why write, with Katherine not here to read it?" Julia kept her gaze fixed on a sweater button. No answer was expected, she knew that, yet she felt Virginia staring down at the top of her head. The sweater disappeared. A match struck, smell of cheroot filled the air again. "You have Mansfield's eyes," the voice stated. "You must come and see me." Julia heard frozen branches crack under footsteps retreating, fading, gone.

"That's nonsense!" Zoe blustered later. "You do not have

Mansfield's eyes! Katherine's were brown, and yours are hazel. There's no similarity at all. She's just trying to, to . . ."

Julia was looking into the mirror, leaning forward then sitting back, then leaning forward again in an attempt to see her own eyes the way someone else might. "Do be quiet, Zoe," she said, moving back again for perspective.

"Oh dammit, Julia! You're not going to fall for that line, are you? 'You have Mansfield's eyes,' " she mimicked in low, sepulchral tones, "George Eliot's nose, Emily Brontë's ears, Sappho's nostril."

"One thing I do not have," Julia was lightly pawing at a frown line on her forehead, "is George Eliot's nose. George Eliot's nose was rather huge and dreadfully misshapen. My own," she turned profile, "tends to refined Roman."

"Psss." Zoe threw herself onto a chair next to the dressing table. She sat with arms crossed and legs sprawling, slouched in disgust. Julia went right on paying attention to her own reflection. "Julia, I have never known you to spend more than twenty-two seconds in front of any mirror either foreign or domestic. What are you seeing in there?"

"Do you think they were lovers?" Julia continued to face the mirror.

"Who?"

"Katherine and Virginia."

"No." Zoe picked up a pair of manicure scissors, "Why?" and looked at them with extraordinary interest while chills of nausea attacked her.

"Just curious." Julia's hand and throat were pleasing each other, the fingers moving in gentle strokes.

Those delicate, dreamy caresses were unbearable. Zoe stood. "Well don't get too curious." The shakes had won and she couldn't fight them back. "For your sake," even her voice was trembling, "I don't recommend it."

"Really?" Eyes briefly appraised Zoe's image, then returned to their own. "I shall certainly keep such objective advice in the very forefront of my mind."

"You. Bitch." Zoe slammed the scissors onto Julia's dressing table and walked out.

How was she to control it? How was she to conquer jealousy? It was destructive, it served no purpose, yet Zoe could not contain it. She couldn't get it to settle, rest, be sensible. How get jealousy to be sensible? If passion knew no reason, then surely jealousy was twice as uncritical. It was impervious to logic; it trampled over best interests; it manifested itself whenever it pleased, taking total control over any moment and ruining it without warning. Or with warning. It didn't much matter once the damage was done.

Zoe could see her reactions pushing Julia away from her, yet she was powerless to stop them. Helplessly, she raged and sulked and played the jealous lover, knowing even while she did it that if anything were guaranteed to threaten Julia's freedom, to send her running, it was the restrictions and demands of possessive love.

Perhaps, if Julia and Virginia had been involved in a physical affair, Zoe might have been better able to cope. But how was she to fight a liaison of the spirit? a communion of the soul? The "inamoratas" hardly ever saw each other. After that weekend in January and everyone's returning to London, Julia had sent a note to Hogarth House only to hear from Leonard by return post that Virginia was ill in bed and seeing no one. Zoe had watched her for some sign of disappointment. There had been none; Julia had merely dropped the letter and strolled away, saying "Of course."

On the rare occasions when they did see each other, Julia would return with a glow about her face that Zoe had never been able to put there. That was the thing. Julia and Virginia were involved in some sort of perpetual courtship. They stroked each other's minds, nothing else. They excited one another with the sensuality of ideas. How easy to become engrossed, with that other sensuality suspended, so that it filled the air with a lush promise which could tantalize forever. Their relationship never descended to the familiar, the everyday, the tiresome. It was never given the chance to.

Go compete with that.

Sexual encounters dwindled from few to none. Zoe had tried, at first, to reassert herself, to force her way into Julia's consciousness via her body, their bodies, accustomed to meetings of intensest pleasure. But Zoe made love with desperation in her now, pushing to prove, to assert, to "be" for Julia. She willed her body to speak; it exhorted and pleaded and demanded and suggested, and sometimes, driven by the terror that Julia was not listening, it brutalized. The roughness she was capable of shocked her, and the realization that Julia's body responded but her mind was separate, inviolate, made Zoe give up. She couldn't stand their union being so diminished, couldn't bear having less than all.

So she withdrew. And there was no solace. Julia retreated from the sight of her wounds. Giles was antipathetic, Zoe having violated one of his cardinal principles: "Don't be tedious," he'd told her, "there's nothing more boring than jealousy." Edward, she would never turn to.

But Julia did, that is she allowed Edward to step in and fill the role of ready companion, left vacant by Zoe's refusal to play the only part left to her. As if having waited in the wings for the lead to fall ill or disgrace herself in some fashion, Edward leaped center stage with practiced agility. Ballet tickets, once for four, were now suddenly available just for two. Invitations which used to come well in advance began to mysteriously appear at the last moment, when Giles was out and Zoe indisposed or occupied or just in from riding and smelling like a horse. Any slide show on walking tours would find Edward, his avid interest in hiking but recently surfaced, hunting down dowdy lecture halls in remote areas of the city so that he might propel Julia there that evening without losing his way. Official functions were harder to deal with; Julia didn't like them any more than Giles or Zoe did, and Edward was only occasionally successful in getting her to accompany him. He always, however, made up for the ordeal by seeing to it a treat followed soon after: an especially long hike at The Crannies, or an invitation to tea at any one of several amusing addresses in Bedford Square. This sort of trade soon became a game between them. "If you go to the reception this afternoon for Bavaria's under secretary of finance," Edward might say, grabbing hold of Julia's hand as she passed him in the hallway, "I will get Ottoline's chauffeur to whisk us up to Garsington tomorrow in time for croquet." "Done!" Julia might reply, "but do make sure the under secretary's head has more hair upon it than the ball, and his balls are more potent than his breath, that his shirt front is crisper than his money, and his money is cleaner than his nails." Still holding her hand, Edward would bow over it and click his heels, promising to "do me very best."

"You know, Zoe," Giles said to her one afternoon in his workroom, "you're even more a fool than I thought." He was making quick, preliminary sketches of her preparatory to the oil he had in mind which would depict a woman from every angle at once. Dressed in a shirt purchased off the back of a Spanish burro driver, Zoe sat across the room from him. The autumn light was striking in yellow shafts, casting sharp, sable-hued shadows of body and chair onto the wall behind. She was posing in profile, face browned by the September sun, dark hair clipped and shaping her head. Her eyelids were drooping languorously; now and then they closed, and long, black lashes rested on the skin; then slowly, heavily, the lashes rose, weighted by abundance.

For a moment Giles' hand didn't move. It hovered above the pad, holding its piece of charcoal without knowing what to do; suddenly it remembered and began sketching rapidly again. "The Woolf isn't your enemy. There's really no threat from that quarter. Never has been. You've wasted all your ammunition on the wrong person, and now you've nothing left to defend yourself with."

"I don't care anymore."

"Balderdung." Giles asked her to turn three-quarters toward him and flipped a page over. "It's quite obvious you do care. Too much for your own good."

"Either way, the result's the same."

"Only if you continue to sulk in your tent. Edward is still a beatable opponent, though admittedly, not nearly so worthy as Virginia. Why not admit to yourself you made a mistake, and come back out and fight?"

"I don't think you understand, Giles. Edward is welcome to Julia if he's willing to settle for part of her, for whatever the Woolf leaves over. I'm not. He can have her, she can have him, they can all have each other for all I care. And I'm surprised, frankly, to find you counseling otherwise."

"Turn please." Zoe faced him. "How little *you* understand. Remember when we finally put several of those salacious skits together into one Grand Performance? I happened to be looking at Virginia when you walked on in your leather breeches, playing Hexsex to my Elizabitch. Her eyes, my dear, coursed up and down your body with, well if not lust, Virginia isn't given to lust, but certainly with decided interest. Julia's not her type, she's too much like her. Virginia likes them tall *and* strong. Witness the strapping lady from Long Barn currently making her presence felt."

"Are they involved? I hadn't heard."

"Not yet, not yet. But Vita Sappho-West will make a move eventually. I've never known her not to."

"I doubt it would change things. Virginia and Julia are above the physical, they're up there in the rarefied air bonded together like . . . Siamese angels. Ethereal twins brushing their wings against each other. I wish they'd come down to earth, and do it like the rest of us."

Giles groaned. "Those images really won't bear scrutiny, Zoe. Lift your chin a fraction, no, too much, there, perfection. I grant you Virginia may be inhuman at times, but her Angelic Qualities must certainly be rated at a minimum. As for Julia . . ." he bent to rummage in the box of charcoal at his feet. Zoe took the opportunity to stretch her shoulder muscles and massage her neck. Giles straightened. "What about Julia, Zoe?" He proceeded to study his drawing.

"What about her?" she continued rubbing the back of her neck.

"Do you think Edward is the best person for her?"

"I don't see that what I think matters very much."

Giles lowered his sketch pad. "Don't be evasive, it's unbecoming. Right profile, please."

"I'm sorry." Zoe moved into position. "You know how I feel about Edward, at least you should after all these years, but if he's what Julia wants, then what's anyone supposed to do about it?"

"Nothing, if indeed it is what Julia wants. But right now I suspect it's still a question of what Edwards wants. It's time he was married, you know. Looks bad at the F.O. for a chap his age not to be getting around to the inevitable. Not that they'd ever say anything; they'd simply never promote him. Bad risk, national security, mumble mumble blackmail y'know. Any man not dutifully performing the functions of a husband must be out enjoying himself, humping either loose women or young boys and blathering the government's highest secrets while he's at it."

"So, they'll marry. What have you got against it? I should think you'd welcome Edward as a brother-in-law."

"Oh, Gordon's a perfectly amiable friend," he noisily changed pages and commanded Zoe to face the wall, "but it's me he wants to bed, not Julia. And it's me he'd rather wed, if only God and jurisprudence would look more kindly upon such nuptials. Since neither activity is possible — I don't know about God, but I, for one, am utterly unyielding — he'll marry Julia. And I'm not at all certain that is fair to her. Nor, for that matter, am I sure it will be good for her either. Among other things, I have never forgotten our conversation that evening at Stone Hedge."

"It seems so long ago. But, surely Julia wouldn't agree to such an arrangement if she were still frightened."

"Of mice? Perhaps not. However, it may be the line of least resistance. Certainly, Edward will press her. And every day she's relying on him more and more for all the things you used to provide, the little comforts and amusements, the practical matters she doesn't want to cope with. She needs these things done for her; she needs someone to care for her, and if you won't, then Edward will."

"How can I, Giles? You're asking me to restore the past."

Giles sighed. "Yes, I admit my motives are not untainted by selfishness. I liked our life the way it was before. When the four of us were comrades. And whatever was between you and Julia, was between you; it didn't interfere. Everything's changed now. You've changed, Zoe. You've become so vulnerable. Really," he tried to make his voice lighter, "if you don't provide a touch of hearty masculinity around here, who will?"

Zoe was unable to laugh. "Aren't you through yet with this rear view? I'm getting tired of talking to the wall."

"Two seconds." He made several deft, black strokes. "There. The model is free to move."

Zoe got up, stretched, and walked to a side table where her cigarettes were. She'd only recently begun to smoke, but inhaled deeply now, watching Giles put his supplies in order. "It seems to me you're trying to protect everyone's interests but Edward's."

"Does it?" He went on puttering with sticks of charcoal and gum erasers.

"Mm."

"Well Edward has Mother on his side," Giles said, sorting through his sketch pads, "he doesn't need me there too."

Zoe turned away. Naturally, Mrs. Carroll would favor the match. Edward had all the attributes of a desirable candidate, but none of them were there to any excessive degree. He was entirely acceptable and absolutely no competition. The union, surely, would be blessed.

And Zoe would be officially discarded. Left outside to make a separate life. To survive.

Could she? Spain, last spring; for a month she'd traveled on her own. Going to the remotest parts. Managing, alone, across a landscape indifferent to her existence. Testing? Yes, and preparing: this is how it will be, this isolation, this aridity; see and smell and feel it, and know.

"Bloody damn!" Giles was trying to adjust his easel and one of the bolts appeared to have stuck.

"Need some help?" Zoe asked, walking toward him.

"I can manage quite nicely, thank you," he said in a tone calculated to stop her. Zoe smiled to herself; this was no time to regain her "hearty masculinity." She must keep it in check while Giles loosened the bolt himself. Then, when he completed the task — childish test of manhood thinly disguised — she'd be free to act his comrade again. Some days there were entirely too many delicate balances to maintain.

She strolled around poking into paint pots and peeking at canvases leaning against the walls. She hadn't realized he'd been so productive. When had he found the time? And where had some of his models come from? "Good Lord, Giles, wherever did you paint this?" Zoe held the large, unfinished canvas in front of her. She was truly astonished. Pastel lights were playing on a graceful body, sprawled in careless regard for both its nakedness and its tumescence, the swollen shaft rising from curls half-hidden by a hand which seemed to have fallen there as if by accident.

"Oh, him." Giles had come up behind her. "I call that

'Queen's Odalisque,' but it's too impressionistic, too romantic. Neither quality, incidentally, the least bit in keeping with the subject's nature. Flagstaff Jack, I believe his name was. Even if I'd painted him the way Gauguin did his island women, I wouldn't have a prayer of getting him exhibited in anything other than some little private show that didn't count." He took the painting from her and rested it on the floor. "I did have a rather marvelous idea for a Cézanne-style rendering of two men ecstatically united, to be called 'Mounting Saint Victoire' . . ." Zoe laughed with more zest than she'd felt in months. "You know, it's nice to see you laughing again. I've missed it."

"So have I."

Eyes were smiling at each other; soon, though, they grew self-conscious and shifted their focus. "Where was I? Oh yes, discrimination against the male nude." He started pacing, gesticulating. "Any bread-baker's daughter can be displayed to the public's eye, but even the son of Adonis wouldn't be given wall space now. The Male Body, Zoe, has fallen into disrepute and lies languishing somewhere in the Dark Ages. The Renaissance chose not to look, but to push forth the Female instead. The result, I suppose, of all those monks scurrying about abnegating their own flesh and transubstantiating Christ while they yearned for the Virgin Mary's bosom. At any rate, Praxiteles turned over in his grave and brave men of impeccable reputation wept."

"What about Michelangelo?" Zoe asked him. "He doesn't seem to fit into that neat little theory of yours."

"Michelangelo was a throwback. He was also bloody lucky not to have been born four centuries later. Can you imagine Queen Victoria giving him a commission? Even had she granted him some Midlands train station ceiling, she'd have taken one look, said 'We are not pleased,' and ordered it draped in black immediately."

"Well, that was Victoria."

"And that is today, too, I assure you. No, if I hope to get a nude into next season's showings, it'll have to be female."

Zoe nodded, reaching for a cigarette. She was lighting it when Giles nonchalantly asked, "Pose for me?"

The match continued to be held against a cigarette already burning.

"You needn't give me your answer today. Anytime in the next month or so will do. See you at tea." He left. Zoe started walking toward the door; she felt dizzy — the result, perhaps, of too much smoke.

Why not, she decided at some point. Posing for Giles would be like having one's brother interrupt one in the bath: nothing extraordinary and something perfectly natural.

However, the first time she stepped out of her robe one morning early in November, she was aware of her nipples puckering and goose bumps prickling her body. Giles, who could always be counted on in a conspiracy, hurried to place more coal in the grate, for of course Zoe was reacting to the cold. His action eased her, and by the time they'd determined on the right pose, she felt much calmer. Total comfort was reached two sessions later, when Zoe managed to shed the last trace of embarrassment along with her clothes, and the modeling hour became, for both of them, an ordinary, everyday occurrence. They never thought how anyone else might look upon it.

When Julia knocked unexpectedly, asking to be admitted, it was natural for Giles to reply "Enter," and go right on painting. They heard the door open and close as Julia came in, hidden by the backdrop which also blocked her view of them.

"Hello," Zoe called, not breaking the pose, "I thought you and Arf were going to a matinee today." She was sitting on a disheveled couch. One arm rested on a nightstand; the other was bent behind her back so the hand, supposedly, could scratch. Surely her last customer had just left and she was exhausted from a hard night's work.

Moving cautiously around the curtain, Julia answered, "We were, but . . ." She saw Zoe's naked body.

Giles, not bothering to look up from the canvas, said, "Hello, Sister, there's a seat to your left, I think."

"But what?" Zoe asked her. She was careful to move just her lips and keep her eyes fixed vacantly ahead.

"Well, speak!" Giles mixed more paint onto his palette. "Has some Momentous Event kept Edward in his cubbyhole?"

Julia sat down. "He's . . . been detained. An uprising of some sort, in Bavaria. Munich. Unsuccessful, the leader's been arrested. Several people were killed; he thought he'd better keep an eye on things."

"An uprising? Did the government cut off their beer or something?" Giles switched from knife to brush and began daubing yellow ocher onto the canvas.

"He did mention a beer hall, but not in any flippant way. It's evidently quite serious — an attempted takeover by the right wing, a 'putsch' he called it. Officials held at gunpoint, private troops marching through the streets, that sort of thing. But this man Hitler, the ringleader, he'll be up for trial and Edward thinks — Aren't you cold, Zoe?"

"Not a bit."

"How can she be," Giles asked, "knowing Edward's at his post, keeping his eyes on world events for jolly England's sake." He peered around the easel, "Doesn't it warm you down to your toes, Zoe?"

"Oh it do, it do."

Julia stood, scraping her chair back noisily. "I don't think that's very amusing. I've obviously interrupted, and won't do so again." Zoe broke her pose to watch, open-mouthed, as Julia made her exit. The door slammed. She and Giles looked at each other; they shrugged, and went back to work.

Later, Zoe went downstairs to bathe and dress for dinner. She was toweling her hair, and did not hear anyone enter. But when she turned around, Julia was in her room, leaning against the closed door.

"I didn't hear you knock," Zoe said for want of anything better.

"I didn't."

"Oh. Do you . . . want to sit down?" She gestured weakly toward a chair.

"No. What's been going on, Zoe?"

"What do you mean?"

"You never told me you were posing for Giles."

"Oh come now, Julia, I've been posing for years!"

"Like that?"

"You mean nude? Well no, I haven't posed in the nude before. This is the first time Giles has asked me to." She sat on the bed. For some reason, she felt compelled to pull her robe closer, making sure no flesh was exposed.

"Are you trying to tell me today was the first time you were naked up there?"

"I didn't say that. But what business is it of yours? I wasn't aware it mattered to you what I did with my time. Or my body."

"I'm not responsible for what you are or aren't aware of. But I do think you might have had the courtesy to ask me if I minded."

"You're joking."

"Most certainly I am not. It was horrible, walking in like that. Seeing you display your body; to someone else."

"Giles is hardly 'someone else,' Julia. As for my body, I'll display it to whomever I please. You can't reject it and claim it at the same time."

"I never rejected you! You turned away from me! I never pushed you away, Zoe. Never."

"Oh not physically, perhaps. But you pushed, Julia, you pushed. I fought you for a while, until I finally realized how hopeless it was. I gave up long after you stopped caring."

"I have always cared! Always!"

"Mmhmm. What I don't understand, Julia, is how you can confront me and not your friend Virginia. Rumor has it she once swam naked with Rupert Brooke; that's much more serious, don't you think? After all, he was a poet, not a painter, and his interest, if he were able to muster any at the sight, could hardly have been professional."

"To hell with that! Virginia's body doesn't exist for me! Yours does! It always has. Zoe, please."

"Please what. You know, Julia, to anyone else in Bloomsbury it's your behavior right now that would be considered unseemly, not mine. You're showing bad form; I merely showed my body."

"Zoe, I can't believe this of you. You have never been cruel to me before. You have never — if I've hurt you, I'm . . ."

"Hurt me?" Zoe got up. "How could you've hurt me?" She yanked at the bedspread; grabbing one of the pillows underneath, she thrust it toward Julia. "How can you hurt a pillow, Julia? And what does it matter if you do?" She threw it violently onto the floor. "There are plenty of others to take its place!"

"No! It's not true!" Julia picked up the pillow at her feet and clasped it tightly. "I need this one, Zoe, this one! It's mine!"

Zoe shook her head in denial.

"Yes!" Her face was distorted. "Mine! I need mine! I need my! I . . ."

"Julia, calm down. Give me the pillow." Zoe held out her hand. "Give it to me." Slowly Julia opened her arms, letting the pillow fall. Zoe caught it and tossed it back on the bed. "You'd better lie down for a while."

"Will you lie down with me?"

Again, Zoe shook her head. Julia seemed dazed; she would have to be led to her room. Zoe took her arm. "Come, I'll put you to bed." Julia didn't move. Her eyes were unfocused; spittle had formed at the side of her mouth. Zoe tried again. "Come on, Julia, you'll feel . . ."

"I hate you, Zoe." She'd said it very calmly as she disengaged her arm. On her own, she opened the door and walked steadily across the hall to her room.

When had Zoe lost the ability to feel? A burst of anger; then nothing. Julia's anguish hadn't reached her, hadn't penetrated those walls she'd built yet somehow hadn't known about, until she was standing behind them. Watching, unmoved, while Julia stood outside and begged. While Julia struggled in front of her, and Zoe hadn't cared any more than a corpse would. She'd been defending a dead thing; Julia had come too late, the blood had already drained from her body. So frightening; she'd only meant to protect herself.

Life in general had a callous way of going on. Giles finished the painting. Edward and Julia announced their engagement. Zoe went through the motions of being alive. Despite the shifts, the cracks, the damage done, the four of them stayed on. They moved more cautiously, though. They were careful of one another, watchfully considerate and polite. They were still a unit, but it was shaky, like a house which seemed to have survived an earthquake, when in fact it could be toppled by a tiny wayward breeze.

It blew in January. Holidays at The Crannies had been quite pleasant, almost as if Julia had never met Virginia on the downs a year before and their relationships had never changed. The marriage decision actually had helped to ease some of the strain by freeing them from uncertainty. Julia and Edward were in no hurry for the ceremony to take place, yet everyone knew it was going to happen, so they could all do what they pleased in the meantime. Often, they paired up in the old way: Giles and Edward playing chess, Julia and Zoe taking walks. Enjoyment was indeed possible, provided they kept away from each other's deep spots, and no one offered or expected anything but surface amiability. Zoe was even beginning to think that things, if let alone, might revert on their own, that nature might take over and do what she couldn't. Every day she felt herself growing warmer; the blood, at least, was back and pumping.

On the evening before their return to Taviton Street, they

were seated around the radio in the living room "about to witness the death of drama as we have known it. And as in all murders," Giles puffed on the Christmas pipe Edward had given him, "we are drawn to the scene despite ourselves, shivering with both excitement and disgust." "Your descriptions are always so level-headed, Giles. I'm surprised the BBC hasn't grabbed you up to broadcast their news reports." "The BBC, Sister dear, will never be ready for my kind of news. Comings and goings of that sort aren't — Can't you do something about the static, Edward?" "Which? The radio's or yours?" "Don't be clever, old boy, we don't expect it of the F.O. Just fiddle with your knobs." "That sounds decidedly obscene." Giles exaggerated a sigh. "Well I know what I should be doing if I were trapped in a Welsh coal mine with all those delicious miners sitting around stripped to the skin with the sweat pouring over their grimy hardened muscles. I doubt, however, the BBC would air the story." "Or promote it as 'The world's first radio drama.' They might still have called it 'Danger,' though — and billed it as a health warning." "Thank you, Zoe. I remind you that one case of summer crabs does not an epidemic make. Furthermore, I left them in Italy, from whence they came." "Ssh, 'ere it comes, 'istory in the makin'.'"

They settled back to listen. Giles full length on the couch, Julia in an armchair, Edward in another. Zoe, hugging her knees, on a footstool near the grate. Fire sounds. The room half-shadowed. Friends encircled, nestling. Life was . . .

Julia shivered. Zoe saw and started up to get a shawl. Edward had already gone. She sat down. He came back. He placed the shawl around Julia's shoulders; she smiled up at him and kissed the hand that had stayed behind to stroke her hair.

He placed the shawl he stroked her hair she smiled up she kissed his hand the hand that stroked the hair that fell the shawl he placed the smile she kissed. The picture, the intimacy. Flashing, repeating, again and again. The smile the hair the hand the kiss. Zoe got up. The hand, the intimacy. It was over. The smile. She would stay at The Crannies, would not go back. The hand. The hair. She would send for her things. The kiss, the closeness! When she knew, the pain! When her plans, the pair, were final.

She rushed from the room. "I think," Giles said, "I'd best stay here with Zoe for a bit. A few days, until she's calmer." Yes, they agreed. Edward mixed Julia a sedative so she wouldn't have to think about it before he could bundle her off in the morning.

Would Zoe have survived without Giles there? comforting, caring, letting her cry and come apart. Giles, unwavering, whether she leaned on him or screamed at him to go away. Patient, kind, willing to see her through the torment, watching from outside, ready to help her come out whenever she felt she'd gone through enough. Not teasing, not judging or moralizing. Not counseling, simply being there.

Was it gratitude that moved her three nights later? Gratitude that made her pull the blanket back when she heard him come into her room? Stand by her bed and whisper "Zoe"? Take off his robe, his pajamas, while she moved over to let him in. To let him in. Gently. Her arms wrapped round his back, her cheek pressed tight against his shoulder, as he moved inside her, tentative, unsure. Of her, of himself, of why. Perhaps it was love. Because they gave. Both of them needed and gave, wondering at the excitement that grew between them. Drawing back for a moment to look at faces. Then plunging, deeper, opening, wider. With tears falling onto each other's bodies. Tears even as they smiled, pleased that they could do it.

Later, they lay resting on their sides, facing one another, the covers drawn. Zoe looked at his delighted, little boy's grin. She reached out and traced a finger down his nose. "You make me feel like an Older Woman."

He laughed. He snapped at her finger and sucked it into his mouth, then let it go. "Mmm, you have tasty fingers for an Older Woman. What other delicacies do you have that A Man should know about?"

"Well, you could try an earlobe."

"Ah, an earlobe." Giles leaned forward to lick the tip of Zoe's ear. "Delicious."

"There's a shoulder."

"Shoulder," he bent his head to kiss it. "Yes, shoulder is very nice."

They looked at each other. Suddenly, Zoe felt stricken by the future. Their limitations, distastes, inclinations. Needs unmet. Pretenses, honesty corrupted. Inevitable withholding. Retreat. The foreknowledge hit her and ran, leaving her so saddened she had to hide her face by quickly kissing Giles on the mouth. Holding his head close, she raised her lips to his fluttering eyelids and kissed them shut. "Sleep now," she murmured, "sleep."

A few weeks, that was all. "Then," Zoe Mohr had told me, "we parted with a great deal of relief. No regrets, mind you. But very glad to be going our separate ways." I recall how she had picked among the pastries while telling me this part, the emotion of reminiscence as dead as the original. "Ironically, I regained my strength rather quickly, thanks to Giles. It always was the helpless female in me that stimulated him. As she began to disappear, the attraction faded too." She brushed some sugar from her hands, briskly, and I had to smile at the correlation. "He took the train to London, I caught a connection to the channel steamer. I was quite sure that should Giles and I ever meet again, we would think those few weeks at The Crannies had happened to two other people. We'd already begun to disassociate ourselves from the affair by the time we parted at the train station."

Which station, by the way, can't have changed very much since 1924. The Crannies, though, is gone, victim of progress

like Sealey's Peak before it. I knew it wouldn't be here, but
I've come to Sussex anyway. I want to walk on the downs. I
want to lie on one of the rolling, grassy hills and wonder if
Julia's, or Zoe's, or Virginia Woolf's body has lain here before
me. In the same spot. Same roots of grass, same earth. I want
to walk along the village's streets and see the four of them
ahead of me, Julia and Zoe, Edward and Giles. I want to
stand outside the wire fence of an abandoned factory and
imagine a country house is here instead, full of strange-shaped
rooms and senseless stairs, a deranged doll's cottage that for a
while sheltered four grown people. And then protected two
who needed to come together, and did, amid nooks and
crannies, nearly fifty years ago. I've come to Sussex because I
want, I think, to remember.

VII

WHEN I TELL Zoe Mohr about my Sussex experience, she smiles. "Good." That's all she says to me. I'm not so sure; I don't know if it's good or not to be so involved, to have someone else's life, her past and mind and memories, supersede my own to this extent. It frightens me more than a little. There's something psychotic about it, except the people who are so real to me are not creatures of my invention; I do hear voices, but they are not of my own making.

That's not entirely true. Often I fill in, add my own details where she has only sketched. Perhaps there are times when I've made too drastic a departure from her outline, when I've forced my conceptions onto hers, intending merely to recall and taking off instead, supplying my own images and interpretations. I'm really not all that clear anymore about what she's told me versus what I think she's told me. It wouldn't surprise me to find myself one day actually arguing with her over what she remembers about her life.

I think she's aware of my growing unease, but she hasn't questioned me. I want her to; I tell her how our interchange has begun to affect me. She seems to get quite excited, yet I'm almost sure she doesn't want me to know it; she hides her mouth behind her hand and tries not to look at me while I talk, but I see her eyes flashing. I finish. She says, "I've ordered up a special kind of cake for tea today. Do try it," and holds out the plate.

I suppose I could turn this into a contest of wills. I won't; much easier to give in, take the cake, let her know she can have the conversation. That's the way it would end anyway; I simply save time, and face, by dropping the subject. So I munch appreciatively.

She cups a hand under her cake to catch the falling crumbs. "Mmm, how nice to really indulge oneself." It is extraordinarily good; I accept another piece while she puts hers aside, saying "I have a vivid recollection of yearning after this while on a steamer in the middle of the Adriatic. I'd been out of England for nearly two years and was on my way from Athens to Rome, when suddenly I was overcome by the most tormenting memory, not of Julia or Giles or anyone else, but of this particular cake, which one can only get in England. It was, I suppose, a rather peculiar manifestation of homesickness." She's off and running; obviously, the important thing to her is not what I have to say, but what she does.

"You see, I had totally cut myself off. I spent more than four years traveling on the continent without returning once; nor did I write. Self-exile is such an extreme form of behavior, but evidently it was something I needed to do. In order to survive, I imagine. To give myself a chance, become my own person instead of someone else's. Perhaps I could have accomplished this without severing all connections, but I think it would have been harder that way, and riskier.

"At any rate, I went about from place to place hoping in each one that a little of the old me would stay behind and something of the new would follow when I left. But I didn't want to concentrate on the process; I was sick near to death of that sort of analysis. What I wanted, and was fortunate enough to be able to afford, was for the outer me to be diverted long enough for the inner me to do what was necessary.

"Of course, there were setbacks. I can remember one morning in Provence, in nineteen twenty-seven. Breakfasting on a sunny balcony off my hotel room and reading about Isadora Duncan's death. I was eating melon. Very carefully I put my spoon down. It was early morning but hot, white hot, and still. Nothing moved, the light glared terribly. I just sat there; totally alone. I looked out over the balcony, and I saw black shapes wavering in the air. Not heat haze, but Julia, whirling, leaping. Free! Beckoning to me, 'You must go against convention, Mohr, look at Isadora.' The loss was unbearable. I couldn't breathe. I couldn't stop crying."

I'm not ready for this. There's a chunk of cake lodged in my throat. My eyes are about to give me away.

"The experience caught me off guard." I know the feeling. Witch. "It showed me that I wasn't strong enough yet to return. I'd been thinking that perhaps I was, but that morning in Provence proved otherwise.

"And it was not a test of my own devising; before then, I'd always prepared my own tests. You know how one does, how one purposely confronts something guaranteed to reawaken the past in order to measure emotions, check on progress. In 'twenty-five, I remember, when *Mrs. Dalloway* came out, I located a copy and read through every page with the hope it would be the one on which Virginia failed. She never did, and I never admitted to liking that book. In 'twenty-seven, though, I was able to read *To the Lighthouse* without hating her; I didn't have to impose an adverse image of her onto every page, I simply read the book. And felt a little freer.

"But, a few months later, there I was on a Provence balcony, feeling desolate and unsure of myself. Wanting desperately to see Julia and not trusting myself to do so. I wasn't on safe ground; I had to leave. Not for England, or even Paris, which had been in the back of my mind, but Italy again. Neutral territory. I had friends in Florence, and I felt much in need of them."

Friends. She hasn't mentioned them before. I'm curious. I feel like Giles wanting to know about Radclyffe Hall, does "friend" mean lover or chum? I don't have the freedom or the impudence to ask.

She's laughing. "Florence. It certainly didn't stay neutral for long." Here we go. "A very 'hot bed' indeed." Yes? "Of all people — but it was good for me." She's smiling. Smirking? no, just grinning. "I knew after that that I'd be all right." Good, let's hear about it.

"Now who," she leans forward as if to jab my knee, "do you think I met in Florence?" I can't imagine. "Late spring, nineteen twenty-eight. Think." I don't know, how should I know? Virginia Vanessa Vita? Gertrude or Alice? Someone fascinating from America? Djuna Barnes? was Djuna Barnes around then? Uh, Carrington? Dorothy Brett? I wish she wouldn't watch me so slyly; she must know a dozen names are flitting through my head and none of them is right. Silly game, this. Why doesn't she just tell me? "My word, can you have forgotten so easily?" Forgotten? well who the hell was it?

"Lawrence! Your old friend Lawrence!"

Oh. Lawrence. Of course, Florence, 1928, the *Lady Chatterley* subscription edition. I know that. But what's he — I don't get it. Surely they didn't.

"Well? Aren't you agog to hear how Lawrence and dear wife Frieda went about hawking private editions of *Lady Chatterley's Lover* to anyone who looked able to afford the exorbitant price?"

Really, she's being a bit harsh. Yes, I'd like to hear about it. I shouldn't have put him so far out of my mind; I've been very bad about that.

" 'Why don't you set up a booth in the Piazza del Duomo?' I asked him. 'Or station yourself outside the Palazzo Pitti with four or five copies under a voluminous coat, and when a tourist comes by you can go "Psst! Mister! You want to buy some feelthy English words?" ' He didn't have much of a sense of humor. But then, living with Frieda — she had a tendency to make one feel as if one had eaten too much sauerbraten, for breakfast."

I'm not going to laugh. That's not funny. It's not. I guess I should be rushing to his defense.

"I bought one, of course. 'I've nothing else to sneak through customs; it might as well be this.' He told me what I could do with my largess; and if that didn't appeal, I could try putting it elsewhere, provided we in Bloomsbury hadn't forgotten how."

She looks at me from under raised brows, as if I could apologize for the man. I would really like to see that first edition. I bet she doesn't have it though, not anymore. There's something not quite right here. Maybe I was geared for a different story; I'm just disappointed, I expected to be hit with something else. Unimportant as that is in comparison, and curse me for feeling let down. The gossip in me is salivating while the academic sleeps; so be it. I can't believe the only hot bed around was Lady Chatterley's.

"All of this is actually rather incidental. I thought, however, you might be interested, considering. I must admit that at the time, securing a copy of Lawrence's new novel wasn't very important to me. In fact I've never revered it as I should, and consequently it's no longer in my possession." I knew it; why was I so sure? "What mattered most to me, selfishly, egotistically, were my reactions to the memories he unwittingly inspired.

"It had been well over ten years, yet I couldn't look at Lawrence, and Frieda, without seeing Middleton Murry and Katherine Mansfield too. The train of association after that is obvious. But there was something else I had to come to terms with which I've not mentioned before: my callous treatment of Lesley Moore after Mansfield died. I was so distraught over Julia's reaction to Virginia, that I never once gave a thought to Lesley; I never tried to reach her, I never tried to find out how she was holding up under Katherine's death, I never offered her comfort or one moment of my time or one fraction of my self. Yet we had been friends; we had shared portions of our lives. And I owed her, even though we were no longer close, had not seen each other for years."

The woman doesn't let herself be human.

"In Florence I faced that, and forgave myself. I think it was then I first started to realize I owed Julia something, too. And Giles. Even Edward, to a degree. I hadn't fully worked it out yet, but at least it was on the other side of the emotions, the attitudes, whatever had sent me away. I felt that I had, in a sense, come through those; I could stand beyond them and look back, with acceptance rather than pain or bitterness. Oh not total acceptance, and there were still traces of the other, but I could look back. With that, I no longer needed to; for the first time in four years there were other perspectives open to me. They were still somewhat vague, and I wasn't completely sure of myself — who ever is — but by September I was in Paris. There, my slow and rather cautious return to England was hastened by what I can only describe as a rude, very forceful shove."

It came, ironically, from Virginia Woolf. Was the world really so much smaller then that one couldn't travel without running into someone one knew? I've been to Paris, too; I've walked its boulevards and past its outdoor cafés, but no friend or acquaintance has ever hurried after me to say hello and urge me to join the table. But then, the circles are not equivalent: I don't have a Vita Sackville-West in my life, nor is it probable I would ever be ushered to any table where a Virginia Woolf is sitting.

Face shaded by a large-brimmed hat, hands gracefully entwined around the base of a wine glass. Her greeting was restrained, yet surely Vita would not have brought Zoe there without her consent, nor immediately summoned the waiter to bring another glass.

The two were on a week's holiday together; halfway through their travel talk Zoe realized that Giles' prediction about them had come true. Simply, unobtrusively, they were a couple. She saw it in the things taken for granted, the private knowledge of one another that kept expressing itself underneath their public words and gestures. They were aware of each other, and there was trust between them. Zoe drank her wine without resenting the envy they inspired. She wondered, briefly, if their husbands felt similarly assuaged.

Conversation turned to "this *Well* business," as Vita put it. Perhaps that too was impelling Zoe back to England; Radclyffe Hall needed friends, and Zoe had been one before even her first novel had been published. She was in trouble now over *The Well of Loneliness*, her lesbian portrayals having outraged censorial minds and vastly disappointed sympathetic ones. The latter, however, were being forced to publicly acclaim the book because the former had leveled obscenity charges, transforming the *Well* into a cause célèbre. "That meritorious dull book," Virginia raised her eyes heavenward. Nevertheless, she was prepared to testify to its literary rather than lesbian merits and was scheduled to appear before the magistrate a week after her return. There were only two problems as Virginia saw it: one, she didn't have a dress suitable for the occasion, and two, she couldn't support Radclyffe's contention that it was a "great novel." "One of the rare occasions when Rebecca West and I have ever agreed on anything," Virginia said. She turned to Vita, "How did she put it?" Vita laughed, cigarette holder clamped between her teeth. "She said," Vita blew a stream of smoke, "that the *Well* is, 'in a way which is particularly inconvenient in the present circumstances, not a very good book.'" They both snorted as if hearing the comment for the first time.

Zoe felt herself getting angry. She would never be called upon to judge John's writing, but if a character witness were needed — Where had these people been when England's men were dying, and the women united to transport their bodies back to safety? These literary personalities, so ready to rally around words rather than human beings.

". . . Julia Gordon?"

"I'm sorry, what did you say?" Part of Zoe had been listening, but the name was too strange. She'd never heard it said before, never thought of her as other than Julia . . . Carroll.

Virginia tilted her head back and peered at Zoe from under the brim of her hat. "I said, 'Why have you deserted Julia Gordon?' " Vita tried to indicate by gesture that perhaps this was an area Virginia should stay clear of. "Nonsense. Zoe will listen."

She did, and was told. Jealousy was not a small self-indulgence on the order of taking one's tea and toast in bed. It was destructive, wasteful, boring and common. The more so when ill-founded. Virginia trusted that by now Zoe was fully risen from its useless depths. She hoped so, because her friend Julia needed her; marriage had not served her well. Zoe ought to be there, yet she wasn't. Why?

Two days later Zoe was checked into a Bloomsbury hotel. She'd written to Julia and was waiting for a reply, having directed the desk to deliver the note immediately it arrived.

The knock sounded, she hurried to the door, turned the knob, dropped the tip, scrabbled to retrieve it, found sixpence and was searching behind a desk leg for the rest.

"That's really not necessary. I came freely, and the very moment I saw your handwriting."

Rising, head spinning, "Julia . . ." blurred.

"In the flesh, what there is left of it. Are you going to stand there gripping sixpence' worth of scone, or are you going to invite me in?"

Stepping back. Door closing.

"You're looking well, Zoe."

Middle of the room, facing. "You . . ." Too much distance to cross.

"Look terrible? Don't tell me. A greying, very haggard thirty-two."

Silence: city noises, carpet creaking, a clock.

"Well," Julia trying, "shall we sit? Or . . . or will you . . ."

They moved toward one another. They met, and held.

"You're back?"

"I'm back."

They kissed, crying.

"Don't leave me again."

"I won't. I swear it."

They hugged and stroked.

"Love me, Zoe."

"I love you."

"Please love me."

"I do, I do."

They lay on the bed and held each other. Shared gentle tear-wet kisses. Reiterated vows. They undressed and pulled the blanket up to lie cozily underneath. They caressed. In time, they made tender, reaffirming love.

Julia was lying with her arm across Zoe's midriff; when she spoke, her lips moved against Zoe's shoulder. "I shall never be cruel to you again."

Zoe laughed. "Not possible."

Julia pushed herself up. "Why not?" Her expression flickered from ingenuous to puzzled to indignant. Zoe watched the features separate: there were brown smudges under her eyes; her forehead had frown lines etched permanently into the skin; creases showed around her mouth, and her cheeks were hollowed far past beauty. Quickly she pulled Julia's head down to her breast. "I love you," she murmured into her hair.

"I'm glad." Julia settled more comfortably on top of her.

Zoe's arm too easily encompassed the narrow back. "I understand now. So much time; I wasn't ready before, in Paris. You were right about the pillow smothering."

"No." Julia struggled to rise, but Zoe held her, caressing.

"Ssh, you must listen. I made a promise that night you knew I couldn't keep. And I couldn't. Any more than you'll be able to do what you just said. It's the nature of things; the best we can do is deal with it when it happens, and carry on."

Julia lay quietly, her hands under Zoe's shoulders and her face turned toward the wall.

"Zoe?"

"Hm?"

"You aren't always going to be so bloody mature, are you?"

"What?" Zoe could feel eyelashes fluttering on her breast.

"It'll be all right if we're irrational sometimes, won't it? Perhaps every third Sunday or so? It's not fair having to be sensible all the time. I would like, occasionally, to be very bad; could I? now and then?"

"Could you? I'd be surprised if you weren't. Julia," Zoe got her to turn her head so that she could see her face, "I've no desire to inhibit you. That's rather what I've been saying. What is this scheduled play-periods sort of talk?"

Julia sighed and rolled off Zoe's body into a sitting position. Her fingers, too prominently knuckled to be lovely anymore, reached into her hair, lifted two handfuls as high as they would go, then let them fall. "Oh," she sighed again, "it comes from four years of . . ." She shut her eyes, closing in the thought.

"Of what?" Zoe sat up too.

"Of being a good little girl, I guess." The look Julia leveled at her then was so hurtful it stunned. You don't know, it said, you weren't here; I've been through things you've no idea of, I've had to accept them, and I do, they're a part of me, but this ugly knowledge is mine not yours.

"I'm sorry," Zoe whispered.

Julia held the look an instant longer, then dropped it and nodded, a weary smile barely raising the corners of her mouth.

To give herself something neutral to do, Zoe checked the traveling clock on her nightstand. "Lord, it's after six."

"Six! Christus!" Julia leaped off the bed and started flinging on clothes as if she'd been caught in a fire drill at school. "Addie's a terror when I'm late, dammit where's me shoe?"

"Under the spread there. Who's Addie, the cook?"

"Addie is Edward, as in Edward Addison — zipper's stuck, can you get it? — Gordon." She knelt so Zoe could free the fabric, "His mother was an Addison," then dashed to a mirror.

"I think I liked 'Arf' better."

Julia was whipping a comb through her hair. "Addie's his idea. Thank God for . . ." she grabbed her purse "short hair," and started for the door. Halfway there she turned back to kiss Zoe lightly on the lips. "You'll come round tomorrow, won't you?"

"Of course."

Already, Julia was across the room. "Good. We'll talk then." She opened the door. "Something tells me we'd never get to that here." Her eyes rolled suggestively, and Zoe smiled; the door closed, shutting her in a room gone depressingly empty.

They'd kept the middle two floors for themselves and rented off the lower and half the top; Giles still maintained a workroom there but his living quarters were elsewhere. "We wanted him to stay, but he wouldn't," Julie said. "He's forever changing addresses now, partly from whim and partly due to circumstance, I'm never quite sure which. I think his lungs are giving him more trouble than he'll admit to; every year he manages to spend several months in some dry climate. Despite his effusive letters about the beauty of beaches and boys, I suspect it's the weather he's really after. I'm sure," Julia looked at Zoe for confirmation, "that's why he goes abroad for holidays instead of to The Crannies." Zoe's expression did not alter; her recollections of Giles were not emotionally charged, and she hoped that his were unemphatic too. Julia merely raised an eyebrow, continuing, "I daresay you'll find him looking older. It's not just his health, of course; Giles is, after all, pushing forty, 'And my dear, I do mean *pushing*. With any luck I'll have moved it back to thirty-seven by New Year's.' "

They laughed. Calling to Clarissa and George, Julia gave

them bits of watercress sandwich. "They are very beautiful," Zoe said. Julia smiled. "I know. George is three and Clarissa's sixteen months. I expect in two years we'll bring another into the house. They're such loves; I can't imagine being without them now." She hugged each individually, then sent them off to lie down.

"Is Clarissa named for Mrs. Dalloway?"

"Yes; Virginia was pleased. 'If it had been a child,' she told me, 'the distinction would've been dubious, but a dog is a downright honor.' And being an Irish setter didn't hurt any. You should see the two of them together some time, both so lanky and aristocratic; Clarissa, though, is much more gentle and not at all a nervous breed." An occasional social event and a hike or two in Sussex were the only contacts between them now; Julia was glad that Vita seemed to be what Virginia needed, and was delighted to hear Zoe had encountered them in Paris. So far, the only sexual tension in evidence had been yesterday's, when Zoe had opened her hotel room door to find Julia on the threshold.

"And George?" Zoe asked. The golden retriever had trotted over to sit at Julia's feet. "Who is he named after?"

"George is Edward's homage, to G. E. Moore. Isn't that right, George?" He placed a paw on her knee and grinned; Julia ruffled his fur. "Personal affection and aesthetic enjoyment are the greatest goods according to that George, and they're marvelously embodied in this one. He's a 'good' dog," she raised his head to look him in the eye, while George's tail thumped ecstatic rhythms on the carpet, "yes, good dog."

Perhaps Julia meant to spend all afternoon skirting the issue. "So, things are, all right then," Zoe offered, hoping to nudge her a little closer to the center.

"I suppose." Julia let the dog return to his rug; she began picking golden traces of his visit from her dress. "Edward has the beginnings of a pot belly and an ulcer; he spends far too much time in that cubbyhole of his for a man who doesn't take things lightly. Father's hearing, unfortunately, has gone the way of his eyesight; he never leaves off grinning now, I suppose because he can neither see nor hear what's going on in the world around him. Mother's a bit difficult; she and Edward don't get on so well as they used to. I try to avoid visits to Stone Hedge, sometimes the two of them make me feel like a patient being argued over by specialists who're more concerned with their reputations than the poor soul lingering on between them." She got up. "Shall we have some sherry?"

Zoe watched her leave. The information about Edward and Mrs. Carroll didn't surprise her one bit. Naturally they would make a competition out of Julia's well-being, and probably destroy it in the process. Selfish people had a way of turning their objects of concern into victims, they . . .

She heard voices raised in another room: one was Julia's, angry; the other was unknown and holding her ground. "I insist! Demeaning. Keys!" "Gordon. Very clear. Call him?" "Not! Fired!" "See. Mr. Gordon. Home." Something crashed. Face burning, Julia strode into the room.

"Dammit! they treat me like a child! They force me to it, they force me! They make me so angry. So frustrated! No wonder I break things. Not to be trusted in my own home! I swear they make things worse by treating me this way. God," she slumped into a chair, "what a bloody vicious circle."

Zoe had risen during the tirade; now she went over and sat on the footstool by Julia's chair. She tried to sound calm. "Tell me what's happened."

"Once, just once," Julia was wagging her finger in Zoe's face, "Edward came home and found me stinking, blotto drunk, and ever since then he's kept the liquor under lock. I forgot to tell him this morning that we just might wish something to drink this afternoon, and Sergeant-Major back there only follows orders, the stupid bitch, so she won't surrender the keys, 'without Mr. Gordon having instructed me to, Madam.' I tried to reason with her, to explain in terms her limited intelligence could grasp, that circumstances had changed, I had a guest to whom I wished to serve a glass of sherry, that she need only poke her head through the door to ascertain this was the truth, and that surely she realized Mr. Gordon would not want to hear of her interfering with his reputation for hospitality. But none of that made the slightest dent. So I broke her mixing bowl. Out of sheer frustration. And when Edward finds out, which he will, because Sergeant-Major's also an informer of the worst order, he'll lecture me about my childish behavior."

Zoe was furious. She got up and marched into the kitchen; within half a minute, she was back with the key.

"Here," she handed Julia a stiff tot of Scotch, "sherry's too mild after what you've just been through. Ridiculous way to be treated." Standing in front of the open cabinet doors, Zoe drank from her own healthy glass of whiskey, not trusting herself to speak further until her anger had subsided. She poured herself another and then sat down. "Why do you put up with it?"

Julia shrugged, sighed. "Because they're right, I guess. I am a child. I do need to be looked after, in many ways. Edward's very kind, really, and Mrs. Craik tries to do her best." Already, Zoe saw, the guilt had crept in. "It's not easy putting up with me, I'm sure many a husband and a housekeeper would've quit over less."

"Sounds to me like they've got you pretty well indoctrinated. Forever in their debt, are you?"

"Yes." Julia sipped from her glass, using both hands to hold it.

"Do you mean that?"

"Life always exacts its price, doesn't it? If I want the good things, I have to pay for them with the bad. I am safe here, protected."

"From what?"

Again, Julia shrugged, signifying that either the answer didn't matter or she didn't care to offer one. "They do have my best interests at heart, I know that, Zoe. And if, occasionally, they mistakenly draw the line, it's not their fault is it? No, don't look so skeptical. You used to have that problem too, remember? overreacting, jumping to conclusions. When I was making those costumes, you said yourself how hard it was to know, to act correctly."

"That was different, Julia. I wasn't, taking away your dignity; I wasn't robbing you of independence."

"Oh? Didn't a lack of trust underlie your behavior too? I thought it did, Zoe. I think perhaps the major difference between you and Edward in this regard is one of style rather than substance."

"Julia!" Zoe was open-mouthed at the comparison. "You can't believe that!"

"I'm not sure, I've only just begun to think about it. In your own way, each of you has overprotected and undertrusted me, not that I haven't given you cause to. The difference is you've acted out of fear, and Edward out of arrogance. You're afraid of the crazy lady in me, while Edward is positive she's merely a willful child. One needs only the proper training, the other needs — what, Zoe?"

"Love. Compassion. The difference is substantive, Julia."

"And hope? On whose side is hope sitting? Isn't it better to have one's rational powers called into question, rather than one's reason?"

"Why are you loading this against me?"

"Because I don't think you realize I need Edward. And I need, therefore I love. You've come back to me, Zoe, for which I'm more grateful than I'll admit. But you must realize Edward and I have something together that suits us. He knows you and I . . . but he doesn't resent you, Zoe, he truly doesn't. He used to, yes, but not now; for several reasons. I don't want you to resent him either."

"Julia, I find it a little hard to believe what I'm hearing."

"You'll have to try harder then." She got up to fix herself another drink.

Same old Julia. This was Zoe's test, that she not respond as the old Zoe would have. Even if the results proved to be the same, her motives, her reasons were going to be different; she wasn't going to act out of fear again, or adoration and the desire to possess. Yes, she had come back to Julia, but this time she would meet her as an equal. To do that she must be fully conscious of the limits of their relationship. And she must deliberately accept its terms. Abide by them, not out of desperation or gratitude, but out of cold-blooded choice; the difference would keep her whole.

And who knows? Perhaps Edward was right; maybe Julia could "learn" to be well, given the proper "training." She didn't look well, but could Zoe be certain she would look any better had the last four years been spent under her care? Julia said that man and wife suited each other; Zoe, for now, would let the assertion stand.

Surprisingly, she was even able to smile. "I'll admit I'm not exactly pleased by what happened here this afternoon." She raised her hand to stop Julia's imminent rebuttal. "But I think your sense of what's good for you is probably more valid than mine. So please, lower your hackles. I'm not about to attack, nor am I going . . ." she lifted her glass "to slink away." Feeling self-congratulatory, Zoe drank. Her empty glass hit the table resolutely. "Now. Tell me about your work. I've missed four years of Projects to Save the Soul and I'm eager to hear about every one of them."

"There haven't been very many. I told you we let the section of the house where my workroom used to be. I miss it, I liked having my things around me. I know the clutter represented failed efforts; still, they were my efforts. I could work among them and feel, I was myself; it was my space, and I was in it."

"Then why ever did you give it up? Surely not for the money."

"Something Edward said, made me see things differently. When the chance came to let it, I didn't object. And we have been trying to free ourselves from the parental purse strings; Edward would rather live on 'our money' rather than money labeled 'his' and 'hers.' "

"Admirable. I'm curious; what did he say to get you to relinquish your workroom?"

"Oh, one day we were up there, and Edward looked around at all my symbols: loom, sewing machine, old ballet practice bar, some easels, a music stand, sculpting tools, that huge picture of the word 'Piano.' He said, 'Julia, this room reminds me of a nursery kept up after the baby has died.' I looked, and suddenly I saw it that way, too. I was the deranged mother refusing to get rid of the crib and the toys and the teddy bear because she couldn't face reality."

Zoe had been shocked at the brutality of Edward's image. "But a dead baby is not equivalent to . . ."

"Don't bother. Equivalent or not, there was truth to what he said. Edward doesn't believe in cushioning his perceptions, or disguising them with frills."

"So I see." Right, wrong or debatable, they would always have the aura of rigorous truth.

"I'm sure it comes from his having been educated in our spartan public schools — so many of his ways do. This one, at least, I can respect."

Zoe wanted to pursue that too, but later. "So you aren't working at all, then? You've abandoned your search?"

A shy, almost sheepish smile crept across Julia's lips. "No, I — may I have one of your cigarettes please?" She lit one, puffing too frequently, obviously unaccustomed to the habit. "I'm involved; have been for several years. Something that doesn't require a great deal of room." Smoke hung around her head; she made no move to dispel it, created more instead.

"Well what is it? Has Giles put you on to needlepoint?"

Julia laughed. "No, thank God; there aren't enough chairs

in the house for both of us to be at it. Anyway, I've no desire to compete with Giles, or to delude myself by thinking just because he has certain talents I should have them too. Actually, for quite a long time I must have resented the fact I didn't have them, or tried to prove that I did; far too many years were wasted on that sort of thing." She killed her cigarette ineffectually, leaving it crushed and smoldering in the ashtray.

"You've found it, haven't you."

Julia had been stretching to reach another cigarette; Zoe's observation made her stop in mid-motion. She resumed it, slowly, and as she struck a match, she nodded, seeming to both confirm and contemplate the words. "Yes," she blew out the match and carefully placed it in an ashtray, "yes, I think I have."

Zoe felt tears forming. She mustn't gush: no tears, no joyful embraces.

"I wasn't aware it showed," Julia was saying. "I should have known, though, you would see."

Zoe nodded in mock sagacity, "Of course. There's just one little detail my powers have failed to tell me. What is it, precisely, that you've found?"

"Precisely?"

"Please."

"Precisely, prose."

"Ah. Prose. A novel?"

"At the moment."

"And before?"

"Oh, things."

"Things."

"Yes, things. Stories, plays, blobs, pieces, snatches: things."

Zoe decided to digest that for a while because she didn't, truly, know how to continue. Julia had always been somewhat mysterious about a project in the beginning, but usually once she was into it her enthusiasm would bubble over into loquacity, she'd insist on showing whatever it was she'd produced, and then, soon after, she'd reject it altogether. This, obviously, was different. And delicate. Zoe felt around for something safe to say. "Well, I remember those skits, and your writing in your diary now and then; but that's about the only recollection I have of your ever . . ."

Julia didn't wait for her to finish. "Right there, all those years. Why did it take me so long? It's all in there, Zoe, it's all there. If I can just . . ." she gripped the air and shook it "set it free."

Zoe waited for her to go on, but she didn't. It would be better not to probe, Zoe knew, yet she didn't want to drop the subject entirely. "Have you, tried to publish anything?"

"Publish?" Clearly the idea startled her. "Heavens no. I've never even shown my work, to anyone. And I won't, until I'm ready."

"Not even to Edward?" The decision to exclude everyone seemed so extreme.

"Oh Edward." Julia waved him away. "He thinks it's just another Project. You know, give her some crayons and a piece of paper, it'll keep her out of trouble." She checked to see how Zoe was reacting to this, then hurried to defend. "Don't believe a word, I'm not being fair. He does encourage me. Both for my sake and in the name of artistic expression." Zoe tried to look sufficiently convinced, and Julia relaxed a bit, sighing. "Mostly, though, it requires a great deal of self-discipline. And discipline is very dear to Edward's heart."

How long was she going to go on merely alluding to the real nature of their relationship? Zoe's suppositions were becoming increasingly unpleasant; she had no desire to be left with them, but she would have to be, until Julia could bring herself to talk about it openly. "Have you discussed it with Virginia?"

"My work? Good Lord, Zoe, Virginia's the last person I'd ever . . ." Julia shook her head. "No, no, too dangerous. Too deceptive."

"But Julia, surely if anyone could help you, V . . ."

Julia flared at her. "Who said I needed help! What gives you the right to assume I need help? Especially that kind! My work is mine, and no one else's! It's me, it's all I have, it's the only thing that is wholly, completely, mine! And when I share it," her entire body was trembling, "when I share it, it'll be with the world. From me, to it; no friends in between, no circle of approval ready-made. No influence mucking things up so that one never knows."

She sat back, still angry but no longer strained by it; slowly, the red receded from her face and neck. "I'm sorry, Zoe." She rubbed her forehead. "I get too intense." Short laugh. "That's hardly news, is it. Tell me yours; did you see the Stein-Toklases on your trip?"

Zoe was ashamed to admit she hadn't. "I intended to except . . ."

Julia wasn't listening. "That evening in the atelier. I didn't understand, but now I do. 'I write for myself and strangers.' I know what she meant now."

"It sounds good, but from what I hear Gertrude is perfectly willing to let her friends intercede. She must have half a dozen of them lugging cartons of manuscript around to editors on at least three continents."

"It's a mistake."

"Not if you're convinced of your own genius."

"Convinced is one thing, genius another. The test must lie outside oneself or it's no test at all. It's an illusion; worthless. Vision, not illusion, that's what counts. My vision and someone's response: that's where the truth's to be found, in that process. It's pure, Zoe; it mustn't be interfered with, it mustn't be sullied. I won't have it corrupted."

"I'm not sure I understand."

"Doesn't matter, I do."

Zoe wasn't offended, but she did feel obstructed. It was a familiar yet uncomfortable sensation; there'd been times during Julia's illnesses when she'd felt Julia was purposely keeping her outside, refusing to take down barriers until in her own mind it was safe. The element of choice disturbed Zoe most, for by locking her out, Julia was also locking herself in. Which might explain why Zoe sometimes got the feeling Julia could emerge from illness if she wanted to; at least, she willingly rather than helplessly succumbed. Cruel suspicions. Yet, now too, Julia could let her in but wouldn't. Quite obviously, she was protecting something again, and only she knew what it was.

"All right," Zoe said. She would wait, time was on her side. Eventually, Julia would tell her things she told to no one else. It had always been that way. At sixteen, Zoe was treating Julia's thoughts like precious gifts; now, she looked upon them as her right. She had as much right to know as to be, because she and Julia *were* a part of one another; too much had been given, too much taken, for that not to be so. "Drink?"

"No. But I would appreciate a kiss."

Julia's face was turned up to meet her; Zoe leaned over the chair, Julia arched her body closer. It was a luxuriously long and intimate kiss that said what each needed to hear.

Wisely, Edward made a great deal of noise on entering the flat. Coming into the room, he looked as Julia had described him, going to Zoe immediately, "Zoe! how good to see you again," kissing her lightly on the cheek. "Hello," he went to Julia and brushed her forehead with his lips, "how's my girl?"

"Fine. We've spent the entire afternoon talking, and drinking, I'm afraid. But don't blame Mrs. Craik, Addie, she . . ."

"Wrestled me for the keys," Zoe interrupted, "and lost. I promised I'd intercede with you on her behalf, however, so please don't demote her to foot soldier on my account."

"Wouldn't dream of it. Scotch, eh? Let's all have one." He headed toward the liquor cabinet, "Seen this?" and passed the evening paper to Julia on his way.

Over Julia's shoulder, Zoe read about the latest development in the *Well* case. Virginia needn't have worried about what to wear. That afternoon a magistrate had ruled testimony on the *Well*'s literary merits to be inadmissible evidence; the book, when it came to trial in November, would be judged on content only. Unfortunately, Radclyffe's characters would have to speak for themselves.

"That's a blow," Zoe said, moving over to the couch.

"Indeed," Edward handed out drinks, "I fear Miss Hall's nasty ladies are going to be condemned for their evil ways, never to see light of day until less threatened minds prevail." Daintily, he tasted his drink and went to perch on the arm of Julia's chair. "Well, at least we don't burn them, we merely consign them to dungeonlike warehouses, where they can rot and wait for some new regime to grant a pardon."

"I feel so sorry for her." Julia set her glass on the table untouched. "To be denied completion. It's the cruelest thing they could possibly do. Writing, presenting, saying here, this is for you; only to have every one of the you's barred from reading it. My God, how futile."

"Perhaps she'll do better in America," Edward suggested, "though I doubt it. So many people there aspire to the puritanical, possibly because so few can rightly claim descent from those boring renegades we managed to get rid of. For a nation which supposedly shuns class distinctions, they're awfully busy proving whose forebears jumped into the melting pot first."

If Edward meant to alleviate Julia's gloom, he did not succeed. She was looking into the void, "What will she do?" dropping questions over the edge, "How can she survive it?"

"Oh, she'll write another, I suspect." He patted her arm.

"No!" Her body jerked with agitation. "Damn them to hell, they've no right! No right to take even one, but all! to take away all!"

"Julia!" Edward's hand was gripping her arm, "you must . . ." the pressure increased "be more reasonable."

There was a pause while he waited to see if she would obey. Silently, Julia fought against restraint though seemingly oblivious to it, as if her goal were some distant object and something, she didn't know what, was holding her back. Then, Zoe saw the exact moment of recognition, she realized it was Edward's hand, on her arm, and she ceased struggling. She relaxed, "Yes. Yes I must," and looked up at him meekly. He smiled down at her and lifted his hand to brush a stray hair from her brow. "That's a good girl."

Zoe wanted no more to drink; it would only make her nausea worse.

"Tell you what," Edward said, the tone of his voice indicating treat-time, "Woolf informs me that Virginia's set to deliver some lectures at Cambridge in about a fortnight. Why don't you and Zoe go up there for a couple of days and take them in? There's a contingent forming already, I hear; word's gone out she intends to light a few fires under some rather venerable arses." Keeping an arm around Julia's shoulder, he turned to Zoe. "It really is good to have you back, Zoe. Julia needs someone."

To play with? Zoe wanted to say.

They decided to join Keynes and Vanessa and the others who were eager to attend. Virginia was known for her residual dislike of Cambridge; its doors had opened to her brothers and all her brothers' friends, but never to her, thanks to her father's adamant ideas about women and education. Far safer to hate the institution rather than the patriarch; her friends were confident Virginia would be superb. What really set them bubbling with anticipation, though, was the publication of *Orlando* ten days prior to her appearance. It was dedicated to Vita, and in a strange, fantastical way, Vita was in it, too, traveling through time and changing sexes as readily as a tourist converting pounds to francs. All unknowing, the officials at Cambridge had invited a respectable literary figure to address their cloistered female students; when she arrived, they were forced to welcome someone who had just given public birth to a hermaphrodite.

Once before Zoe had seen that rapt look on Julia's face. Now, however, instead of a short, heavy-set body striding to and fro against a backdrop of brilliant colors, there was a tall, somewhat stiff woman on a bare stage not daring to move from behind her lectern. The room was huge and glaringly lit, that other had been small and dimming into shadow at the corners. There, masterpieces had been visible, touchable; here, words created pictures, but they were just as real. Though this performer was cool, and she had a sense of humor, stinging her listeners into awareness rather than bludgeoning them for lack of it, both were magicians. They made one believe.

Who cast the more potent spell? Stein, discussing men and art? or Woolf, portraying women and fiction? Zoe had been saddened by an account of Matisse's suffering. But for Judith Shakespeare, she mourned. Despite misfortune, Matisse had fulfilled his potential and the world was richer for it; Shakespeare's sister had never been allowed to try. An incalculable loss, more real than imaginary; Zoe felt it, and so did everyone in the room.

Friends, students, strangers, they all rose when Virginia had finished. Clapping and cheering, some of them crying, they wanted her to know what she had done to them, what she had done for them. They were a community of exposed souls who would close up soon after, but for now, they were touching, impassioned, together in paying homage to the one who had brought such a thing about. Obviously embarrassed, Virginia wanted to leave the stage, but they wouldn't let her. She would have to stay there and accept their offering, a reluctant god who had merely shared with them some words on women, and writing, and needing a room of one's own.

On the train back to London, Zoe and Julia were surrounded by the high spirits and rampant speculation of Virginia's friends. *Orlando* and Cambridge within two weeks of one another! think what it meant! Vanessa. The *Times*. The world! She was a better artist, she was A Major Artist, she was this and must do that, she'd proved that and should do the other. Money. Reputation. Lytton. Morgan. Right to, responsibility for, one ought.

Julia got up and moved into the corridor. Zoe managed to follow and stood for a moment watching her look out a window. Though the train was barely swaying, Julia had a tight hold on the handrail.

"What's wrong?" Zoe asked quietly.

Julia didn't answer.

"Is it Virginia?"

Julia nodded, once.

"Are they . . ."

"They are making her into something she is not." The words were evenly spaced and tinged with anger. "Virginia is a writer, not a Literary Figure. She must write, she needs to write. But not for the reasons they're saying. Those things are all outside Virginia, they've nothing to do with her. None of them knows, except maybe Leonard, what it's all about."

"You make it sound like a conspiracy. They mean well. They're enjoying her victories. Maybe they're going a bit overboard on planning strategy for more, but it's done out of affection and enthusiasm, not malicious misinterpretation."

"I'm not accusing them of maliciousness, not this afternoon at any rate. They simply do not understand, and stupidity can be dangerous."

"One thing these people are not, is stupid. You can accuse them of all kinds of failings, Julia, but not that one."

"Sorry, but I think all this comparing of Virginia to Vanessa is stupid, and about as meaningless as matching her royalties against Lytton's. Does anyone really think she writes out of a desire to make more money than Strachey or to be more famous than her sister?"

"Of course not. The thing between Virginia and Lytton is

superficial, but it's there. And it's not unreasonable to assume it goes much deeper with Vanessa; you can't deny the sisters have been more than a touch competitive over the years."

"Lord, Zoe, what does it matter? Vanessa's . . . like Giles, she's extremely skillful and has a great deal of flair. Tell her she could never paint again and she'd grow plants, or take up weaving, as easily as Giles went from potter's wheel to paintbrush. But prevent Virginia from writing, and you'd destroy her."

"Julia, if Giles had been told he could never again express himself artistically, in any way whatsoever, I don't think he'd have come through the war quite as well as he did. He was extremely upset as it was, you do him an injustice if you think otherwise, and it was the very versatility you're disparaging that saved him."

"I don't doubt for a moment that Giles was 'upset.' But versatility is no guarantee of survival. Tell Virginia she could still write reviews for the *Times*, and books of criticism, biographies, that she could do everything she does now except for one thing: write novels. D'you know what would happen? She wouldn't be 'upset,' she'd bloody well go to pieces!"

"How do you know that?"

"I know, Zoe. It's her refuge, and her defense, and the only weapon she has."

"Against what?"

Suddenly, they were assaulted by noise and thrown back from the rail. Whistle screaming, wheels racketing double time, the train raced through a tunnel. Julia's mouth opened, but Zoe couldn't hear. She lurched forward, shouting "What?" "Tear her!" Julia seemed to yell back. "What?" Zoe cupped her ear. "Terror!" she may have shouted, clutching the handrail. Zoe couldn't be sure, and it was useless asking again.

VIII

"You have to expect it when you've got friends who are older," Edward attempted to comfort. All three needed it. Friends were gone. Years had disappeared. The house itself was moaning, buffeted by wind.

"Carrington was thirty-eight. Two years older than I am," Julia said flatly. "Lytton was fifty-two. I don't consider fifty-two old. Do you consider fifty-two old?"

"Julia," Edward said her name patiently, "he was riddled with cancer, riddled with it. That sort of disease has no respect for age. Why must you insist on death operating rationally?"

Julia stared at his tentative smile. "I have known it to before," she told him quietly.

"You know I don't like to hear you talking like that." He moved as abruptly as he'd spoken, getting off the armrest and walking toward the mantelpiece. On the way he made a half-bow in Zoe's direction. "You try, Zoe."

"Yes, Zoe, you try," Julia said mockingly. "You tell me what disease Carrington died of. Tell me, Zoe. Try."

For the past twenty minutes Zoe had been sitting in her chair saying nothing and watching Julia for signs. Death, Julia had said that afternoon in her workroom years ago, death connected them all; it made the wave come and suck her under into a world of dim green madness. Was the wave building now? Growing offshore, rolling steadily toward her? Zoe couldn't be sure, yet she felt Julia might not be in danger. Somehow, these deaths were different; they were separate, they didn't "belong" to Julia. She was upset, yes, but so were they all.

Zoe wanted to counter Julia's bitterness as calmly as she could. "I don't think Carrington was sick, necessarily. I have never considered suicide a manifestation of sickness. I believe it can be a sane and valid alternative."

"Sane," Julia repeated.

"Selfish is what I would call it," Edward offered from his vantage point by the fire. "You leave everyone behind to clean up after you. Friends, family — they have to deal with the mess you've left, they have to carry on. The suicide has no thought for anyone else, only himself. He's the coward who runs from battle."

"By that you impute weakness," Zoe countered. "I think there are times when suicide can be seen as an act of strength. I should think it takes quite a bit of courage, actually."

"Oh really, Zoe, what a lot of romantic twaddle. There is no courage born of desperation, only fear. We're all of us attacked by fear time and time again," Edward went on, "but most of us manage to keep a grip on ourselves."

"Hooray for most of us," Zoe muttered.

"Yes, dammit, hooray for most of us." Edward was still lounging against the mantelpiece, but his voice was tense. "There is something to be said for 'seeing things through.' That is the harder path; how much easier to throw up one's hands and abdicate responsibility. I've no respect for those who surrender voluntarily."

"You'd prefer we were all beaten to a bloody pulp first."

"Don't be facile, Zoe. I simply refuse to surround the suicide with 'an heroic aura,' that's all. As for Dora Carrington, she was a dear sweet child, wastefully dramatic and utterly egotistical. I'm sorry she's dead; I shall miss her at parties; but it's Partridge, it's the survivors I must reserve my feelings for."

"I feel for Ralph, too," Zoe said, "though I doubt he needs my feelings, or that they'll be of any use to him. Frances Marshall can help; he has her at least. Carrington must've felt she had no one after Lytton died."

" 'What is the use of Adventures now without you to tell them to?' " Julia quoted softly. She'd been so quiet during the disagreement that Zoe thought she'd drifted away, and was listening, perhaps, to other voices. "She wrote that in her diary, Her Book. Clearly she saw her life as a story to be told, and Lytton was her only audience. With him gone, why bother going on with it?" Julia stopped, frowning. "I have heard something like that before, Zoe, haven't I? Where have I heard that before?"

"I don't know. Perhaps . . ."

"Oh yes." Julia nodded. "Virginia. 'Why write with Katherine not here to read it?' That was different, though; Virginia could replace Mansfield. No, she went on with Mansfield's place empty. Carrington couldn't do that; there was no one else but Lytton. The emptiness . . . spread. It took over, there was nothing. She would have to live with no one there to see her." Julia looked around at them. "Are any of us, do you think, that dependent on another?"

"It is to be devoutly hoped we are not." Edward took out a pipe and began scraping the bowl with sharp, angry little twists of his knife.

"I like the way she burned his spectacles and pajamas. That was good," Julia might have been commenting on a cinema plot, "treating Lytton like some Viking king. Or a Greek warrior. If he'd been an Indian raj, you know, she could have thrown herself on the pyre. But he wasn't; the fire was quite small. She watched it burn. She threw in his pajamas. She threw in his spectacles. She watched the fire take them; keep them; preserve them for her." The tone, the image put Zoe on alert; out of the corner of her eye she glanced at Edward to see if he was worried. He was cautiously tamping in tobacco, staring at his wife while he did so. "Later, she took a shotgun, and . . ." Julia turned first to Zoe, then to Edward. "It was her greatest artistic achievement, don't you think?"

Zoe could do nothing but blink her eyes; Edward, however, was able to draw on his pipe and light it to his satisfaction. "I can't say that I understand," he spoke between deep measured puffs, "what you're referring to, dear. You must try to remember not to talk in private symbols."

"Blowing her heart out," Julia was surprised the point needed clarification. "The perfect metaphor. She transformed herself into poetry. Surely you see that. Surely you see the artist, turning herself into art?"

"No," Edward replied calmly, "I don't see anything of the sort. I see an inconsiderate, silly young woman who always had to be the center of attention; she couldn't even do away with herself without turning the event into another one of her gaudy splashes. In death as in life, foolish and dramatic to the end."

"You are devoid of sensitivity, Edward. Totally without any aesthetic sensibility whatsoever." Julia's voice was cold, controlled, and still, it seemed to Zoe, intent on reactions to a cinema.

"If by sensitive you mean sentimental, then I gladly stand as charged," Edward told her. "Aesthetics really have nothing to do with it. Into what grand scheme would you place Carrington's first attempt, or should we label it one of her earlier efforts? Let's see," he tapped the pipe stem against his teeth, "locking herself into the garage, turning on the car motor, lying down next to the exhaust: does any superb metaphor come to mind yet? Perhaps if we take into account the fact Lytton was still alive while she did all this, perhaps then its true creative essence would make itself clear, at least to someone of my limited sensitivity. How unfortunate old Partridge had to break in and save her, thereby destroying what might have been the greatest — the greatest what, Julia? Any ideas?"

"You are talented, Edward, there is no one who can be quite so heartlessly sarcastic as you. I give you that. But you have not changed my mind. Chance has its part to play, that's all you've proved."

"Ah yes. Chance. Close relation to your dear acquaintances, the Fates. I should've known we'd get to them eventually, those temperamental friends of yours around whom we all must tippy-toe lest we offend. If you don't pay them their due, they'll desert you just when you need them. They sound very predictable to me, Julia. There must be a contradiction in terms there somewhere."

"You are pitiable. There's no room in your universe for mystery, is there Edward? Everything is right out in the open, clear-cut, ascertainable, or else it doesn't exist. Chance, Fate; because you can't grasp them, they aren't real. You're talented, Edward, but you could never be an artist; you insist on everything being under your control."

"Fortunately, my dear, I've no desire to be an artist. I leave such occupations to people like Carrington, and yourself. Though I must say I think I know a good book when I read one." His pipe had gone out; he looked up at Julia from under his brows while he brought it to life again.

"Meaning?" Julia asked, the strain visible now in her face gone pale and her hands gripping the armrests.

"Meaning you are, supposedly, the artist in the family, while I am, without question, the critic. You respect my critical acuity, we know that; you don't put on a dress without asking me is it suitable. You wouldn't dream of sitting even six around the dinner table without checking the arrangement with me first. On every little detail of your little, protected life, you ask for and receive my opinion. Except for one, little detail. Your Art. Your precious book. Or is it books? We've been married for eight years and I've still to see a word, let alone a series of words put together for the purpose of . . . whatever one decides the purpose is. Yet I have let you have your artistic way. And under its guise you've been allowed to indulge your bizarre habits, your moods and silences and your shrieking sensitivities. Indeed, Julia, you ought to be the artist. You have all the trappings of the artist. It's the substance I worry about. Don't you?"

"Edward, please!" Zoe was on her feet.

He kept his eyes on Julia. "Stay out of this, Zoe."

"No, not anymore. I won't allow this cruelty of yours to continue."

"Won't allow?" Edward faced her. "You, won't allow? You're not important here. You're nothing but my wife's playmate, her little friend in fantasy. This is between my wife and me. You don't count, not here, not right now in this room. If you can't bite your tongue then go away; she'll come out to play later."

"You bastard." Zoe spoke the words quietly. "You small-minded, envious, son of a bitch."

Julia was sitting like a corpse propped up, her visionless eyes taped open for the occasion. Edward brushed past Zoe and went to stand in front of her. "Julia?" He leaned toward her. "Darling?" He took her chin in his hand. "Julia." Her eyes came into focus. "Dear," he said, "you . . ." She spat in his face.

Slowly, Edward drew himself up; he stepped back and reached into his pocket. Zoe moved, rushing to Julia, helping her up, trying to steady the body that was shivering now as if a thousand tremors were coursing through it.

"Put her back, please, Zoe," Edward said politely, refolding his handkerchief into neat squares.

"Oh get out of the way, Edward." She tried to walk by him. He sidestepped, blocking their way.

"I said, put her back, please." The 'please' demanded.

"Go to hell." Zoe was standing with her arm around Julia; pulling her even closer, she moved forward, attempting to shoulder him aside.

His fingers were incredibly strong on her arm. "Zoe. I forbid you, to take her, from this room!"

For a few seconds, they glared at each other. Then, before Zoe could comment, Edward regained most of his composure. He raised his hand in a gesture that tried to be reasonable; from somewhere, he summoned up a voice to match. "Zoe, Julia has got to learn that she is responsible for her actions. And it's high time she learned to accept criticism, too. Now provoked or not, that was a willfully childish thing she did, and it should not be rewarded with tender ministrations. Rewarding will only encourage repetition. For her own good, Zoe, she ought to be punished. For her own good." Edward nearly smiled at her.

"Edward," Zoe nearly smiled back, glad to be unleashing her contempt, "I know all about your fondness for punishment." She saw his startled look, his face twitching and falling into bloodless pieces; if not for Julia, she would have stayed around to watch more.

It was the first time Zoe had ever used it against him, though for years she'd known the nature of Julia's and Edward's sex life. At first Julia hadn't talked about it except to assure Zoe she needn't worry. Then, months after Zoe's return, on an afternoon when they were dreamy and soporific from lovemaking, Julia had told her. Keeping her face averted, she'd asked, "Do you find it horrid?"

"Yes."

"Some people think that what you and I do is horrid."

"Yes."

"I think it's horrid the way missionaries do it."

"Yes."

"Do you still love me?"

"Yes of course."

"Wouldn't you rather he did it that way than, other ways? The normal way?"

"I don't know."

"Well, I'd rather." She'd snuggled closer and Zoe had absentmindedly stroked her hair. After a while Julia dozed, but Zoe still lay looking at the ceiling and stroking her hair; listening to voices, seeing images. You have been a naughty child, Julia, you shall have to be punished. Go to your room and wait for me. Yes, Addie. Julia stripping the clothes off her slender, small-breasted body, pulling a long cotton nightgown over her head, pushing her arms through, letting the gown fall to her ankles. Meekly sitting on the bed, waiting. A· small light shines dimly in a corner. Edward comes in, he wears an old-fashioned nightgown too, but wrapped around his shoulders is an old woolen shawl. He stands over Julia until she looks up at him, he is standing very close and she must strain her neck back to see his head. Were she to move forward instead, her face would be pressing into his belly. His right hand holds a large silver-backed brush, his left grips her shoulder, he says, Come. Obediently, she walks in front of him to a chair and waits for him to sit. He spreads his knees, pulling her down over them, his brush hand sliding up under her gown, fingers trailing on the quivering buttocks. The brush comes down on them, stinging, You are a naughty child, stinging, A naughty child, stinging, Bad! stinging, Bad! Bad! Under her stomach she feels his erection crawling. It hardens, it pushes up at her through both their gowns. She waits, buttocks burning, for it to finish, waits, tearless, for the shudder to come, for the wetness to seep through, the punishment to end.

Zoe Mohr is silent, letting me linger on the scene. When she speaks again, I have to force myself back from a distance immeasurably longer than the few feet which separate us. "No more today," her voice is weary, "no more."

There are questions I have which will have to wait. I leave dissatisfied, knowing from the weeks we've been at this that she must tell the story her way, with little regard for lapses, empty spots, things left unexplained. She is content to let me fill in; she wants me to, for never yet has she allowed me really to interrogate her about details or anything else she hasn't

chosen to present. At first I resented this; it made me
suspicious and want to challenge her. Now, I'm not sure why,
maybe it's because of the time we've spent together, I don't
feel that way. I know that on my own, I'll be able to ease my
dissatisfaction. I'll supply what I need, I'll think and dream
and make it whole, no longer caring which part is mine and
which is hers. Because the two aren't separable anymore.
And it doesn't matter if what I've added is imagined; it's real
enough to me, and just, quite possibly, the truth.

Of course I realize that later, once Zoe Mohr has finished,
I'll have to be more rigorous. A really tedious period of
authentication will have to begin if the biography is to bear up
under any kind of scrutiny. It may not get me a Ph.D., but
the commercial market's demanding, too. Like it or not, she'll
have to answer my questions. And I'll have to drag out my
white index cards, take stacks of notes on the period and the
people in support of what she's said. At least I won't have to
get my footnotes right and my subheadings in order; I won't
have to bury everything under an acceptable format until only
the respectable shows through.

I'm glad Julia won't be disappearing into that, into
Lawrence's moon imagery. I like her this way; I want her, to
stay the way she is. So I can see her. Maybe I shouldn't —
My Dear, we mustn't go on meeting this way! But why not?
What's the harm? I'm not taking her from Zoe Mohr; she
offered to share her. Well, I've accepted.

And I think both she and Edward have treated Julia too
much like a child. I've come to agree with Julia about that:
Edward, for all his overplaying the part of strict parent, was
no more guilty than Zoe, who overindulged her while
constantly avowing love and best intentions. They neither one
let her "be." They allowed her no independence, no respect,
no existence apart from their own. Obviously, Edward got his
kicks from perverting their relationship; I'm beginning to
believe Miss Innocent Zoe got what she wanted too, suffering

and sacrificing and sinking her claws in so deep Julia didn't have a chance to break away.

Poor Julia, she must have beaten herself with guilt for not appreciating them. There had to have been times when she resented her need for them, and hated herself for resenting. Especially if she realized who was behind it all. Big Mama, The Great Earth Mother and General, Rebecca Carroll. Julia never got away from her, not really; she had to latch on to substitute parts of her wherever she could find them. Miss Pitt, Zoe, Giles, Edward, Virginia Woolf, Mrs. Craik: put together they made one super giant-sized MOTHER.

Zoe Mohr may not see these patterns, but I do. Lately I've had to hold myself back from using them against her. When she gets imperious I'm tempted to shake her up, confront her with a few things. But what would be the point? She's a frail old woman who has lived her life. It's her past, her story, so why should I say to her, "Look, you made some big mistakes a few decades ago. If you hadn't done thus and so, then thus and so probably wouldn't have happened, the hurt or the damage wouldn't have been done. You were wrong here and weak there, and because of it Julia . . ." My comments wouldn't change anything, they wouldn't affect what she has to say, they'd only make her feel bad. The days she talks about are gone; I've no desire to ruin those she has left. I keep these things to myself, but I intend to use them later, when the time comes to get it all down on paper.

It's not very hard for me to wait, keep my counsel, it's just that when I think of Julia — I don't know. I'd like to have done something. I know I've got the benefit of hindsight, still, if it had been me, with Julia, I'd have pressed more. I wouldn't have given up so easily, or given in so soon, I'd have pushed a little; Julia was strong enough to take it. No one ever gave her enough credit for her strengths, they always concentrated on her weaknesses. I would have played to that strength, made her use it, exercise it, give it a chance to grow.

That nasty scene over her work — it could have been prevented; the entire conversation could have been turned into something constructive. But Julia was always able to deflect Edward and Zoe whenever they got too close to what was inside her. Mentally ill people can be very cunning when protecting their secrets, and Julia had lots of them. So she set up a part of herself as a decoy in order to save another, more precarious part: the one in hiding, afraid to show what she knew about suicide, the Fates, death and responsibility. Jennie Hilbreth, brother Jordan. They were all hidden in the basement of Julia's mind, while over them stood the Artist, bravely submitting to Edward's attack. Neat? Neither he nor Zoe saw the defense. Whereas I, I'd have been on the lookout; I wouldn't have let the Artist get close enough, I'd have kept on about Death until the Julia in hiding was forced to come out, and claim what she thought belonged to her.

"What about Jennie Hilbreth's suicide, Julia? Weren't you glad she killed herself? You were, weren't you. You were hoping she'd find some way to do it, to save herself the agony of a tortured life, give herself release from having to look in a mirror every day and vomit at the reflection. You were with her when she did it. Yes you were. It would have made Byrnes' flesh crawl to know that you actually kissed Jennie's face, you were so sure of what she was about to do, and glad for her. You were happy. You'd asked the Fates to be kind, and they'd listened to you; they would do that sometimes if you asked them long enough, or hard enough, or with the right words. Everything would have been fine except that as Jennie fell, she screamed No! She'd changed her mind, the stupid girl, she wanted to live after all, but it was too late, and you were the one who'd gotten the Fates to intervene. If it weren't for you, Jennie might have lived, had magic surgery, become a Princess. Isn't that right? Don't you know that to be true?"

She'd have denied it. She'd have closed her eyes, clenched her fists, yelled at me to stop. But she would have heard.

"And your brother Jordan? Hadn't you talked to your Friends about him, too? Didn't you want him to be so far away he'd never come back? Remember the child's voice, 'I wish my brother Jordie was dead. I wish a big wave would come and swallow him up, or a mountain fall on top of him. Then he couldn't make me do things anymore.' But for years and years nothing happened; you'd almost forgotten about your private wish. Until . . ."

She would have seen the horror exposed. At first to light, and then, given time, to reason. We would have worked together, stripping away powers. Every day, together, we'd have made a little more horror disappear, until eventually nothing was left but an impotent fantasy. "And that's all. This old decrepit thing is all there is, Julia. This is the truth, just what you see here."

She'd laugh a little in relief, and — reach out to touch my cheek, her fingers . . . No, she'd laugh a little in relief, then look at me, until I got up from the couch to . . . She wouldn't laugh, she'd just take my hand. Press it to her lips.

She looks so much better. There's life around her eyes; she's put on a little weight; her wrists are lovely again. She's strong. We smile at each other. We've done it! We've conquered the damn thing, and by God, we're going to celebrate. In bed, with champagne cooling where we can reach it. The afternoon's ahead of us, and spring air is making the curtains flap, ever so gently.

Sure.

The next day I'm the one depressed; Zoe Mohr is fine. She perks, she bubbles! If only she could get up from her couch and do a dance or clean the silver. She's got far, far too much energy; she has to expend some of it in twitches and tics, in picking things off her blanket that aren't there, in letting her words rush about with no control over their volume.

I'm not in the mood for any of it. Why can't she be having one of her quiet, teary spells today? A subdued bout of melancholy — I could identify with that. I'd much prefer it;

both of us could sit here and be morose for a while, let sadness lap till we were soothed; maybe have a drink or two. It's the kind of afternoon I'm in the mood for, not this.

"AhHa! caught you, didn't I? You didn't ask! You didn't ask!"

What's she going on about? She's got too much powder on, she looks grotesque. What does she want from me?

"Not yesterday, not today. My my. I've had my answer ready just in case, but now I needn't worry since you haven't brought the question. You don't seem to care where Zoe, where I lived during those years. Where was my home? With Edward and Julia? Elsewhere? By myself? did I live by myself? In a flat? A hotel? Perhaps a house. In Bloomsbury, or out? City or country? What? Well? Doesn't it matter?"

Now that she mentions it, no. It's not really very important; the relationships are clear enough, the way things were between them. It doesn't much matter whether six blocks or three feet separated them, Zoe was obviously a part of the household.

"It's only a detail, am I right? Yes, you see that, don't you. You see how dispensable it is, as so many of them are. I am right about details, the first day we met I told you what I thought of them, and now you see, you understand. Don't you? Yes, you do."

The old girl is having quite a day, supplying my questions and my answers, too. What does she need me for? She might as well be sitting here talking to herself. Would she notice if I got up and left?

"Briggs! Briggs! Briggs!" Her bell's gone berserk; awful, strident jangling. "Let's have some tea, Briggs! Some tea!" Please, Briggs, take the damn thing out of her hand and give us some relief. Don't look at me, I don't know what's going on.

But Briggs does. The gentleness, one doesn't expect it. A woman her size, such a blank exterior. Beautifully gentle, removing the bell; she took a toy from a well-loved child who didn't understand why. Well done. She knows what she's doing, there's more than practice behind her actions. I've misjudged her, I think.

"Can you see? Is she getting our tea? She's so slow, I don't know why I — not like Julia, not at all. Did I tell you how quickly she recovered? Did I, yesterday, how quickly she got over the attack? A few hours' rest, that's all she needed. Amazing, how quickly she . . . how quickly, when one has to. Thank you, Briggs, goodbye."

Wait, Briggs. Why not stick around this afternoon? What if . . .

"We all had to. There were so many blows in those years." She drinks; the cup's fairly steady in her hand. "So many deaths. A horrible fad, everyone was doing it in some fashion or other. Lytton, Carrington, Lowes Dickinson. Poor Morgan Forster was undone when that man died, undone. So much love, and esteem; and then, you know, when the mentor dies the pupil sees his own death coming next, like the son once the father has gone. Generations can feel that too." Perhaps the tea is soothing her; she's certainly quieted down. "The stars Dickinson had touched at Cambridge, those bright young men who'd brushed against him and been the better for it. Think how they must have felt, knowing they were the last. Think how frightening: a friend, and an era, dead at the same time. And you are left behind, but for how long?

"The worst, was when Roger Fry died, two years later. In September; it didn't help, his going with the leaves. The world stripping itself of color; color fading, dying. A man who had loved it, gone. The rest of us had relied on Roger, it was Roger who'd shown us what to look for, how to see. I remember . . . an autumn funeral, the chill." Her face is immobile, as if frozen by memory.

"One must bury the dead," she turns stiffly toward me, "and be buried in turn. How much easier to cope with the death of others, than confront the inevitability of one's own. Are you perhaps too young to know that? No, age doesn't mean much. The century was in its thirties, and so were many of us. Burying. The Lindbergh baby, John Galsworthy, Leonard Woolf's sister.

"Deaths needn't be of friends or kindred souls, though then the knife goes especially deep. They all matter. An innocent, a luminary, a person neither guiltless nor famous. They are dead, and you are not. Is there something to be learned from that? Something that will bring the secret closer, or make the meaning clearer?

"Of course not. That's why one always winds up grieving for oneself. A moment for them, and for oneself, a lifetime. One can mourn for a lifetime. Unless everything one does becomes a diversion, a trick to take the mind off death. That's the business and busyness of life. Waving the magic wand. There's nothing else. We invent. To keep going. And we pretend we are not pretending."

I have changed my mind. I preferred her manic perkiness to this onslaught of cynicism and gloom. I wish she'd change the subject.

"That is why I have always been so fond of artists. They twist necessity to their own advantage. They do their tricks in public, and we applaud, we're enchanted. Why it's Art! not artifice. The everyday is risen, gloriously transformed. An aura of significance surrounds it; we need only lift our eyes to see, to partake. And we do, we worship style, revere technique, exclaim over truth and beauty. Because through Art, our pain becomes communal. Our futility is shared, and made to look like something grand."

I don't want to be around this, I don't need it, and I would like to get up and say goodbye. Five minutes, I'll give her five more minutes; if she hasn't reperked by then . . .

"Has your tea gone cold? Such a simple, unassuming comfort, hot tea; pity it's not enough. Do try a sweet, the package says they're fortified with nine different vitamins; but I imagine you're like me, you'd prefer the tenth. Should I have Briggs light the fire for us? turn on some lights?

"Look there, it's the neighbor's cat outside the window, on the ledge. Can you see her? Strange, she usually visits in the morning, when the sun makes a nice warm patch for her to sleep in. I used to have a cat of my own, great source of companionship, such an interesting creature. Violet, I called her Violet, and she had quite the largest whiskers of any cat I've ever seen; a calico. Briggs had to . . . It's not fair, the life span of pets. I never got another."

That's it. I'm going. Dead cats, Jesus.

"Let's have a gin, shall we? Why don't you make us one. Perhaps it will help; I'm finding things a bit hard today. I know it's Julia we should be — but we are, we are, though it may not seem so. I promise to get to her directly. That is, very soon. I am trying. It's difficult, you understand, bringing her back, knowing she has to . . ."

I don't want to hear about it. Not until I have to. And we're not there yet, we can't be.

She takes the glass I hand her but can't keep a grip on it. It drops, clattering, onto the tea cart. Not too much is spilled, but the noise was startling. I think her hands actually are getting palsied; she seems to be crumbling, breaking apart, a little every day. Maybe I just never realized her true condition in the beginning, though how I — unless she was doing a good job of hiding it from me.

What, is she crying because she dropped a glass? Where the hell is Briggs?

"Sit down," she says, gesturing me back. "Sit down. You must, let me finish. I am, in control, you see? I am, perfectly capable. I will finish what I intended to cover."

All right, though I still think those were tears I saw. But I'm sitting. In awe of something I'll call stubbornness for now.

"From nineteen thirty-two to nineteen thirty-four we experienced, as I've indicated, a series of crushing deaths. Each one of them, seemed to take something away from life as we had known it. Not only people, but things, the way things were — We'd reach out, and nothing; the familiar had disappeared.

"Of course the entire world was changing, but we didn't see that, we didn't see the patterns, the shock waves and repercussions outside our own circle. We were living our private lives in England. When, for example, Hindenburg died, it didn't mean a great deal to us. Not at the time it happened. It was part of Edward's job to watch what was going on, but even Edward couldn't have been expected to know. One needs clairvoyants, not analysts. A foreign government went fascist, its dissidents were purged, its president died — we noticed, but hardly applied such things personally. After Hitler had been Reichsführer for a month, our lamentations could be heard, but they were for the dying leaves and Roger. Those were the changes we felt, and remarked upon.

"Saxon Sydney-Turner had a better understanding. It needs to be personal, you see; the blow must pierce one's selfish sphere of interest. Saxon's was music, and he was hit earlier than the rest of us. Nineteen thirty-three, when Schönberg got jackbooted out of the Prussian Academy. Saxon was tremendously upset; it wasn't what the Nazis had done to a man, but what they'd done to music. The country of Bach, Beethoven, Wagner, silencing a composer 'because it didn't like the sounds he created? Good Christ, if a government can decree aesthetics,' he said, 'you just watch what they'll be in control of next.' "

Is it me today? She's so hard to follow, I don't understand her purpose, what she means me to get from all this. If only she wouldn't fluctuate so; she's never been this bad before. I should leave and come back tomorrow. If she's just the same, then at least I'll be ready for it.

"He tried to warn us. We listened with half an ear. We were used to having Saxon around, he was an old friend of Lytton's and the Woolfs', but no one placed much faith in him anymore, or bothered to take him seriously. He'd been the man with a brilliant future for far too long, in fact everyone suspected his future had been over for years. Though he talked about his music beautifully, no one ever heard the notes. They were never finished, never played; all of his compositions deteriorated into words eventually. In a way, his warning was the same: Saxon could describe the danger, but he couldn't make it real.

"Except to Julia. She must have listened better than the rest of us. Schönberg's fate seemed to haunt her, she'd go into bizarre little moods over it. 'It's because he renounced his Judaism. It's punishment for that,' she decided one afternoon. 'Oh good Lord, Julia,' Edward told her, 'it's not your Fates at work, it's the Nazis. And they're taking jobs away from the Jews first of all.'

" 'Then he shouldn't have surrendered his religion since he lost his job anyway. We mustn't abandon what we've been chosen to carry.'

" 'We, Julia?'

" 'You married a Jew, Edward.'

" 'Did I indeed. Your religion looks to me like a discarded cloak you've suddenly decided to wear again. Frankly, I find it most unbecoming.' Very dramatically, Julia wrapped an invisible garment around her body and strode out of the room. Edward put his paper down and said, 'Really, Zoe, I very much doubt it was Saxon's intention to create a religious revival with all his going on about injustice. The man never did have much control over his material.'

"But Saxon had an effect on Julia even if it wasn't the one he intended. Without doubt, he was special to her; not as a man, or even a friend. It was what he represented, I think. For a while they were quite close. He would come to the house and they'd hole up to debate things like, what is the first duty of the artist, to communicate or to create. And, if revelation is the essence of art, then which is more incomplete, a book that's never read or a symphony that's never played. Julia was always agitated after he left; within half an hour she'd invariably get depressed and retreat to her room.

"I didn't want to interfere in her relationship. But one day I found her sitting by a window and looking out with such a forlorn expression, I had to ask her what was wrong.

" 'Saxon is dead.'

" 'What? He just left the house twenty minutes ago!'

" 'You're so literal-minded sometimes.' She didn't look around, went right on staring out the window.

" 'Your choice of metaphor was very strange, Julia. Saxon is full of enthusiasms and vitality; he has a thousand talents and twice that many causes to keep him going.'

" 'He's got no core left. There's nothing inside anymore.' She was unusually composed for being so low. 'He's like a marionette, pulling his own strings. Lots of movement, activity, bouncing around; all of it futile, artificial. It's senseless, and sad. I don't want to be like him, Zoe.'

" 'Darling, whoever said you were?'

" 'I don't want to become another Saxon, brilliance burned out and only the vapors remaining, nothing accomplished, nothing tested or proved. He *is* a dead man, Zoe, a former artist of great promise; what could be more hollow than that?'

" 'Does he see himself that way?'

"She dismissed the question, got up from her chair and began pacing the room. 'How is it,' she asked, 'that self-conviction can become self-delusion without our knowing it?' She stopped, rubbed her chin, then started walking round again. 'I used to think the act itself was enough, the making. But it wasn't. So I decided that one must finish the thing to attain full satisfaction. But one doesn't. I see now that one must offer it up, for verification. Book, painting, symphony — it must be given to others to make real. To validate, not just it, but oneself.' She stood in the middle of the room. 'One must make the offering, it's the only way.'

" 'But what if it's rejected?'

" 'Then one must try again.'

" 'Julia, please don't place too much dependence on a perfect world. You talk as if the artist and his art and his audience were involved in a simple equation, an honest relationship. Surely you know how easily sullied that is, how much room there is for error. Whim, fad, the dictates of commerce, how is any of that to be avoided?'

" 'It can't be. Yes I know, I used to insist on purity: from me, to the world. That's not possible, I see that now. I was merely justifying, deluding, when I insisted on it. There are so many traps one creates, in order to avoid the true test.'

" 'How true can the test be? What about all the artists who died penniless, unknown, totally devoid of outside verification? Are you saying they were less than artists? Van Gogh only sold one painting in his lifetime. There must be thousands and thousands of artists whose work has never been seen or heard or accepted, by anyone but themselves.'

" 'One must still make the offering, Zoe. Otherwise, it's the tree falling in the forest with no one to hear it.'

" 'Well it's still a tree, Julia, and it has made a sound, whether or not anyone verifies it. One knows that by having heard other trees, falling in other forests.'

" 'But there's no way of comparing the sound, is there, Zoe? There's no way of knowing its quality.'

" 'The tree could know, if it had heard other . . . Oh this is silly, Julia, you're not a tree. You've read tons of books, you must have some sense of your own work in relation to them, some idea of the quality.'

" 'Perhaps. But my opinion is not to be trusted anymore. I must go beyond it to be sure. Of all those thousands and thousands of artists you mentioned, there may have been one, possibly two, who knew, and had no doubts that they were right. Even Van Gogh had his Theo, Zoe, someone who believed along with him.'

" 'There's still no guarantee. Look at Virginia. All the verification an artist could want, yet she always works herself into a horrible state waiting for the critics to react. Do you think she is ever sure?'

"Julia walked to the window, splayed her hands along the sill. She was silent for a while. Then she said, very softly, 'Virginia. Van Gogh. Me. There's got to be more than the torment. The talent, even a portion of the talent; I must know if it's in there, too.'

" 'Well, I don't know why I'm playing devil's advocate. What do you intend to do?'

"She traced a finger around one of the panes. 'I've been told there's a critic in the family; perhaps I'll start with him.' Turning halfway toward me, she smiled.

"Like this," Zoe Mohr says, twisting the upper part of her body slightly to the side and gifting me with a small, rueful grin. It fades; she goes back to her usual position and pulls at the blanket over her legs. "Something in me made me argue with her that day, something. Oh well," she sighs, "I probably couldn't have prevented anything anyway. Things take their course, don't they, and there's not a great deal we can do about it.

"Take Carrington. Virginia and Leonard visited her at Ham Spray the day before she died. People always said Virginia disliked her; do you think it possible she said or did something, inadvertently of course, that helped Carrington pick up the gun?" She shakes her head emphatically. "No. The point is there was nothing she could've said or done that would have stopped Carrington. I doubt Virginia blamed herself in any way; we know how much she knew about suicide. And if Leonard was as smart as I think he was, he didn't waste much time blaming himself for failing to save Virginia, either, when her time came. It's tempting to think he might have found her note a little earlier than he did, and rushed to the right spot on the riverbank, and emptied those heavy stones from her pockets, and given her a good shaking before taking her home to a nice pot of tea by the fire. But the fact is, he didn't. Both those ladies did what they were going to do; no one else was responsible. It's the insidious need to feel guilty that makes one think otherwise."

I'm not so sure about that. It sounds pretty self-serving. Makes me think that Julia, too — is she trying to prepare the way? Set up excuses for herself so I . . .

". . . forgot to tell you an interesting theory about Virginia. I'm not sure anymore how much of it's Julia's and how much mine, but I meant to go into it. You must ask me about it tomorrow. When you come back tomorrow, you must ask me. I have to stop now. I'm very tired, suddenly. Very tired." The bell sounds, one feeble jingle-jangle is all she's capable of. Briggs must have been listening for it, because she comes in just as I'm stretching out of my chair. I leave Zoe Mohr to her, gladly; I've just realized I'm exhausted too.

IX

THE LADY'S RIGHT: how quickly we recover. Next evening, I grab a quick pub dinner and hurry home. The theory about Virginia Woolf won't stop working in my head; I've got to get it down, see it better. I fumble with the lock, the lights, the typewriter cover; prefer to think it's excitement, not indigestion gripping me.

Three drafts later, my stomach's unknotted and I'm able to lean back, satisfied with what I've got:

"It's known that Virginia Woolf rarely if ever finished a novel without suffering a serious bout of mental illness during the period between completion and publication. These illnesses have been ascribed to tension over the ensuing critical response to her work; but if it were simply that, worrying about whether or not her work was good, she ought to have broken down after submitting every literary review, each of her books on criticism, and her biographies. Strangely, the illnesses coincided just with her novels. Perhaps this peculiarity can be explained.

"Psychotics have extensive, detailed fantasies that often supersede reality, or the world as it is commonly accepted. When they cease making concessions to reality altogether, the rest of us, who are busy at it, become threatened. We call the people 'mad' and lock them up, or if they're rich, we say 'incapacitated' and send them to the country in the care of hired keepers.

"Talent aside, there's but one discriminating difference between the psychotic and the artist, and that is the distance between the person and her fantasy. The artist manages to externalize her fantasies, to get them out of her psyche, often by disguising them, and into a poem or painting. There, if not always appreciated, they are at least acceptable; they may threaten aesthetic values, but not society itself. Should an artist become incapacitated as an artist, there are still other social roles she can play, the dysfunction isn't total; this is because she is not involved in a fundamental conflict between her fantasies and society, merely a controversy over her art and its appreciation. So, though the artist may be only one step removed from the psychotic, that externalizing step is significant.

"Complexity becomes extreme when the psychotic and artistic personalities are combined in one individual, as they were in Virginia Woolf. Then externalization is only intermittently possible, distancing suffers from erratic fluctuation, and distinctions between fantasy and art, and art and therapy, become dangerously blurred. This is particularly true when the artist is all too aware of her psychotic fears, and attempts to control them through her art, by creating a structure in which they can be either neutralized or resolved. It's an impossible task; the effort must fail as therapy, though it can succeed brilliantly as art. But if, in addition, it doesn't succeed as art, the work is worthless, the devastation total.

"For a time, Virginia Woolf was able to externalize her madness through the artful manipulation of fantasy, the writing of a novel; on completion, however, the madness was still inside her, and only the structure which she had produced to deal with it remained, 'out there.' Though that structure was cohesive, she was still scattered and diffused. The inner life had been treated, but it belonged to someone else. As therapy, the novel failed.

"But as art? She must at least have that. There had to be assurances. The tensions became enormous. Despair and fear grew; she collapsed under their weight. Then the critical responses came in; by acclaiming her work, they restored her perspective. Virginia recovered: the artist, triumphant, climbed over the psychotic, and even kept her down for a while. Until it was necessary to go through it all again.

"Why did the process have to be repeated over and over? Perhaps another artist gives the clue: 'I have this funny thing which is that I'm never afraid when I'm looking in the ground glass.' That's Diane Arbus, and Virginia Woolf would have understood her, though most likely she'd have hated her photographs. Both women, both artists, both ill and suicidal; each able, for a while, to conquer her fear of life through her unique focus on life as an artist. Unfortunately, when fantasies refuse to be externalized, the camera lens and the pen aren't strong enough to force them. Then there is only one last thing the artist can do to prevent the psychotic from ruling forever: she must sacrifice the individual."

I've put in the quote from Diane Arbus myself, because it fits; I'm certain now that the word Julia screamed on the train coming back from Cambridge was 'Terror.' So I've added my bit, hoping Zoe Mohr will agree. This way the theory, as it stands, is part hers, part Julia's, and, at least a little, part mine. I like the company I'm keeping. I like the theory, too. A literalist might look for an exact replica of the psychotic's fantasies in the artist's work; a fool might think the individual was totally aware of the forces she contended with. I am neither; I can simply hold the theory and enjoy how good it feels.

There's no way of proving it, perhaps that's why it appeals to me. The seductiveness of armchair conjecturing. Much more alluring than any finite test. Embrace a grand theory. Take one to bed tonight.

It's all I've got. My sensual experiences have been very limited of late; I seem to have been making dreams and little else. Usually, if I think very hard about Julia right before falling asleep, I can get myself dreaming about her. I don't remember the dreams, but I know I've enjoyed them. Sometimes I wake up with an emotional carry-over, a warm feeling wrapped around me. A sense of being loved. Once I woke up climaxing; said to myself see? women have wet dreams too. But then I opened my eyes, and I wanted to be asleep again, with Julia; not awake and empty, alone. It's better not to do that, just to have a wonderful dream and a cozy, enclosed feeling in the morning. It fades, but there's always the next night. That's why I look forward to going to sleep; nice things can happen.

Which I have never mentioned to Zoe Mohr, naturally. At the end of our next session, however, I suspect she knows. Not only knows, but understands.

I'm undone, and I don't do a very good job of hiding it. I feel her eyes on me while I struggle into my coat, keeping my back to her on purpose, praying she won't say anything more. But she does. "Will you be all right?" Very gentle. "Tonight, will you manage?" Not trusting my voice, or my face, I nod once, without turning around. I walk to the door. "You're sure?" she asks. I nod again, back still to her. "I'm sorry," she insists on continuing, "if I've spoiled . . ." I can't listen, I wave my arm to indicate I've heard and accept and am leaving, and I go.

From her apartment, to my own. Where I can think about what's happened. Go through it again. As many times as I have to. Feeling as Zoe must have, when Julia told her what Edward did to her at night, hearing voices, seeing faces. Sitting, lights on, coat on; mind on.

"I wish you'd written to me about it earlier, Zoe." Long legs crossed, Giles occupied the chair matching hers, one on either side of the sitting room fire. Zoe was only mildly shocked by his appearance. A drooping mustache aged him more than he'd have liked to know; she remembered his starting it after Roger died, saying he felt the need of more protection against the world. Evidently, the need had grown. There was a permanent sheen of perspiration on his face now;

the strands of hair he ceaselessly pushed back from his forehead were greyer than last time, and his eyes shone too brightly from their hollows.

Zoe knew why Giles' appearance wasn't upsetting her too much: Julia, the last time she'd seen her, had looked worse. "My reasons seemed very good to me at the time. I'm sorry, Giles, I guess I was more confused than I realized."

"I'd have come back immediately, you know."

"Yes, of course." But what could he have done? Why endanger his health, unless there were something he could have done about Julia's?

"If only to share the trouble, I'd have come."

"I know. I just . . ." She shrugged, spread her hands.

"Just had to go through it alone. Stoic Zoe, the last of the independents. I don't think I ever fully realized how difficult it is for you to turn to someone for help. You're always so stiff upper lip; more English than the English."

"Not always." She didn't look at him. She wanted to avoid significant stares, emotional reminders of that time when she hadn't been as Giles described. Then why had she said, 'Not always'?

"Ah yes," Giles must have smiled, "I seem to remember an exception." He waited for her to say something; when she didn't, he laughed. "Oh do look up, Zoe. It's perfectly safe. Surely at this stage we should be able to enjoy a pleasant recollection from our impetuous youth. Shouldn't we?"

Zoe grinned. It was good to have him here. "Thank you," she said, sinking back against the cushions.

He didn't ask her what she meant. "D'you think we might have a spot of something?"

"Certainly, sherry? scotch? Or shall I ring for Mrs. Craik to put on tea."

"Is that old battle-ax still around? Sherry, please. If she had to be anywhere, why is she here? Why isn't she down at The Crannies, with them?"

"Because Edward insisted. Just the two of them, that's all

he'd allow. You've no idea," she finished pouring their drinks, "what a tyrant he's become."

"Doesn't surprise me in the least. You should have known him at school. He'd have been a bully if he'd owned a better body. Had to content himself with 'mothering' instead. Even then, though, he knew a fine sherry; I'll have to grant him that."

"The worst of it is, everything he does, he does in the name of Julia's health. I don't doubt his sincerity, at least I don't think I do, but I find his tactics deplorable."

"Lord save us from men of honorable intent. Give me a good North African carpet dealer any day; open dishonesty is positively the only thing one can trust. That, and a certain guileless amorality still to be found in the better class of beach boy."

"I apologize for taking you away from all that."

"Nonsense. In the flesh, Tangier's pleasures aren't nearly so delectable as their reputations would have them be. I was quite glad of the excuse to come home. And after all, Zoe, it is rather nice to be needed. Are you sure *that*," he reached for the decanter, "isn't part of the problem?"

"What do you mean?"

Giles took his time refilling their glasses. "Well. Either Edward has pretty well managed to cut you out; or Julia is no longer cutting you in."

"Thanks for the admirable appraisal, but that isn't why I wrote you."

"Now, now, don't be angry. It doesn't hurt to check out the simpler things first. Especially when one's been gone so long."

"You have been, Giles, that's just it. If you hadn't, you couldn't have said what you did, you'd have seen how badly off she is. I don't know how I can get you to believe that it's not me I'm worried about, it's Julia."

"How about my just taking your word for it, which I do. How long have they been away?"

"Nearly a month."

"And you've heard nothing?"

"Oh no, Edward is very good about sending along little progress reports. Such as 'Monday, February 12th: Julia was able to sit up for three hours today.' 'Wednesday, February 21st: Julia ate an adequate tea.' No one down there has seen hide nor hair of them, despite the fact that 'Sunday, March 4th: julia was permitted to take half an hour's walk this afternoon.' I've written to the Woolfs, others in the area; but when they call, Edward greets them politely at the door, thanks them for their concern, and sends them on their way. I've been forbidden to write directly, forbidden! There's no point anyway, Julia would never get the letter. Short of showing up on the doorstep with a constable in tow, I don't see how — What am I to do, go down in darkest night and sneak in the window? I just don't know what to do, Giles!"

"Most peculiar. Glass, please."

Zoe held it out, not caring what or how much he poured. "I'm glad you agree. There's no question Julia needed a rest. She was very ill, very disturbed. I tried — She had a teacher, Miss Pitt, taught art and was, quite fond of her. She and her sister run a convalescent home in Cornwall now, a good one, highly recommended. Edward wouldn't hear of it. 'I'm fully capable of nursing my own wife back to health, thank you.' Fully capable! Giles, he is the cause of it! He's to blame for Julia's attack! And the bastard knows it, too."

"Just what, did the bastard do?"

"That bastard." Zoe gulped her drink. "That . . ."

"Bastard," Giles supplied, filling her glass again.

"Exactly. A real fully fledged, fully capably fledged, bastard." She looked closely at the sherry and then put it down. "I don't think I want any more of that. It's making me sick."

"Sorry. I thought it would do you good."

"It's not. Where was I? Oh yes. Bastardly Edward. D'you know what he did?"

"No, but I am trying to find out."

"I'll tell you. He made her promise — Why she ever trusted him with her work I will never know. It was a horrible, foolish, wrong decision. But she made it, and I'm sure Edward is thanking God that she did." Zoe stopped; bitterness contorted her mouth and chin.

After watching her through a minute of silence, Giles felt impelled to prod, "Zoe dear, I remain unilluminated. Do please continue."

She looked at him with hostility, then visibly shook it off as she realized who was sitting across from her. Her head cleared, and she was able to go on. "Julia decided, it was time to show her work to someone; for reasons I'm not entirely clear about and won't go into at the moment, the someone was Edward. They made an agreement: he would read everything at his own pace, and when he was through, they would discuss all of it at one time rather than each piece by dribs and drabs.

"Well, he really took his time. Damn him, he took it, even though he saw Julia getting more and more tense every day. More and more worried about what his reaction would be. She got incredibly wound up, tighter than . . . Anyway, finally he called her into his study. I don't know what he said to her. I still don't. All I know is, she came out absolutely drained of color. Edward followed right behind, he came out and put his arm around her, kissed her hair, the picture of tenderness, and said 'It *is* for the best, darling. Just remember that, and be a brave girl.' Then he squeezed her shoulder. 'All right?' he asked. Julia nodded, but she seemed oblivious, really, to anything that was going on.

"For a few days she was very quiet, very subdued. I asked her what had happened; she wouldn't speak. I asked Edward what had happened, and all he did was preen his feathers and utter something about 'a private agreement' between them. I admit, I was more than a bit pushed by all the secrecy, and yes, I did feel excluded. I'd never been allowed to read . . .

and here they were . . . But, I accepted it, I really did, Giles. Until I saw that Julia was not coming out of her lethargy, but sinking into it, deeper and deeper. At first she wouldn't leave her room; then she wouldn't leave her bed; then, it was as if she wouldn't leave some secret place in herself. So, I . . .''

"Had it out with Edward."

"Yes. He told me Julia was simply indulging herself, but that he was allowing it because she'd had to give up something very important to her, and it seemed only fair to let her carry on for a while. 'You mean,' I said to him, 'this odd behavior of hers is really a form of treat?' 'You could put it that way if you like.' 'A treat. Well don't you think it's time you took it away from her? Got her to stop? I assume you think you can put a stop to it any time you like.' 'I can begin to. But I've no desire to be ungenerous, Zoe; I think she should have her way for a little while longer. There's no harm, really.' 'No harm? My God, Edward, don't you realize she is totally out of touch? Completely unreachable? I can't even get her to eat! I have to spend two hours every meal just getting the barest minimum into her! How can you call it harmless?' He looked at me in that awful, pompous way he has, and said, 'I assure you I have every bit as much concern for Julia's welfare as you do.' 'Then for God's sake go up there and tell her treat time is over!' 'I don't intend to be bullied by you, Zoe.'

"I realized my anger was making him that much more obstinate, so I tried, I literally begged him, 'Please,' I said, 'please, Edward, if you can bring Julia out of this mood, or whatever it is, please, please do it now.' He stared at me as if I were some sort of strange creature performing an exotic ritual before his very eyes, and then — this was incredible; he looked at his watch! Just like someone checking to see was it time to take the roast out! 'Very well,' he patted the fob, 'I suppose a few days more or less . . .' And he went upstairs, after commanding me to stay where I was. So I didn't see or hear what went on in that room, either. But whatever happened, it didn't work. Thus, The Crannies. Where no one can be a witness to his failures; and no one else can take the credit, when he succeeds. If he succeeds."

"Did you ever find out, before they left, what precipitated Julia's collapse?"

"Not directly, but I've a bloody good idea. One of the first things Edward did after their talk in the study that day was to lock up every scrap of Julia's writing. Her novels, her plays and pieces, even her diaries. Everything, and he took all of it with him to The Crannies. Perhaps he thinks I'm not above picking locks in his absence."

"Why take everything she's done, unless there were some assurance she wouldn't write more? But that couldn't be the agreement; it's not credible."

"And it's immaterial, too. You don't seem to understand how incapacitated Julia is. She can't even write her name, whether or not Edward would like her to. Anyway, I'm fairly certain that's not it. What I do think, is, he's forbidden her to publish." Zoe let that sink in, seeming to enjoy the distaste which was slowly appearing on Giles' face; he turned his head aside slightly, as if Zoe herself were the cause of it.

"That . . . is a most unpleasant conjecture."

"It gets worse. Edward hasn't forbidden her exactly — he knows Julia's quite capable of rebelling against such a dictum — but somehow, he has gotten her to agree to it voluntarily. I think Julia has made him a promise not to publish anything, for whatever reasons Edward has managed to make palatable."

Giles grimaced. "Doesn't make sense. Whether he's forbidden, cajoled, or threatened her in some way, why would Julia first go along with it, and then break down?"

"Stress? I don't know, maybe a part of her really agrees with what Edward had to say, and another part doesn't, it hates the agreement or hates the person who agreed; so to get away from both, Julia withdrew? I don't know, Giles."

"Hm." He played with his mustache, twisting bits of it between his fingers, smoothing the bits he'd twisted, twisting them again. "I suppose the two of us might go down there and see what's happening." He glanced at Zoe to see if the idea was being well received, and had to smile at how relieved she looked. "Well then. What would you say to a little weekend at The Crannies? It's been ever so long since we were there together. Even Edward would have to grant us our nostalgia."

Zoe sighed, almost happily. "Thank heavens you agree we have to go. But Giles, I've never told either of them anything about . . ."

He stood up, and reached for her hand. "Wasn't necessary. Nor will it be."

Taking his hand, Zoe allowed herself to be pulled from the chair. She accepted his brotherly kiss on her forehead, knowing it was all she wanted and all he intended to give.

Giles released her with a flourish. "We'll show up with absolutely tons of luggage, and old Gordon will be so flustered he'll have no choice but to let us in."

Obviously, Giles was still top god in Edward Gordon's pantheon. If Zoe hadn't known him better, she would have been amazed at how quickly Edward altered his features and his manner the moment he opened the door wider and saw who was accompanying her. She left them to their ecstatic reunion, quite sure Edward would have loved to consummate it on the spot.

Julia was outside in the back garden, bundled up, attempting to sketch flower stalks with her mittens on. If she heard footsteps, she didn't bother turning around. "Hello," Zoe said quietly, forcing the eagerness and tension out of her voice.

Julia looked up; her face was pale, but healthier. "Oh, hello, Zoe." She went back to sketching.

Zoe moved to stand in front of her. "How are you feeling?"

Julia carefully erased a few lines; she answered, speaking to the pad, "Fine, I guess."

"You look much better."

"Do I?"

"Yes. Much."

She went on drawing the remains of last year's plants. "That's nice."

Giles and Edward came out to a silent tableau: Zoe standing, head bowed, Julia sitting, eyes down, hand making tentative arcs over a half-filled sheet. "Julia?" Edward was beaming. "Darling? Look who's here!" He grabbed Giles' arm and pulled him forward to stand by Zoe.

"Hello Sister Dear." Giles gave the top of her head his most ingratiating grin.

Slowly, Julia looked up. "Giles?" When she saw his face, her own reacted; for the first time, Zoe saw motion and life there. "Giles!" She pushed the pad off her lap and threw herself into his arms. "Giles! Giles! Giles!"

Laughing, he swung her around, careless of Zoe's shins; she saw his grinning face over Julia's shoulder, his crinkling eyes with the moisture seeping out at the corners. She was happy for them. Yet sad, too. A little jealous. But, mainly happy; then guilty, because she hadn't called on Giles sooner. Perhaps he actually was the answer. She glanced at Edward; he was enjoying the scene, his delight at Julia's response was genuine.

There were too many doubts. Zoe turned away, closing her eyes. She didn't want to look at the possibility she might have been wrong. The three of them together, it was Paris all those years ago, when she'd felt excluded, separate, watching a trio that balanced so well without her. She'd overreacted then, blaming Edward for her own inadequacies, resenting Edward for the natural way he'd fitted in. It had been easy making him a villain; easy, never to stop seeing him as one?

Zoe wished she knew how to faint; how blissful it would be to lose consciousness. Not to think for a while, not to be burdened. To withdraw, as Julia could; have time to sort things out. "Aren't you coming, Zoe?" one of them called. "Yes!" yes of course, nothing could keep her away. Brain thrumming, she had to follow them into the house.

Apparently the stimulation of her brother's presence was not enough to keep Julia steadily aroused. Over dinner, she started to retreat again. Edward paid no attention, but both Zoe and Giles watched Julia grow paler, quieter, motionless: an obedient child putting up with company she'd lost interest in, staying at the table until excused. After dessert, Edward rose without comment and calmly pulled back her chair, freeing Julia to go to her room if she wished. They watched her leave. Giles and Zoe exchanged looks; he shifted his eyes toward the kitchen just as Edward turned to ask, "Port?" "Naturally," Giles replied. "No thank you, Edward, I believe I'll start clearing," Zoe said; in a few minutes she was able to leave the two of them alone.

It was after midnight before Giles could get to her room and tell her about "The Pact," as he called it. Evidently since coming to Sussex Edward had been forced to ease the terms somewhat, as an incentive for Julia to pull herself together. "And it's worked, too, because almost from the day he revised their agreement, Julia's been improving." Giles seemed convinced.

"She's got a long way to go yet, Giles. She may be better, but she's far from well."

"He insists that this new proviso granting posthumous publication has turned the tide."

"Oh really? First he sinks her, then he saves her. What kind of power is the man after? It's brutal, and disgusting."

"Just a moment, Zoe. He didn't show me any of her manuscripts, but from what he says about them, I gather Julia can be pretty disgusting, too. And very brutal."

"I don't believe it. What could she possibly have written that would make Edward move to suppress it in this manner? Forbidding her work to be published in their lifetime! how absurd."

"Remember Julia has agreed to it. She must have a good idea of how devastating her material is. It's not just Edward's reputation at stake, either, I can assure you. He's acted to preserve the best interests of many people, Julia's most of all. There are things she's exposed that should never've been brought out; we'd all be better off not knowing them."

"You're very trusting, Giles, to take his word on this. Don't you think it suspicious that he won't let anyone see Julia's words?"

"No. He's trying to protect the family, and I believe him."

"Well I don't. I see self-interest shining all around the man. Either Julia's told the truth about him, and he can't bear for it to be known, or she's written something truly great, and he can't bear for that to be known either. It wouldn't do for a middle echelon clerk in the Foreign Office to be married to a genius, would it?"

"Careful, Zoe. You'd be well advised to look into your own objectivity before attacking his."

"Would I? What about yours? How is it Edward always manages to get you into his corner? What does he do to you to make you so soft and pliable, Giles; lick your *boot*?"

She knew immediately she was wrong to say it but was too angry to apologize; she kept mute while Giles' eyes grew colder by the second. "Your common streak seems to have broadened with age. Try exercising a few manners; it might keep the slut in you down."

"Get out. Goddamn it, Giles, get out!" Wordlessly, he rose; picking a piece of lint off his suit, he let it drift to the floor, and then he walked out. Zoe grabbed a cushion to throw at the door; instead, she threw it on the bed and herself after.

The next morning, Edward was alone at breakfast. As Zoe came in, she thought how smug he looked, though he was simply reading the newspaper and munching on his marmaladed toast. But she expected him to look up at any moment and snicker something, like "Lovers' quarrel?" He didn't, of course; he barely broke his concentration to nod good morning. Maybe Zoe was the real sick one in the house, not Julia. If she didn't get more control over herself, she'd never be able to do what she'd decided she had to: repair the damage with Giles, and talk Edward into letting her see Julia's manuscripts.

Bringing an especially strong cup of tea to the table, she sat down across from him. "Giles about?" Her tone was carefully disinterested.

Lifting the paper, he neatly folded over a page. "No, he isn't."

Zoe's stomach churned. "He hasn't gone back to town, has he?"

Edward flipped the paper in half and looked at her over the top. "Now why would he do that?" Mock astonishment, surely.

"Oh . . ." Zoe let a vague gesture answer for her; she sipped her tea.

"He's gone," Edward raised the paper again, "on an appetite-inspiring walk with Julia."

"Oh. Good." She moved her cup a little closer. "Edward . . ."

"Mm?"

"Edward, I'd like to talk to you for a moment."

He put the paper aside. Daintily, he wiped his hands and replaced his napkin in its ring. "What about?"

"The manuscripts, Julia's. I'd very much like to read them. May I?"

"Certainly." He pretended not to notice the look of shock on Zoe's face. "If Julia agrees."

That was something Zoe had never thought of; she assumed them to be in Edward's control. "Oh, Julia. Yes." She tried to get more comfortable in her chair. "I don't want to, risk upsetting her. Wouldn't it be possible for me to read them first? And then . . ."

"Tell her afterward? Don't you think that's being a bit dishonest?"

"She need never know, that is, I so much want to read them, if there's even a chance that my asking would disturb her, it might be prudent not to. Not to put her through anything unnecessarily."

Edward acted as if he were considering this. "I don't know, Zoe. They are hers, after all; I'm merely holding them in safekeeping for her. I'd certainly hesitate to break that trust." He frowned. "No, I'm afraid I couldn't do that. You'll have to risk asking her. She must have had her reasons for keeping them from you all these years. But," his bright smile almost succeeded in looking genuine, "perhaps she'll change her mind."

Perhaps, you clever son of a bitch; she forced herself to smile back. There was nothing she could do now but wait until the hikers returned, and then face each with what were probably impossible requests.

When they came back, Zoe was in the garden breaking up stones for a new retaining wall. It was good to swing the heavy sledge, hitting the wedge so squarely it vibrated in her hand with a resounding ring; the stone would crack into usable pieces, she'd shove them aside, then lift another whole one into place. For over two hours she'd been at it, dressed in boots and an old riding outfit, jacket discarded, shirt beginning to cling with perspiration. Nothing but her own labor existed; she could have gone on and on, purified.

Motionless by the corner of the house, Julia watched her for several minutes. When Zoe stopped for a moment, she stepped forward, and came up quietly behind her. "You're a workhorse." Zoe turned around. "A beautiful workhorse." Julia placed her fingers on Zoe's arm, where the sleeve was rolled above the elbow; slowly, she kneaded the muscle there, then ran her fingers lightly down to Zoe's wrist. "Beautiful."

Zoe couldn't read the expression on her face; it didn't seem to belong with what she was saying, and doing, both hands now caressing Zoe's arm, shoulder. "Julia, please. I'm, all sweaty and unattractive." She stepped back, gently lifting the hands from her body. Her jacket was somewhere. "How was your hike?" She brushed it off and put it on.

"What's the matter, Zoe? Are you frightened of me?"

"No, of course not. It's just the chill, the air, you don't feel it until you stop working, you get clammy and the air . . ."

Julia placed the tips of her fingers on Zoe's mouth. Her own lips were parted while she scanned Zoe's face. "Zoe. You're so tense. Don't be afraid." Zoe wanted to say she wasn't, but Julia's fingers were still pressed against her mouth. "Zoe, I'll make it up to you, I promise."

Zoe moved the hand aside. "Julia, there's nothing . . ."

"Ssh, don't say it. I know better. It's all my fault. Just please don't hate me."

"Darling, I don't hate you, I love you. You haven't done anything to change that; you're not guilty of anything."

"I know about guilt, you don't. Anyway," she turned away, stepping over the broken stones, "let's not talk about that." She went to one of the benches and waited for Zoe to join her. The moment she did, Julia said, "I'm sorry about Giles. Aren't you?"

"Yes I am. Very."

"He looks so sickly." Zoe wasn't sure they were talking about the same thing. "Poor Giles. It's a pity he's never had someone to look after him, as I have. Two someones; one of them should've been his."

"Really? Which one?"

"Be good to him, Zoe. Please? Especially after I'm . . ." Julia let the thought go unfinished. Now Zoe wasn't sure just what they were talking about.

"After you're . . . ?" she tried to see Julia's face. But Julia had laid her head on Zoe's shoulder, and put her arms around Zoe's waist; agreeing to the closeness automatically, Zoe had allowed her arm to encircle, holding Julia to her. "After you're what. Hm?"

"Hm?" Julia repeated dreamily.

"You said, 'especially after I'm . . .'"

"Zoe, I can't remember everything I say. My memory floats in and out, like a ghost," her hand swayed slowly in the air, "trailing from room to room in an abandoned house."

Zoe had to smile at the effortless dissembling. "That's very poetic."

"Thank you." Her hand went back to Zoe's waist.

"You are getting stronger, you know. Every day. You're much better than you were on Taviton Street. You'll be well soon."

"Perhaps in an eon or two."

"Don't be silly." Zoe hugged her closer.

"I'm not. I know the Jews are the Chosen People. Suffering for thousands of years so that the pain of others can be milder. That's all right though; it's the price for being first in God's eyes."

Zoe shook her head as if to clear it. "Uh, that's very interesting. You see yourself among them?"

"I'm trying to. I would like to suffer justly. To know, there was pain because of goodness. To carry pain as a sacrifice, instead of punishment."

"Darling? Who's punishing you? What is it you've done?"

Julia drew away from her. She rummaged in her coat pocket. "D'you know what I've got? Look," she held out a small piece of yellow, crumpled felt.

Zoe took it and straightened it out. 'Julia, what are you doing with this?" She held up the Star of David. "Where did you get this?"

"Why are you angry?" Julia took the Star from Zoe's hand. "I made it. I'm only being prepared for when I'll have to wear it. They're making everyone wear one, Zoe, don't you know that?"

"But that's in Germany, not here, not England! Darling, those are German Jews; it won't happen here."

"I suppose you're prepared to guarantee that."

"Yes."

"Well fortunately for me I'm not crazy enough to believe you. I'll be ready, when the time comes. I have my Star, Zoe, just remember that."

"All right," Zoe sighed, "I'll remember. Can we please talk about something else?"

"We haven't done anything bad, you know. It's persecution. It's in our history, our blood, it's nothing we've done. We're innocent. You believe that, don't you?"

Zoe was puzzled and frustrated, yet about to agree hoping the topic would be dropped; she changed her mind. "I think so, yes, but it's very hard for someone outside to understand. I want to understand, I know how important this is to you. So important, I imagine you've even written about it, used it in your work. Am I right?"

"Yes! Yes I have, though for a long time I didn't realize why. But it's there. It's as if I knew, before I knew."

"Perhaps, if you were to let me read what you've done, it would help me to understand."

The eagerness faded from Julia's face. She lowered her head, started playing with the buttons on her coat. "Edward's got them all locked up," she said in a sad little singsong.

"I know, but if you tell him you said it was all right for me to read them, I'm pretty sure he'd let them out."

"All locked up, in the dark. Forever."

"Not forever, Julia. Don't you remember he's . . ."

"It might as well be forever."

"Darling. Look, first things first. I can't do anything unless you tell Edward it's all right to open the box."

Julia giggled. "Pandora's box, Addie thinks it's Pandora's box. But it's not." Sudden melancholy. "Hers had hope at the bottom. Underneath the evil. Mine doesn't." She looked at Zoe, brighter again. "He's bloody weak on mythology and strong on rectitude, isn't he."

Zoe nodded, grinning. "Will you do it, then?"

Julia shoved her hands in her pockets; she scuffed the gravel, kicked a small stone down the path. "I don't know. If you want me to. It doesn't matter anymore. It's futile; you ought to have learned that by now. Perhaps you will, if I tell him."

Edward had no choice. Zoe took three novels, four red-bound diaries, and a large carton of assorted "things" up to her room, and for the rest of the week, no one saw her. She closed herself in, breaking only to eat or exercise at odd times when the others weren't about. She didn't want to have to react, or explain, or comment to anyone, until she was through. Fortunately, privacy was one of their respected values; no one came to her room, no one disturbed her or interfered.

She couldn't pry into the diaries right away, had to set them aside. Arbitrarily, she picked an early story to start with, titled "Next Door to Medea." In it, Julia transposed literature's most dreadful, possessive woman to twentieth-century London. The effect was hilariously bizarre, until one realized Medea looked exactly like Rebecca Carroll, and the cockney chorus were amiable witnesses to atrocity.

Julia's view of human nature was uncompromising; in story after story, the grotesque became horrific, the people repellent. Gradually, however, Zoe could see Julia struggling to make it otherwise, to carve a space for compassion, and let it breathe. As her characters became enmeshed in webs they had not willfully created, her work became more powerful; one read them shuddering with recognition, rather than with horror.

Years of effort preceded, and went into, Julia's novels. In them, her mastery of form and vision became complete. *The Children of Rhea* was an awesome trilogy. Again, Julia wove the excesses of Greek tragedy into contemporary society, but here there was no cynical observer standing back. There were characters so anguished, so racked by the horrors of existence, that one wanted to scream along with them for release. And just at that point, just when the reader, too, could withstand no more, Julia provided it. Passages of such strength and beauty one must stop and replenish oneself among them. This, too, was the human condition; that knowledge, the moments in between, kept one going.

Immersed in Julia's world, unable to separate himself, Zoe read on. She finished; exhausted and convinced of brilliance.

After looking at Julia's diaries, she clung to her conviction even more; she needed to hold on to something, and Julia's talent was the only certainty she had. As for everything else: she believed and was incredulous at the same time. The conflict was tormenting. Edward must have felt it too; that's why he'd locked everything away. Not sure what contained the truth, he'd taken no chances, and hidden it all. Zoe understood; she sympathized; with Edward. Julia was more distressing and unknowable than ever.

In contrast to her work, Julia's diaries were impenetrable. There were so many lapses, coded entries, and seemingly flagrant violations of fact, that Zoe was hard put to make sense of them. There was no controlling vision, only outrage and disorder, ugliness in the extreme. Hideous fantasies, acceptable in fiction, were shocking and intolerable distortions here.

There was no mitigating beauty in hating her brother Giles. In willingly committing incest with her brother Jordan up until the year he died. In killing Jennie Hilbreth. There was no truth, either; these were the ravings of a plagued mind. Yet, in the novels, Zoe had seen a fictional Julia resenting Giles for his intrusion on her sexual monopoly over Jordan. Unprotestingly, she'd followed a Julia who was furious with Jordie for agreeing to his graduation cruise when they were to have spent those months together on the Continent. She'd read of their horrible fight, Jordie wishing to break away, Julia hysterical, vituperative, a Harpy shouting curses as he left.

Then, Jordie's death; Julia's guilt. Added to the incest guilt already in her. Incest and guilt. The fear of mice, the fear of sex with other men. A suicide pact. Both girls to leap off the peak together, hand in hand; but Julia pulled away without warning at the last second, let Jennie go over, alone.

Guilt and death. Jordan's death. Jennie's death. Julia's own death in the novel. Destined as any tragic Greek, she could not escape from the violation of taboos. Inner Furies hounded her, and for the fictional Julia, no mental illness offered shelter. No persecuted race welcomed her. No resolution was possible but that she die.

Zoe was sure Julia's "real life" had been radically different, yet her sense of guilt seemed equally as strong. At the same time, both Julia's saw themselves as victims, driven by forces too powerful to control. She had to sort it out. She tried making a chart; dividing a sheet of paper into "Fact" and "Fantasy," Zoe wrote down what she could ascertain of both, hoping to see, in black and white, what the patterns and relationships were. Perhaps Julia believed that when her character was punished, so was she; or that Julia the character was able to be honest about her "sins" and accept punishment for them, while Julia the author must hide them and escape. Except she wasn't escaping, Furies were pursuing the real Julia, too; and at times, her fate seemed worse than the retribution she'd invented.

In less than half an hour, Zoe had crumpled up the paper and thrown it away; it was impossible, nothing was one-to-one. She couldn't reduce Julia's mind, her life, to tidy summations on a page. It didn't matter, anyway; there could be truth in fantasy as well as fact. The important thing, she realized, was that when Julia wrote, she somehow freed herself from her fantasies by putting them to work. They worked, her novels worked, and Julia should be working again, too. No one had any right to stop her. The handful of people who cared how close Julia's work was to her life would just have to deal with their fears, and let the novels go.

Zoe went to bed convinced of two things: Julia had dramatized not the events in her life, but her view of life. And she'd done it brilliantly. Her imagination might be a plague to her, but to others, it was a gift. And if Zoe had any say at all, she would see that the world received it.

Sleep proved to be difficult. Hearing Edward's unmistakable tread, she decided to bathe, dress, and go downstairs to have it out with him. Further delay would only allow Julia more time in which to brood and acquiesce to guilt. Edward's reaction had strengthened her belief that she was "bad"; and a bad girl needed to be punished, even if she hadn't meant to be bad. He had done a good job of training her. The thought made Zoe angrier than she wanted to be.

Both of them knew a fight was inevitable, but neither expected it would be so vitriolic. Alone in Edward's study, the door locked, they killed civility with surprising swiftness, turning to attack with a ferocity neither one admired yet was able to control. Their behavior was outrageous; they didn't care; this wasn't a Bloomsbury drawing room, and no one was there to see them.

But anyone passing the study would have heard. Julia did. She was frightened, repelled. Responsible. She couldn't listen, had to hurry away.

Room after room; no good, the voices followed. Who could help her? Giles? He was at Charleston, he couldn't stop the voices from bouncing against the walls, into her head. She was alone in the house except for those two screaming at each other, arguing over her, what she'd done, hadn't done, ought to do. She ran to her room, locked herself in; but the voices went after her. They burst through the door, they climbed all over the furniture and up the walls; they got in her clothes, her hair, she had to spit them out of her mouth. Air, they wouldn't survive in the air, the cold; she raced outdoors, leaving jacket, scarf, boots behind, filled with voices. She ran.

She ran until she could hear her shoes crunching the

frost-crusted ground. She ran until the blood boomed in her ears. She ran until her head was filled with the sound of breath gasping to renew itself, until her heart pounded on the wall of her body to be let out. She kept on running, she kept on, until she ran the final, consciousness-killing lap.

When she came to, the stars were out. She lay on her back, in a hollow between two small hills, and looked at the dark, clear sky. So many stars. How beautiful they were. How lovely it was, to be on the downs, lying against the hard earth and looking up at the night sky. She didn't mind the cold, her clothes stiff with frozen sweat, the cuts on her legs and hands. How could she mind them, exposed to so much beauty?

She turned her head away. She had to cry a little.

Later, she opened her eyes; her vision was bleared, an ugly scum lay between her and beauty. Why did she have to ruin things? Why even a simple, night sky? How quickly she'd stopped seeing it, enjoying it; how easy it was. Would she always have to ruin what was good? Oh yes. The hated stayed with her, the loved . . .

She let herself cry again, for a while.

Afterwards, she tried putting her arms behind her head but was too stiff, so she lay very straight. That was all right. There was no point and she was tired of trying. Why had she tried so hard? What could have meant so much to her? She had to smile; she couldn't remember. Nothing, there was nothing. And it would never change. She'd tried before, it had never changed; it never would. Why had it taken her so long to know that? No matter, she knew it now. Again, she smiled. There was no point. Everything she needed, was here.

Dawn, dusk and night repeated themselves. Still she smiled.

They found her covered in white; she was grinning at them, through layers of hoarfrost.

X

IT DIDN'T HAVE TO BE that way. Maybe it wasn't that way at all, it was an accident. She tried to get up, go back, but couldn't; she was too weak. That doesn't account for the smile, the rictus of happiness frozen into her features forever. Better to think she wanted it to happen and didn't struggle. Better to have her last moments free from terror, her life in order, as it should be, with everything the way she wanted it. Better to think that, than imagine her lying lost on the downs, unable to save herself and terrified at the steady encroachment of death.

Damn Zoe and Edward for their selfish entanglement. So busy arguing over what was best for her they couldn't take time out to save her. A few seconds, that's all it would have taken, to check, see if she was in the house, see what their words were doing to her. But no, they had to prove which of them was right, even though it meant arguing over a dead person. What would it have taken to open the door and see her running down the hall? Or look out the window and see her running across the downs? To follow, catch up with her, exhausted but alive. Take her hand. Talk quietly. Hold her; bony narrow shoulders, damp hair. Talk and soothe.

Walk slowly back, arms interlocked for warmth, heads together. Build a fire, bundle her up, pour hot broth into her poor racked body. Lead her to bed and put her in under lots of comforters and quilts; maybe climb in with her, hold her through the night. Keep her warm, warm the life in her. Wake up the next morning, a winter sun edging through the shutters, the light making her eyes blink open; luminous hazel, glad to have survived. A kiss? A gentle caress, then snuggling closer to sleep again. Steady breathing. Life pumping. Her body is warm, alive; she makes little sleep noises. The sun falls on her hair, there's honey in it, flowing through the silver. Press her closer; doze until she wakes.

Keep her there. Dream, eyes closed, head back; dream and make it true. Stay with me, Julia. Don't go, don't fade. I'm losing you, don't. Come back in the bed, we'll start again, come back and let me hold you. Oh please come back, please. I want you. I want you. Please. Come back. Don't go. Come back!

"Julia, please!" My voice. I'm half out of the chair. My eyes are wide open, staring and burning with tears. Me. I'm alone, my coat is still on, I'm straining like a fool with my mouth open and my eyes streaming, refusing to accept, I am alone!

It's not fair! It's not fair. Back and forth I rock, huddled to myself, crying with no attempt to stop.

Eventually, the tears ease off. Who am I feeling sorrier for, Julia or me? Not Zoe. Why not Zoe? It's not right to blame her, she couldn't have saved Julia. Any more than I could have.

My pain is minor, compared to what hers must have been. The memorial service, the cremation: she had to live through those. I have a choice, I don't have to experience those events unless I want to, and I don't. The words are sufficient; I needn't acknowledge anything beyond them, I don't have to watch that part.

I get up, take off my coat, put on some water to boil. I never liked tea before coming to England. I seem to have adopted everything I've found here; other people's customs, other people's lives. Their lovers. Was my life so blank before? I hope not; there's no excuse for a barren existence, at my age, with my opportunities.

Count your blessings, she said, sitting down to drink her tea.

Count your blessings. You have youth, intelligence and good health. You've loved. You're involved in a fascinating project, thanks to chance and the gods, and Zoe Mohr. Look at her, look at what she's done with her life. Surely you can do as much, if not more. Perhaps you'll learn something from her, about how to live. So that when you're seventy-six and crippled, you can look back on a full and happy . . .

Crap. Full and happy. Fairy tales.

She had to go back to Taviton Street. Pick up clothes, other things that had found a home there over the years. Edward wasn't expecting her, but she had told him she'd be over soon to do what was necessary. She let herself in, thinking, "I must leave the key this time, before I go." She looked at the key, the years of opening a door knowing Julia was behind it. Unable to stop, she listened for a footstep, a hoot of laughter. No Julia. Just an absence of her, hollowing the house. To allow such an irrational hope — Zoe unfastened her key ring and slapped the key onto the hall table.

It didn't take her long to get her things together, going from room to room double-checking but refusing to linger. She turned herself into a mechanical person, searching, picking up, packing; no thoughts, no emotions, just empty, steady movements that took her through the house.

The sitting room was last. Probably nothing of hers was in there, but she opened the door to make sure. Edward was bending over the fire; he whirled around to see who it was. Zoe willed herself not to react; there would be no more scenes with Edward, ever. But he didn't know Zoe had entered with no expectations, that she'd interrupted merely to do a chore; angry, and frightened, he gripped the firepoker like a weapon.

". . . and looked at me so suspiciously, so tensed for battle that it was ludicrous, because I wanted nothing from him, nothing. Yet he was crouched there in front of the fire, ready to spring. I almost laughed," Zoe Mohr had said. "Almost laughed. But then I saw what it was, what he'd done, and I could only gape. There were no words. I don't even know what I felt, what I could've said if my voice had worked."

Curling in the fire, turning ocher and black and then disappearing, were pages of manuscript. Pages, burning to ash. Grey scraps of it fluttered over the flames. Pieces of white, singed and indecipherable, protruded from a glowing mound. In the center, something red, redder than the fire: a cover from Julia's diary. Zoe watched it start to smoke, saw the first tiny flame spring up and eat its way into a cover which protected nothing, because its soft insides already had been ripped out and consumed. Nothing was left; the box by the grate was empty.

"I couldn't move, I couldn't talk, I couldn't even look at him accusingly. There was simply no response equal to the crime. The entire time I was there, not one word was exchanged. It took every bit of energy I had just to get myself out of that room."

And out of the house, never to go back. A past destroyed. A life — accomplishments, relationships, everything that one had made and nurtured — nothing more than ashes in a grate. Julia was dead, she couldn't start over; Zoe was forty, and had to. How? How go back to zero and start to fill one's life again?

She'll never tell me. She's finished her story. Her eyes, her shrug, indicated as much when I looked at her as if to say, "And then what?" "And then, nothing," she might just as well have said, but didn't, because I should have known. It's all over, there is no more, it's up to me now.

Tomorrow, when I — no, today, when I see her, I'd better know exactly what to ask. Perhaps a list.

I go to bed, thinking about it, making lists over and over until sleep whirls my head.

What about Giles? That's going to be my first question. I practice it on the door while waiting for Briggs to let me in. After all these weeks she still leaves the safety chain latched, checking me out first and then opening the door wide enough for me to get by. I'm always tempted to call her Briggsy just because she's so ill-suited to the diminutive.

Nodding her usual wordless greeting, she ushers me into the front room; for the very first time, Zoe Mohr isn't here on her chaise waiting for me. I turn to ask if something's wrong, but Briggs is already gone. The tea cart isn't set either. Perhaps I'm not staying.

I look around. Everything else is the same, my chair opposite the chaise longue, a lamp nearby should twilight come before we're through. It's a handsome room, one I've been in so many times I no longer see the books, the telescope shrouded like a birdcage, the dusted, wood-grained surfaces free of clutter. I'll miss this.

When Briggs comes back a few minutes later, I'm all ready for work, pad out, questions jotted, pen literally poised and waiting to proceed. "She can't see you."

What? Why?

"She's not a well woman."

Spare me the clichés, Briggs. What's the matter, is it serious?

"I've had to sedate her."

But why?

"She needed rest."

I see. I don't, really, but Briggs is obviously not about to tell me more. Is she sleeping?

"She's resting. I only gave her enough to quiet her, any more and it's dangerous for a person her age."

Do you . . . often have to do that?

"Often enough."

I start to put away my reporting paraphernalia.

"I've been directed to offer you a drink."

No thanks.

My refusal seems to fluster her. "But you must have a drink. A gin, you've never turned down a gin before."

I'm not thirsty, Briggs, I'm disappointed. And very concerned. Are you sure she's all right?

Briggs nods. "I've seen her worse."

I guess that's some comfort, but the session's still — Listen, you don't think she might be up to one little question, do you?

"She can't see you."

Yes, I know that. But suppose I were to write down a question, just one. Do you think you could take it in to her, and see if she's up to responding?

"I don't know. I'm just supposed to fix you a drink."

Yes, yes, I'll be happy to have a drink, if you'll just — I've whipped out a sheet of notepaper and am scribbling "What about Giles?" — give this to her. I hold out the paper; very reluctantly, Briggs extends one of her huge hands and takes it. Thank you, Briggs, thank you. I promise, I'll make the drink while you're gone.

I don't know what's made me so nervous. I find I really do want a drink now. It must be the disappointment, not seeing Zoe Mohr, and then, the uplift, hitting on the note idea. That Briggs, she's not exactly a gold mine of information. I guess this drink's supposed to compensate for a canceled . . .

Briggs comes back with the slip of paper, and I practically tear it out of her hand. Below my question, either she or Zoe Mohr has written, "Giles died." Just that? I turn the paper over and upside down, looking for more; that can't be all. But it is. Briggs, this — dammit, this isn't enough! Furiously I write "How? When? Apology? Ever seen again?" Take this; no, no, this is the last time, I promise. Just, please, take this in to her and, see if she'll reply.

Stoically, Briggs accepts the note. Her stolidity makes me realize how silly and frantic I must seem. But damn it all, I'm ready, I'm the one who has to tie everything together and I want to get started. If Zoe Mohr were here I wouldn't feel so tense about it; Briggs is such a blank wall, she just exaggerates my touchiness, or whatever it is that's wrong with me.

She comes back again, hands me the note. At the very bottom, there's just one word in answer to everything I've asked: "Details." I slump onto a chair. Details. It's all very well to say they don't matter when they don't, but sometimes they do. To me at least. I shake my head; the woman's impossible. All right, Briggs. There's no point sending you back in there again. I crumple the note, put it on the table, and get up to go. Tell me, is there any point in my coming back tomorrow? Will she be better tomorrow?

"No telling."

Really, I've just about had it with her. Well should I come back or not?

Briggs looks down at the carpet for a minute; she is the slowest . . . And I am the stupidest: when she raises her head I see how close to tears she is.

"You've been good for her. But now I don't know."

What do you mean? I put my jacket down. Have I done something? She's not ill because of something I've done, is she? I search Briggs' face for an answer. Is it the sessions? Have they been too taxing? What is it?

Briggs sits down then, and so do I. She frowns.

Briggs, please. I'm fond of her, too. You know that.

She nods. "I know." Then she looks up at me, such a tortured expression, like a dog who's powerless to help an ailing mistress and is aching. To do, to be, to make the world right. "I'm not sure what's best for her anymore. If it's right to keep on."

What can I do? Does she want support? I've never seen this Briggs before.

She sits hunched over with her knees spread, her hands joined nervously between them. "For a long time, she just used to lie there." She jerks her head toward the chaise. "No energy, no life. I did what I could. I've always tried to keep her spirits up. That telescope," she points to it, "that was my idea. But mostly they were hers. And I've always gone along.

Anything that helped. Even if it seemed crazy. Even though some people might think it was crazy, I've always done what she asked."

I want to reach out and comfort her somehow, but I can't, I don't, I don't know what the problem is. "When all this started," she gestures to indicate the room, "it was good to see the life in her again. She was, so full of life, I got taken in by it. I stopped worrying, it seemed so good for her. Even when she got too agitated, too worked up. I thought, better that, than the other, the depressions. They still came on, but they didn't last nearly so long. I should've seen, I should've. They were deeper than the others. She was up too high and down too deep; I should have seen that." She lifts a giant hand; it slides through her hair and squeezes the back of her neck, trying to comfort on its own.

Don't blame yourself, Briggs. I'm sure you've done what's best for her. She speaks so highly of you. She values your service, really she does.

"My . . . service?"

Yes. What is it, over ten years you've been with her? That's a long time, it says a lot about your worth to her.

"Do you know how old I am?"

What an odd time to ask. No, I don't. She could be close to thirty or to fifty, she's got one of those faces impossible to judge.

"I'm forty-eight. I'm one year older than she was when I first came here. That was twenty-nine years ago. You think it's 'service' made me stay. You think I stayed here all these years out of duty. That I could live with her, day and night, without . . . loving her?"

I . . . God, I'm sorry. Please, I thought, that is I assumed, when she lost . . .

"She was the handsomest woman I'd ever seen. I was only nineteen. Fresh to London. No real education. I had . . . a gift though." She holds up her hands, "These. They have a feel for life. They can find it, hiding in muscles and bones. These, are what I had to offer." They quiver in the air between us. "And she gave me, everything in return. Life, for me too. I didn't know how to read, to listen, to look. She showed me, she taught me. Galleries, plays, everything; I'd go for her. Then come back here, and between the two of us — That's when I really saw, and heard, when she did. When we shared. Her mind, my body."

Wait a minute. I don't understand the timetable. I distinctly remember Zoe Mohr telling me, the very first day when she saw me looking, that she'd lost the use of her legs over a decade ago. And that it had something to do with aging. So. What were you hired for? Originally.

"For these. To massage, exercise. Like my aunt before me; she got me the job."

Briggs. I am afraid to ask. There is something very, very wrong here. I am suddenly . . . very, very, fearful that . . . all is not quite right. Briggs, how long has she been paralyzed?

"Fifty years. More. Over half a century, living, like that."

No! Now listen, that's just not true. It's not possible. Not, possible. What year? What year did it happen?"

"Nineteen eighteen."

No, no! you're wrong! mistaken.

"I'm not. Nineteen eighteen, the year the flu struck. Except it wasn't the flu, with her; it was something else, meningitis I think."

No! This is a ghost story! It just can't be!

"They were too late. She might not've been bedridden, if they'd known it sooner. She's lucky, though, she didn't die. I've always told her that. Tried to make her feel glad that she lived."

You're lying! Why are you lying to me! What's going on? Why are you doing this?

There's pity on her face. For me! She's sitting over there shaking her head from side to side, pitying me!

Stop it! My fists pound the chair. Stop looking at me like that! I've leaped, my fists are pounding on her shoulders. She gets up grabbing my wrists. She hurts them, there's pain. God damn you! Struggle to free my hands. Damn you let me . . . I can't, go! I wrench away, turn my back, rub the pain.

She walks up close behind me, I feel her breath in my ear. "I'm sorry. I had to." I won't talk to her; poor wrists, they're burning, they're all mottled red and white. She'd better move away from me or I'll . . . "I'll take you home," she says. "I'll walk with you." Her touch is light on my arm; I yank it out of reach.

Get away from me. I stumble toward my jacket. She follows, tries again to touch me, again I pull my arm away. I don't need a goddamn keeper, I know how to walk! I push past her and get out.

On the sidewalk, I stop to do up my jacket. Across from me is the fence, the parking lot, the entrance to the British Museum. I give it the finger. Arm straight up, an obscenity for everyone to see; stupid. I wheel around and search the building for a window with a telescope shrouded behind it; when I find that, I give it the finger too. Then I jam my hands in my pockets and stomp down the street, wishing all the people I pass would go bugger themselves.

After I've slammed enough pots and pans around my apartment and intermittently licked my wounds, I start dealing with it. I expect a lot of emptiness but there isn't any, there's too much to mourn and too much to puzzle over.

I know it's going to be a long process. Every day, I try to free myself a little. I take rambling walks, and let whatever mood is strongest take over, so that I can have a chance to work through the emotion. Anger is the easiest to get rid of, though it turns itself into hurt pride, and that's tougher. Sadness is something I should have given in to all at once; after a while my conscience starts acting up every time it comes around again, and I know I'm indulging myself more than grieving. Bewilderment is hard, because I don't have any answers, I only have suppositions or theories, and their plausibility fluctuates drastically from one moment to the next.

After five days, my sorrow and hostility are down to a level I can live with, but my bewilderment is still as strong as ever. I can't do away with it on my own. I've no way of proving anything once I think it's right, and armchair theories won't do this time, not with me part of the equation.

What I cannot figure out is, why have I been so grossly manipulated? The whole thing has to have been a setup from start to finish. From Briggs' luring me out of the Reading Room right down to her saying so much in the living room. I'm convinced that was no accidental revelation: Zoe Mohr sent her in there to do a job, just like she'd sent her to the British Museum to find me. But why? That's what I can't figure out.

Nor can I go through the rest of my life being puzzled. I have to go back, and I'm sure Zoe Mohr knows it. I wonder how much time she's allotted me to reach this conclusion? It's got to be in her grand scheme; the tea cart's probably been set for days. She's just sitting on her chaise, waiting for the knock at her door. If not, then I'm a little ahead of schedule, that's all, I'm not expected until later. Well, she'd better put the kettle on, because here I come.

Briggs opens the door; she can't look me in the face. That's something at least. Any apology I may owe her is minor compared to what's due me. Though I guess she didn't have much choice — it wouldn't have done for me to hit a cripple.

How're things, Briggsy? The best she can come up with is a wan smile before turning to walk ahead of me into the room.

Zoe Mohr is dozing in a patch of sun. I don't remember her being so wizened, tiny. She's all lines, liver spots, sagging skin. Perhaps it's the light. Or her blouse, it's too big for her; it didn't use to be. Her hands are curled on top of the blanket;

how could one of those hands have gripped my own with so much strength only a few weeks ago?

It's hard keeping up a tough guy act in front of this. Is she sedated? A whisper.

"No, she hasn't let me the last few days. Said she needed all her senses, for when you came." Briggs crosses the room and shakes her gently on the shoulder. I turn away; too intimate, watching someone come out of sleep, it's between Briggs and her.

I wander away, scan book titles, keep their muted voices behind me. So many shelves. Big section on Bloomsbury, naturally. For reading about friends or boning up on strangers? Is it just books she's collected, or people too? Perhaps everything she knows comes from these. Or maybe it's time she were in one of them; she's been overlooked and it's all been a plot to get herself a footnote somewhere. But then, why choose me? There are plenty of others, with reputations, who would have welcomed the chance.

"Thank you for coming." Her voice is weak but it calls me back to where she sits, propped up and supposedly feeling fit. "Sit down." She gestures to my chair. "You look tired."

My goodness, consideration at this stage? I notice she has a little trouble looking me in the eye, too. Well, that's only right.

"As you can no doubt see, I've not been well lately. It's been . . . very difficult, worrying about you. Waiting to see if everything worked out."

Double-talk. She hasn't worried about me, not Me; maybe some person who happens to be me, but not me, as I am.

"So many people in my position — that is, in something close to my position — have suffered for lack of someone like you. Briggs did well in her search; how unfortunate for others that they can't go out and do the same. But then, they don't think in such plastic terms, they content themselves with molding in only one dimension, instead of three."

I really do think it's time to stop playing around. Why not try telling me what this is all about.

She leans forward. "Be assured, neither of us is going to be denied the satisfaction of an explanation."

I'm glad to hear that.

Slowly, she settles back against her cushions. "I have cared about you, very much. You've been good to me, and I'm grateful. I've relied on you, on your strength; your imagination."

Gullibility's a better word.

"You have a beautiful imagination. I admire it; most certainly I needed it. You're sensitive, and I required that too. You're also intelligent, which was grand, because I would've settled for educated; but you, aside from just knowing certain things, were willing to entertain the possibility of others. Actually, my dear, you've been near perfect. And in return, I think I've treated you . . ."

Abominably, go ahead, admit it. For all my imagination, sensitivity and intelligence, you've treated me abominably.

". . . brilliantly." She beams. She really believes it! "You see, dimension," her finger's up in the air emphasizing the point, "is the key. It's what makes the form unique."

That's fascinating; except I don't know what she's talking about.

"You've read those children's 'pop-up' books. The kind where you open a page of cleverly folded paper and out pop bright little characters in bright little scenes. Of course it's only the paper that's three-dimensional; everything on it is flat and painted quite unimaginatively."

I've seen them; so?

"As a child, I always wanted to jump into a book, rather than have the characters jump out. I wanted, to live in it. Along with the others, to be where they were, doing what they did. When I succeeded, it was uniquely exciting. But the strain was tremendous, and the effect short-lived. I was always terribly disappointed on finding I'd come out again. I can remember, even then, feeling there must be some way of controlling my ability to stay. I was never afraid that one day I might go in and never come out, because at that time, when I was young, there was always the next book for me to visit."

This is creepy. She's talking so matter-of-factly.

"A child's imagination is such a beautiful, powerful force. It frightens adults; they always want to limit it, to force it down and pile huge blocks of reality on top until the poor thing can barely breathe. You have to be very careful if you want to keep it alive; you have to hide it from them, protect it. Most children don't realize the danger. I did.

"And I managed to live where I wanted. But the older I got, the less satisfying it became. When I was in there, immersed in whatever life the book revealed, I wanted to change things around. But I couldn't. It wasn't my imagination's fault, I knew that, so it had to have been the books'."

Of course.

"It was only natural that I start making my own. At first, I tried writing them; very soon I realized how silly that was. After all, with other people's books, the hardest part was getting myself beyond the printed word, into the life behind. So why not do away with the page, the word, altogether? And go right into, living it?"

Why not? Doesn't she realize? Presenting each step so logically. The whole idea is bizarre, dangerous.

"I was getting to be quite good at it, when this happened." She rubs the blanket covering her legs. "Punishment which I accepted too readily. I thought reality had found me out; it was paying me back for all the years I'd only pretended to regard it. So now, it was getting me to pay attention by making me suffer, to a point where I could experience nothing else."

Her hands stop massaging; they'd stimulated memory, but that was all. "How quick we are to assume our guilt, bow our heads to the sentence life hands down. It's either that, we think, or death. For a long time I lay in my bed wishing for the latter. I even tried to hasten it; several times." There's no apology in her voice.

"Then for a while I became a model prisoner, doing exactly what was expected of me; stupidly, I hoped that any day the judgment against me might be reversed if only I were good. Of course that wasn't possible in my case.

"Finally I realized there was little else life could do to me, so it was safe to take up my old habits. Except I couldn't, I'd forgotten how. Years of being afraid, of going along, had done that, and I shall always resent having to start all over. It was much harder, I'm sure, than had I been learning to walk again.

"Time, though, was something I had an overabundance of, and at least the years were filled. I devoted myself to work, to mastering my craft. But by the time Briggs came, I was into a stage of severe depressions: I thought I'd reached the limits of my art."

She has me following right along; if I'm not careful, everything will start making sublime sense to me, too.

"Briggs has a limited intelligence, but she's served me well; without her, I doubt I should ever have made my discovery. She's always fetched, carried, coped, watched, listened, enjoyed, and all for me, on my say-so. I used to send her out, oh, to an art gallery, and have her describe everything to me when she got back. It never occurred to me until much later that I could get her to react to something that didn't exist, as well as to what did.

"The first time I practiced on her, I sent her to a concert saying I used to date the oboe player when I was seventeen, that she was to keep her eye on him and tell me if she thought he was happy, married to the woman he'd left me for. A simple exercise, but effective; Briggs responded to this man, whoever he was, entirely in relation to the frame of reference I'd created. And that, is when I first began to see the possibilities."

I bet. I suppose it also never occurred to her that Briggs might've been smarter than she thought and was just telling her what she wanted to hear. Though either way, delusions kept her going.

"I worked as hard as any writer could, perfecting my technique, but I still didn't realize the full import of my discovery. All I knew was that if I could 'write' a book, someone should be able to 'read' it; basically, it was a question of equivalency, of finding the right method so that someone else, under my direction, could live my book, too.

"Eventually, I was ready to put my theory to the test. And by then I knew I had to prove it for Art's sake as well as my own." Why not? The world's breath was already bated. "I knew my methods were more than revolutionary. I knew I had discovered a new art form. That I had developed the power to put author, book and reader into a dimension where they'd never been before. It had to be demonstrated, but I knew!"

And I know that lunacy disguised as literature isn't really new. This brand just victimizes.

"I promised you a book. I have given you one. A living book. You've been an ideal reader, for which I thank you."

No, no, thank *you*. You've messed up my life. Ruined my work. Played with my emotions, made me suffer. Worse, you made me believe. Thanks for that; now I have to deal with coming back from your world. Your world doesn't exist, mine does, only I don't know where it is anymore. So thanks awfully for the experience. If I should ever get my head back together — but why give a damn about that.

She blinks in amazement. Obviously, my feelings are totally beyond her comprehension. "But how can you be bitter, when I've given you so much? Don't you understand how fortunate you've been? This is new ground we've explored, you and I together! Why, even the moon is nothing compared to where we've been!"

Well, I'm sorry to be ungrateful, but I think your manipulation of me has been inexcusable. And it's not your having sent me all over southern England that I object to, it's where you've sent my mind.

"But dear girl, that's precisely what makes this such a success! It's what every writer hopes for. And what every reader wants, otherwise they'd never go beyond cookbooks and motor manuals."

You're overlooking something. I didn't know what I was doing. And readers do know when they're reading; it's not necessary to tell them afterwards what they've been up to.

"It's just a matter of timing. I get the illusions working *before* the book is opened, that's all. Everything else is comparable, everything! Except my readers must use their bodies as well as their minds, because my books are for living in."

Why stop with the reader? Next time why not manipulate people into being characters, too? Think of the fun you could have sending them all over the world satisfying your plot requirements.

"That would be absurd."

Indeed, it would.

"Besides, I'm an artist, not an army general maneuvering troops. I've no desire to control anybody's destiny."

No, you just take their heads; their destinies can be left to God. Or the Fates. My stomach doesn't like that word; I take a deep breath and wait for the churning to subside. It doesn't. I have to ask her.

Tell me. Was it *all* made up?

"No more than any other novel. I have tried for a strict transliteration. Otherwise I could be accused of all sorts of things." And committed for them, too.

Why say it? I'm wounded, but not vicious. The longer I sit here, the less my desire to get back at her. I guess I feel loss more than anger. Loss I can't fully cope with yet.

The Bloomsberries? A mournful question.

She chuckles; it veers into a cackle. "Weren't they marvelous? I did well with them, you must agree."

Oh yes.

I hate to ask the next. I'm not sure I really want to know; I don't know I'll be able to accept the answer.

And Julia? I want to shut my eyes. Is Julia a fiction too?

"Julia." Such a fond smile creases her face. "I loved her very much." She looks at me and I nod. This is the way to handle it, for both of us. "You won't forget her, will you?"

I'm not likely to. But, I think I should try.

She puts out her hand as if to touch me. "Please don't. After . . . I'm gone, you'll be the only one who's known her."

Now wait . . .

She runs a trembling hand across her forehead, Julia's gesture. "I haven't the strength, I can't go through it again. And I've . . . no way on earth of preserving it. I should have thought of that before."

Strange her delusions haven't come up with an answer. From grandeur to immortality — I shouldn't have thought that was a difficult leap.

"My work. All that effort." Her chin is quivering. She pulls a handkerchief from her sleeve. I wish she wouldn't.

Why must I be subjected to this? It can't be my pity she wants.

"I'm sorry. It . . ." she wipes her eyes again, "it would be best, if you left now."

Now? But I . . .

Keeping her face averted, she waves me away. "I'm sorry if I've interrupted your work. But," she jerks her head up; her eyes have their old snap, "I don't for a moment regret having taken you away from that man Lawrence."

I have to grin. The woman is really too much.

"He can have you back now. Give him your best. He's supposed to be worth it. Goodbye."

I guess this is it. Goodbye. We shake hands; hers rests limply in mine and then pulls away.

On my way out, I look for Briggs to say goodbye to, but she's not around; no need for messenger service anymore. I leave. Outside, I look up at their window, then start walking down Great Russell Street toward home.

So that's over. I turn up Bloomsbury, skirt the bus stop queues. Then why can't I shake the feeling it's still up to me? Pass Bedford Square, cross Montague Place. Why do I feel this way? Up Malet Street. Something's unfinished. Over to Gordon. What? Not Julia; she's safely tucked in memory.

I stop. The rush hour crowd has to detour around me; they probably think I'm bonkers because I'm standing in the middle of the sidewalk and laughing. But I can't help it: to the very end, Zoe Mohr was setting me up. It was never Julia's story she wanted told, it was her own.

I walk on, through Bloomsbury. Lawrence never had a chance.

A few of the publications of
THE NAIAD PRESS, INC.
P.O. Box 10543 • Tallahassee, Florida 32302
Phone (904) 539-9322
Mail orders welcome. Please include 15% postage.

MURDER AT THE NIGHTWOOD BAR by Katherine V. Forrest. 240 pp. A Kate Delafield mystery. Second in a series.
ISBN 0-930044-92-4 $8.95

ZOE'S BOOK by Gail Pass. 224 pp. Passionate, obsessive love story.   ISBN 0-930044-95-9   7.95

WINGED DANCER by Camarin Grae. 228 pp. Erotic Lesbian adventure story.   ISBN 0-930044-88-6   8.95

PAZ by Camarin Grae. 336 pp. Romantic Lesbian adventurer with the power to change the world.   ISBN 0-930044-89-4   8.95

SOUL SNATCHER by Camarin Grae. 224 pp. A puzzle, an adventure, a mystery—Lesbian romance. ISBN 0-930044-90-8   8.95

THE LOVE OF GOOD WOMEN by Isabel Miller. 224 pp. Long-awaited new novel by the author of the beloved *Patience and Sarah*.   ISBN 0-930044-81-9   8.95

THE HOUSE AT PELHAM FALLS by Brenda Weathers. 240 pp. Suspenseful Lesbian ghost story.   ISBN 0-930044-79-7   7.95

HOME IN YOUR HANDS by Lee Lynch. 240 pp. More stories from the author of *Old Dyke Tales*.   ISBN 0-930044-80-0   7.95

EACH HAND A MAP by Anita Skeen. 112 pp. Real-life poems that touch us all.   ISBN 0-930044-82-7   6.95

SURPLUS by Sylvia Stevenson. 342 pp. A classic early Lesbian novel.   ISBN 0-930044-78-9   7.95

PEMBROKE PARK by Michelle Martin. 256 pp. Derring-do and daring romance in Regency England. ISBN 0-930044-77-0   7.95

THE LONG TRAIL by Penny Hayes. 248 pp. Vivid adventures of two women in love in the old west.   ISBN 0-930044-76-2   8.95

HORIZON OF THE HEART by Shelley Smith. 192 pp. Hot romance in summertime New England.   ISBN 0-930044-75-4   7.95

AN EMERGENCE OF GREEN by Katherine V. Forrest. 288 pp. Powerful novel of sexual discovery.   ISBN 0-930044-69-X   8.95

THE LESBIAN PERIODICALS INDEX edited by Claire Potter. 432 pp. Author & subject index.   ISBN 0-930044-74-6   29.95

DESERT OF THE HEART by Jane Rule. 224 pp. A classic; basis for the movie *Desert Hearts*.   ISBN 0-930044-73-8   7.95

SPRING FORWARD/FALL BACK by Sheila Ortiz Taylor. 288 pp. Literary novel of timeless love.   ISBN 0-930044-70-3   7.95

FOR KEEPS by Elisabeth Nonas. 144 pp. Contemporary novel about losing and finding love.   ISBN 0-930044-71-1   7.95

TORCHLIGHT TO VALHALLA by Gale Wilhelm. 128 pp. Classic novel by a great Lesbian writer.   ISBN 0-930044-68-1   7.95

LESBIAN NUNS: BREAKING SILENCE edited by Rosemary Curb and Nancy Manahan. 432 pp. Unprecedented autobiographies of religious life.   ISBN 0-930044-62-2   9.95

THE SWASHBUCKLER by Lee Lynch. 288 pp. Colorful novel set in Greenwich Village in the sixties.   ISBN 0-930044-66-5   7.95

MISFORTUNE'S FRIEND by Sarah Aldridge. 320 pp. Historical Lesbian novel set on two continents.   ISBN 0-930044-67-3   7.95

A STUDIO OF ONE'S OWN by Ann Stokes. Edited by Dolores Klaich. 128 pp. Autobiography.   ISBN 0-930044-64-9   7.95

SEX VARIANT WOMEN IN LITERATURE by Jeannette Howard Foster. 448 pp. Literary history.   ISBN 0-930044-65-7   8.95

A HOT-EYED MODERATE by Jane Rule. 252 pp. Hard-hitting essays on gay life; writing; art.   ISBN 0-930044-57-6   7.95

INLAND PASSAGE AND OTHER STORIES by Jane Rule. 288 pp. Wide-ranging new collection.   ISBN 0-930044-56-8   7.95

WE TOO ARE DRIFTING by Gale Wilhelm. 128 pp. Timeless Lesbian novel, a masterpiece.   ISBN 0-930044-61-4   6.95

AMATEUR CITY by Katherine V. Forrest. 224 pp. A Kate Delafield mystery. First in a series.   ISBN 0-930044-55-X   7.95

THE SOPHIE HOROWITZ STORY by Sarah Schulman. 176 pp. Engaging novel of madcap intrigue.   ISBN 0-930044-54-1   7.95

THE BURNTON WIDOWS by Vicki P. McConnell. 272 pp. A Nyla Wade mystery, second in the series.   ISBN 0-930044-52-5   7.95

OLD DYKE TALES by Lee Lynch. 224 pp. Extraordinary stories of our diverse Lesbian lives.   ISBN 0-930044-51-7   7.95

DAUGHTERS OF A CORAL DAWN by Katherine V. Forrest. 240 pp. Novel set in a Lesbian new world. ISBN 0-930044-50-9   7.95

THE PRICE OF SALT by Claire Morgan. 288 pp. A milestone novel, a beloved classic.   ISBN 0-930044-49-5   8.95

AGAINST THE SEASON by Jane Rule. 224 pp. Luminous, complex novel of interrelationships.   ISBN 0-930044-48-7   7.95

LOVERS IN THE PRESENT AFTERNOON by Kathleen Fleming. 288 pp. A novel about recovery and growth.   ISBN 0-930044-46-0   8.50

TOOTHPICK HOUSE by Lee Lynch. 264 pp. Love between two Lesbians of different classes.   ISBN 0-930044-45-2   7.95

MADAME AURORA by Sarah Aldridge. 256 pp. Historical novel featuring a charismatic "seer."   ISBN 0-930044-44-4   7.95

CURIOUS WINE by Katherine V. Forrest. 176 pp. Passionate Lesbian love story, a best-seller.   ISBN 0-930044-43-6   7.95

BLACK LESBIAN IN WHITE AMERICA by Anita Cornwell. 141 pp. Stories, essays, autobiography.   ISBN 0-930044-41-X   7.50

CONTRACT WITH THE WORLD by Jane Rule. 340 pp. Powerful, panoramic novel of gay life.   ISBN 0-930044-28-2   7.95

YANTRAS OF WOMANLOVE by Tee A. Corinne. 64 pp. Photos by noted Lesbian photographer.   ISBN 0-930044-30-4   6.95

MRS. PORTER'S LETTER by Vicki P. McConnell. 224 pp.
The first Nyla Wade mystery.   ISBN 0-930044-29-0   7.95

TO THE CLEVELAND STATION by Carol Anne Douglas.
192 pp. Interracial Lesbian love story.   ISBN 0-930044-27-4   6.95

THE NESTING PLACE by Sarah Aldridge. 224 pp. Historical
novel, a three-woman triangle.   ISBN 0-930044-26-6   7.95

THIS IS NOT FOR YOU by Jane Rule. 284 pp. A letter to a
beloved is also an intricate novel.   ISBN 0-930044-25-8   7.95

FAULTLINE by Sheila Ortiz Taylor. 140 pp. Warm, funny,
literate story of a startling family.   ISBN 0-930044-24-X   6.95

THE LESBIAN IN LITERATURE by Barbara Grier. 3d ed.
Foreword by Maida Tilchen. 240 pp. Comprehensive bibliography. Literary ratings; rare photos.   ISBN 0-930044-23-1   7.95

ANNA'S COUNTRY by Elizabeth Lang. 208 pp. A woman
finds her Lesbian identity.   ISBN 0-930044-19-3   6.95

PRISM by Valerie Taylor. 158 pp. A love affair between two
women in their sixties.   ISBN 0-930044-18-5   6.95

BLACK LESBIANS: AN ANNOTATED BIBLIOGRAPHY
compiled by J.R. Roberts. Foreword by Barbara Smith. 112
pp. Award winning bibliography.   ISBN 0-930044-21-5   5.95

THE MARQUISE AND THE NOVICE by Victoria Ramstetter.
108 pp. A Lesbian Gothic novel.   ISBN 0-930044-16-9   4.95

LABIAFLOWERS by Tee A. Corinne. 40 pp. Drawings by the
noted artist/photographer.   ISBN 0-930044-20-7   3.95

OUTLANDER by Jane Rule. 207 pp. Short stories and essays
by one of our finest writers.   ISBN 0-930044-17-7   6.95

SAPPHISTRY: THE BOOK OF LESBIAN SEXUALITY by
Pat Califia. 2d edition, revised. 195 pp.   ISBN 0-930044-47-9   7.95

ALL TRUE LOVERS by Sarah Aldridge. 292 pp. Romantic
novel set in the 1930s and 1940s.   ISBN 0-930044-10-X   7.95

A WOMAN APPEARED TO ME by Renee Vivien. 65 pp. A
classic; translated by Jeannette H. Foster. ISBN 0-930044-06-1   5.00

CYTHEREA'S BREATH by Sarah Aldridge. 240 pp. Women
first enter medicine and the law: a novel. ISBN 0-930044-02-9   6.95

TOTTIE by Sarah Aldridge. 181 pp. Lesbian romance in the
turmoil of the sixties.   ISBN 0-930044-01-0   6.95

THE LATECOMER by Sarah Aldridge. 107 pp. A delicate love
story set in days gone by.   ISBN 0-930044-00-2   5.00

ODD GIRL OUT by Ann Bannon   ISBN 0-930044-83-5   5.95
I AM A WOMAN by Ann Bannon.   ISBN 0-930044-84-3   5.95
WOMEN IN THE SHADOWS by Ann Bannon.
    ISBN 0-930044-85-1   5.95
JOURNEY TO A WOMAN by Ann Bannon.
    ISBN 0-930044-86-X   5.95
BEEBO BRINKER by Ann Bannon   ISBN 0-930044-87-8   5.95

Legendary novels written in the fifties and sixties,
set in the gay mecca of Greenwich Village.

VOLUTE BOOKS

JOURNEY TO FULFILLMENT	Early classics by Valerie	3.95
A WORLD WITHOUT MEN	Taylor: The Erika Frohmann	3.95
RETURN TO LESBOS	series.	3.95

These are just a few of the many Naiad Press titles—we are the oldest and largest lesbian/feminist publishing company in the world. Please request a complete catalog. We offer personal service; we encourage and welcome direct mail orders from individuals who have limited access to bookstores carrying our publications.